Silent Waters

Murder on Boulder Creek

Silent Waters

Murder on Boulder Creek

Crime Thriller

by

Mark R. Beckner

Becknerbooks Publishing
Becknerbooks.com

First Edition: October 2023

ISBN: 978-1-7369607-6-9 (paperback)

Credits

Sally Beckner – Copy review and editing

Writing companion – Roxy

Preface

After retiring from the Boulder Police Department following 36 years in law enforcement, I began my new career as a writer of fictional crime dramas. My stories evolve from my imagination, as well as from my time as an investigator. While each story is fictional, the police and forensic work are based on reality. I rely on my knowledge and experiences gained over my long tenure and from continued interest in actual cases to add realism to my stories.

I was somewhat nervous about my new adventure. Would people like what I wrote? Would my stories be interesting enough for readers? Well, this is now my fourth book and eighth crime thriller. My three earlier books comprised more than one story. My latest book, **Silent Waters**, the one you are reading now, is my first full-length novel. The feedback and reviews of my first three books have thus far been positive. Maybe I'm doing something right.

The setting for this book is Boulder, Colorado, the town I worked in for so long. Boulder Creek is an important waterway that runs through the middle of the city and provides beauty and recreation to residents and visitors alike. Because of its prominence in Boulder, crime sometimes occurs along its banks or adjacent parks. This story transforms the creek into a haunting dumping ground for the suspect's victims. I hope you are riveted by the intricate web of clues and shocking revelations. As you will find, the first chapter captures your attention. Follow along as primary detectives Caroline Shaw and Tom Nichols try to unravel the mystery and find the suspect before anyone else gets hurt.

Thank you so much for your support. Independent authors rely on readers willing to take a chance on our work. Finally, please leave me a review, as it would be much appreciated.

Please visit my website for additional information.

Becknerbooks.com

Or email

becknerbooks@gmail.com

Other books by Mark R. Beckner: **Behind The Lies**; **Death From Desire**; & **Naked Evidence**

Chapter 1

"Why are you doing this to me?" screamed Della. "I'm freezing and hungry!"

"I want to know how much you can take," replied the man wearing a white hood while looking through the metal grate above.

"I hate you! Get me out of here!" Della shouted as she looked up through the black metal grate that imprisoned her in the eight-by-10-foot wood-lined walled enclosure. She estimated the walls to be about eight feet tall. They were made of thick wooden timbers designed to prevent escape and limit her screams from being heard outside the chamber. Her only sight from the chamber was through the two-by-three-foot opening at the top, covered by the black grate. In her estimate, the bars on the grate were approximately three inches apart. Della could not tell which way was north, south, east, or west. One sixty-watt light bulb hung through the grate, providing her with light whenever her captor turned it on. In the middle of the concrete floor was a five-inch round drain.

The only furniture provided was a small metal cot with a thin mattress along one wall and a thick wooden chair sitting in a corner. The chair had wide wooden arms on each side with buckled leather straps attached, often used to buckle her to the chair for what he called "experiments." Similar ankle straps were attached to the front legs of the chair. In the middle of the opposite wall across from the bed was a two-foot-wide solid metal door. In one upper corner was a small camera pointing into the room toward the chair. A metal bucket sat in the opposite corner and served as Della's toilet. Toilet paper was provided, but there was nothing with which to wash her hands. The bucket was only emptied every four to five days. The smell reminded Della of the old wooden outhouses used in state parks when camping with her parents as a little girl.

Della did not know how long she had been a prisoner and could not remember how she got here. She estimated she had been captive for approximately thirty-some days. Della could not distinguish day from night. Her last memory was being at a bar with a young male. From there, everything became hazy, like trying to look through a thick fog. Della referred to her place of containment as her dungeon. There were times she thought of ways to overtake her captor whenever he entered the dungeon. At other times, her disorientation and depression made thoughts of escape challenging to comprehend. Thoughts of suicide sometimes crept into Della's head, although she didn't know how she would go about killing herself.

The temperature in the room was cold. Della believed it to be about 60 degrees most of the time. Of course, 60 degrees would feel more like freezing whenever he sprayed her with water. The cotton shirt and shorts provided were no comfort against the cold. Della would sometimes lie in bed under the only blanket, shivering to the point of making it difficult to sleep.

Della was fed minimal food, usually a dry peanut butter sandwich with bottled water once a day. She would sometimes get a sandwich of lunch meat, if lucky. The sandwiches were relatively dry without mayonnaise or other condiments, but the meat was a refreshing change. To deliver the food, a bucket would be lowered into the room containing whatever sandwich was served that day. It was the same type of metal bucket used as her toilet. She hoped the buckets were never switched out for one another. Most of the time, she would drink all the water. At other times, she would save a small amount for cleaning her hands and face.

"You are not leaving here until you transition," he told Della.

"Transition to what?"

"Back to who you really are, Amy."

"My name is not Amy. You want me to go crazy, don't you?"

"I never said that."

"I'm sure people are looking for me."

"What people?"

"The police."

"No one has even reported you missing."

Della knew he was probably right, which further depressed her. At seventeen, she had run away from her home in Erie, Pennsylvania. Now nineteen, Della was no longer a juvenile runaway, but her mother had little idea where she was. She had only been in Boulder, Colorado, for a couple of weeks before being imprisoned in a hell-hole wooden room. She doubted anyone even knew she was missing.

"What day is this?" Della asked.

"What does it matter? You no longer have days. You only have time, so you might as well make the most of what you have left."

"What does that mean?"

Without answering, he stared at Della through the metal grate for several seconds. She stared back. He then got up and left. The lightbulb in her wooden tomb shut off. Della was left in total darkness. She had no way of knowing what time it was or whether it was day or night. Della sat on the edge of the metal-framed bed and listened. She knew there was another woman somewhere nearby. Sometimes, she would hear muffled screaming from another room, possibly another wooden dungeon like hers. The voice was that of a female. Della tried to call out to the other woman.

"Hello," she shouted. "Can you hear me?"

Della was afraid to call out too loudly for fear of her captor hearing her and punishing her for it. Della called out again. Still no response. *She's probably too afraid to respond,* thought Della. *Who is she? Does she have blond hair like me? Is she in a similar room?*

Della slowly lay down on the bed and positioned herself in a fetal position. She pulled the musty blanket to her neck as tears trickled down her cheeks. *How did I get into this situation?*

Chapter 2

Boulder Detective Caroline Shaw arrived at the police department on an unseasonably warm Tuesday morning, May 9th, at 8:10 am. As usual, she walked upstairs to the break room to get a coffee from the vending machine before returning downstairs to her desk in the Detective Bureau. Her first order of business was to see if any fresh cases had landed on her desk. Before she could even set her coffee down, Detective Sergeant Luca Martinez walked by.

"Come see me in my office right now," ordered Martinez.

"What is it?" responded Shaw.

"We have a dead body."

Detective Shaw quickly followed the sergeant into his office. "What have we got?" asked Shaw.

"Patrol got a report of a female body found in Eben G. Fine Park this morning. One of our transients called it in. Patrol officers are there now securing the scene. I'd like you and Nichols to respond. See what we have there."

"Sure thing," responded Shaw. "Is it a homicide?"

"Right now, I don't know. I only know that we have a confirmed dead female."

"Got it," said Shaw as she walked out and headed toward the desk of Detective Tom Nichols. Nichols was not at his desk. Shaw retrieved her cell phone and called him.

"Hey Caro, what's up?" answered Nichols.

"Where are you?" asked Shaw.

"I'm downstairs talkin' trash with some patrol guys. Why?"

"We have a dead female body at Eben G. Fine. Martinez put us on the case."

"Okay, I'll be right up."

"Gotta go. Dead female found in Eben G. Fine," said Nichols to no one in particular as he walked away. Nichols hustled to the detective bureau, where he met Detective Shaw.

"You ready?" asked Shaw.

"Geez, give me a minute. I need to find my notepad and put my jacket on."

Shaw stood and watched as Nichols fumbled around on his desk until he found his notepad under some spread-out reports. He then grabbed his blue sports coat off the back of his chair and put it on. "Now I'm ready," Nichols said.

Shaw rolled her eyes and led the way out of the building to her assigned detective car, a white Ford Explorer. It was a simple drive to Eben G. Fine Park. All Shaw had to do was head due west on Arapahoe from 33rd Street and follow it to the west side of town (the police department is on 33rd Street, just north of Arapahoe).

Boulder, Colorado, is a vibrant and picturesque town nestled at the foothills of the Rocky Mountains 25 miles northwest of Denver. It is known for its stunning beauty and active lifestyle. Boulder sits at an elevation of approximately 5,400 feet, surrounded by beautiful open space with plenty of parks and trails. Boulder's skyline is partially defined by the Flatirons, iconic rock formations southwest of the city. The town's location is ideal for outdoor enthusiasts for hiking, biking, running and various other outdoor activities. The University of Colorado sits in the center of town, creating youthful energy and a vibrant academic atmosphere in the city. Boulder also has a thriving cultural scene and hosts various festivals and events throughout the year.

Eben G. Fine Park is located off Arapahoe Avenue on the far western side of Boulder, snuggled along Boulder Creek, which flows east from the mountains. The tree-lined park has a wide-open area for picnicking, playing frisbee, or lounging. Along the park's north boundary runs Boulder Creek, nestled between tall trees, many of them majestic maples and cottonwoods. A paved walkway and bike trail run parallel to the meandering creek that gurgles and babbles as it cascades over rocky boulders. This trail continues through Boulder and connects with other walkways and bike trails. It is very popular with heavy traffic in the summer. In high water runoff, the creek provides some whitewater for tubers and kayakers. In Eben G. Fine Park, the city has created a unique whitewater play park for kayakers and tubers to enjoy. During calmer times, people can often be seen wading in the cool waters of the creek.

Many enjoy the park, but it's also known as a popular spot for the homeless, often referred to as transients, especially during the warmer months. While mostly peaceful, the transients can sometimes cause problems after drinking too much or being too aggressive in asking for money. Therefore, the Boulder Police frequently patrol the area.

Shaw and Nichols arrived at the park at 8:38 am. They could see three officers and a patrol sergeant congregated near the creek bed on the far west side of the park. Yellow crime scene tape cordoned off an area along the creek, and several bystanders were milling around. Nichols grabbed the camera from the backseat. They exited the car and walked toward the gathering, approximately 300 feet away. As they walked up, Patrol Sergeant Jean Wilson stepped forward to greet them.

"Hi, Jean," said Nichols. "What have we got here?"

"Not sure," responded Wilson. "Deceased young white female. She doesn't look to be in great shape. May have been dead for a while."

"Any indication of the cause of death?" asked Shaw.

"Possible suicide."

"Why do you say that?"

"The first officer on the scene checked her vitals. He saw that her right wrist had been sliced."

Detective Shaw shook her head. "Who found her?"

"One of our transient friends, Chris Shilling. He goes by the nickname of Grizzly."

"Ah, I remember Grizzly from my patrol days," offered Nichols. "Even arrested him a few times on minor stuff. You know why they call him Grizzly, right?"

"Yeah, because he's so hairy," answered Wilson.

"He sure is," said Nichols. "He's got hair all down his back, his chest, beard, he has it all. When he hasn't showered in a while, that hair carries quite an odor."

"Okay, that's enough about his hair and odor," snapped Shaw. "What did he tell you?"

Sgt. Wilson continued. "He told me he had gone down to the creek a little after seven this morning to splash some water on his face when he came upon our victim. He said her legs and lower body were in the water, with her head and upper body on the rocks. Grizzly pulled her out of the water to check on her and found her dead."

"Great," said Nichols. "So, we have a contaminated crime scene."

"Most people would have checked on her," responded Shaw.

"Officer West was the first to respond," continued Wilson. "He checked her vitals and immediately knew she had been dead for some time. That's when he saw her right wrist had been cut. The coroner has been called, and someone is en route."

"Okay, let's look the body over and get some pictures," suggested Shaw.

"I've got the camera," replied Nichols. "You look things over, and I will take the photos."

Shaw stood back while Nichols took multiple photographs of the body and surrounding area from various angles. Once he finished taking overall pictures of the victim and crime scene, Shaw moved in to examine the body. Shaw noted the victim appeared to have been dead for at least several hours. She could see the cut on the victim's right wrist but did not want to move the body to check the left wrist tucked under the victim's left side.

The victim appeared to be a young white female, possibly around twenty. She had long blond hair and pale skin. Shaw estimated her height to be between five-foot-four inches and five-foot-six inches. The victim was very thin, and her face had an emaciated look. *This woman was not in great health*, thought Shaw. On the right hand, Shaw noticed the fingernails were broken and worn.

"Her right hand may have been damaged from the rocks," suggested Shaw. "Be sure to get some photos of her hand."

"I will," responded Nichols.

Shaw noted the victim was scantily dressed in a gray T-shirt and white shorts. She did not have any shoes on. While it was a warm day, Shaw did not believe the women had dressed appropriately for the weather, especially for the night or early morning hours.

Shaw then searched around the body, looking for anything out of the ordinary. Other than the body, Shaw found nothing unusual. Once Nichols finished taking photos, Shaw suggested they talk to Grizzly. They both approached Chris Shilling, commonly known as Grizzly, sitting at a nearby picnic table with a patrol officer. Grizzly wore a red plaid flannel long-sleeved shirt and well-worn blue jeans. A pair of dirty brown construction boots adorned his feet. He wore a blue bandana on his head of thick, long, dark hair. Underneath the bandana, his hair was tied back in a ponytail. A dense, bushy beard covered the lower half of his face and hung down below his neckline. He looked to be middle-aged. Shaw detected the body odor Nichols had mentioned as she got closer.

"Hello, Chris," said Shaw.

"Just call me Grizzly," Shilling replied.

"Okay, Grizzly. I'm Detective Caro Shaw, and this is Detective Tom Nichols. We understand you found our victim this morning."

"I did."

"How did you find her?"

"I was just going down to the creek, like I usually do in the morning, to clean up some. When I got there, I found this woman lying in the creek. I pulled her out to check on her and found she had already drowned."

Shaw believed she could detect an odor of alcohol on Grizzly's breath. It was tough to distinguish from the body odor. "Why do you think she drowned?"

"She was face down at the edge of the creek when I found her."

"What did you do next?" asked Shaw as Nichols scribbled notes in his notebook.

"I pulled her out."

"You pulled her out of the creek after you determined she was dead?"

"No, I pulled her out first. She was cold and not breathing."

"Did you see anything else in the water?"

"No."

"What else did you touch?"

"I didn't touch anything else on her. I just grabbed her arms and pulled her out onto the rocks."

"Who else was with you?"

"No one."

"Did you see anyone else in the park?"

"Umm, just a few people walking by on the path."

"Who were they?"

"I don't know. Just some people. There are usually people on the path in the morning."

"Didn't they see the body?"

"I guess not. I didn't see her until I got to the creek."

"Do you know this woman?" continued Shaw.

"No."

"Have you ever seen her before?"

"Not that I remember."

"How much have you had to drink today?"

Grizzly looked at Shaw for several seconds. "Nothing."

"I can smell alcohol on your breath."

"I haven't had anything today."

"Yesterday?"

"Yeah, I was drinking yesterday. Am I in trouble?"

"No, not at all," assured Shaw. "We just need to know all the facts. When did you last have a drink?"

"Last night sometime."

"Before or after midnight?"

"I don't know."

"Do you feel drunk right now?"

"No, I'm fine."

"Do you know what time you found the woman?"

"Early. Probably around seven."

"Did you take anything off the woman?"

"No. Why are you asking me these questions? All I did was find the body."

"We are just being thorough. The more information we have, the better our investigation will go. We appreciate you reporting this. Thank you."

Grizzly nodded.

"Here is my card. If you think of anything else, please call me. Every bit of information may be important."

"Okay."

"Is that your backpack?" interjected Nichols as he pointed to a medium-sized blue backpack on the picnic table.

"Yeah."

"Do you mind if we look inside just to be thorough?"

"You want to search my backpack?"

"Just look inside, that's all."

Grizzly reached over and grabbed the pack. He then handed it to Nichols. Nichols unzipped the top and looked in. He found miscellaneous items inside, including cigarettes, a half-empty bottle of Jack Daniels, a half loaf of bread, a couple of dirty T-shirts, a folding jackknife, and some matches.

"You going to bust me for an open container?"

Nichols looked at Grizzly. "No, we don't care about your open bottle of whiskey. We're just making sure you had nothing to do with this woman's death. Your cooperation is appreciated."

Grizzly nodded.

"Where did you go to call the police?" asked Nichols.

"I used my cell phone."

"I don't see any cell phone in here."

Grizzly reached into his shirt pocket, pulled out a small cell phone, and waved it at Nichols.

"That's your cell phone?"

"Sure is. Government-issued."

"May I see it?" asked Nichols. Grizzly handed Nichols the phone.

Nichols checked the phone log and found a call to 911. He then handed the phone back to Grizzly and thanked him. "Where are your bedroll, jacket, and other items?"

"I keep them stashed where I sleep. And I don't tell anyone where that is. I've lost too many items over the years."

"I understand," nodded Nichols. He then turned to Shaw. "I don't have anything else."

Shaw looked at Grizzly. "You are free to go now. Thanks again."

"I can leave?"

"Yes, you may leave now."

Grizzly stood up, grabbed his backpack, and walked away.

"I think he's our guy," said Nichols.

"Huh?" responded Shaw.

Nichols laughed. "I'm being sarcastic. Grizzly is not the type to do something like this. Besides, he wouldn't have stuck around if he was involved."

"I agree. It looks like the coroner has arrived. Let's go see what he finds."

Shaw and Nichols returned to the creek's edge where the body lay. The coroner, Ron Larsen, was a large, middle-aged white male with dark hair parted and combed to the left. A thick, dark mustache adorned his upper lip. He stood at six-foot-two with a large physique, and black-framed glasses sat on the bridge of his nose. His eyes were dark brown, almost black. Larsen wore dark pants and a blue nylon windbreaker with "Coroner" emblazoned across the back. Blue latex gloves covered his hands.

"Good morning, Ron," said Detective Shaw as she walked up beside him. Nichols remained quiet as he looked over the body.

"Homicide?" asked Larsen.

"We don't know, but there is a cut on her right wrist," answered Shaw.

"Do I need to take pictures?"

"No, Tom took plenty from all angles."

"Good. Let's get her out of here and onto the gurney."

Shaw and Nichols stepped forward to help Larsen lift the woman up and out of the water. The body was partially stiff, indicating rigor mortice, the stiffening of the muscles, had already begun. Shaw estimated the victim had been dead for at least several hours. Once they got her out, they lifted her onto the gurney.

"Look at this," said Nichols. "Her left wrist is also cut. She must have been very intent on killing herself."

"Maybe," responded Larsen. "But I find it strange there is very little blood."

"It probably washed out in the creek," Nichols replied.

"Possibly, but I would still expect more blood, especially on her clothing. It would be faded, but there should be some blood stains somewhere. I'll know more when I get her to the morgue and do a thorough inspection and autopsy."

Once Larsen had the body covered and strapped down, he wheeled it toward his waiting van. Two nearby patrol officers assisted Larsen in loading the body.

Shaw and Nichols then took the time to search the rocks and water where the body had been found. Neither of them could find anything of evidentiary value. They both noted that no blood was visible on any of the rocks or surrounding dirt.

"If only these waters could talk," pondered Nichols.

"That would be nice," agreed Shaw as they stood listening to the bubbling water flow by.

As they were completing their search, Detective Commander Stella Greenberg arrived on the scene. Greenberg started with the Boulder PD when she was twenty-four years old. She was now fifty-four and had been the detective commander for the past three years. Her short, brown, wavy hair covered her ears, and she wore her typical outfit, a women's business suit. Today, she was in gray. Under the jacket, she wore a white open-neck blouse. As always, Greenberg wore a solid gold pendant around her neck. The pendant comprised three circles of gold, each engraved with the name of one of her three children. "What have we got? Please tell me it's a simple drowning."

"I'm afraid we can't tell you that, Commander," replied Nichols. "We don't know what we have. Our victim was found by a transient, Grizzly, who said he stumbled across the body this morning. There were no obvious signs of trauma other than a deep cut on both wrists."

"Sad, but good. All we need is another homicide on the creek path. Boulder would go crazy."

"We aren't so sure this is a suicide," advised Shaw. "There's no visible blood anywhere. Larsen believes there should have been some blood evidence, especially on the clothing."

"She was found in the water. The blood evidence is likely gone," replied Greenberg. Neither Shaw nor Nichols replied. "Let me know as soon as the coroner has a finding."

"We will," Shaw assured her.

It was 10:45 am by the time Shaw and Nichols had completed their investigation at the scene. "Have you had breakfast yet?" asked Nichols.

"I usually only have coffee in the morning."

"Well, it's almost eleven already. It will be eleven-thirty by the time we get there and get served. You can call it lunch. Let's go to the Village Coffee Shop."

Shaw chuckled. "Yeah, I am getting a little hungry, but not for breakfast food."

"You know they serve lunch food as well, right?"

"Of course. I've been there before."

"Great, then you know the way."

Shaw chuckled again at the insinuation that she might not have known where the iconic and Boulder favorite Village Coffee Shop is located. It is centrally located on Folsom Street, just north of Arapahoe Avenue. Anyone in Boulder for any length of time knows of the Village

Coffee Shop. Its website advertises itself as "890 square feet of reality, surrounded by Boulder." It is the place to go for comfort food, and the servings are plentiful. Fluffy pancakes are one of their specialties. The lunch menu consists primarily of burgers and a variety of sandwiches.

Before leaving, Shaw and Nichols walked around the park to see if they could find anything out of place or suspicious. Finding nothing, they packed up their equipment and headed toward the Village Coffee Shop. Shaw pulled the Explorer into the parking lot and quickly found a parking space. "There doesn't seem to be many people here today."

"It's only eleven-twenty," laughed Nichols. "The perfect time between the breakfast crowd and the lunch crowd. By noon, it will be hard to find a table."

They both entered the small restaurant and found several tables available. As cops often do, they chose a table in the back that provided a view of the entire restaurant and the front door.

A waitress, a forty-something motherly-looking type, handed each of them a menu. "Hi, Tom. How are things going today?"

"Well, it's only eleven-thirty, and we've already responded to a dead body call," answered Nichols.

"Oh. That doesn't sound good."

"No, it's been a busy morning. We've worked up an appetite."

"Do you know what you want already?"

"I do."

"I'm going to need a minute to look over the menu," said Shaw.

Nichols interrupted. "Mary, this is my partner in crime, Detective Caroline Shaw. We call her Caro for short. Caro, this is Mary, the best waitress in Boulder."

"Pleased to meet you," said Mary.

"Same here," replied Shaw. "I've been here a few times."

"You look somewhat familiar."

"She's also been on TV a few times," announced Nichols. "Caro's been on some major cases recently."

Mary smiled. "Would you like something to drink?"

"Coffee, please," replied Shaw.

"Iced tea for me," said Nichols.

After Mary walked away, Shaw looked at Nichols. "You didn't have to tell her I've been on TV. That's not something I advertise."

"No, but that's where she might have seen you."

"Or maybe when I've been here before."

Nichols changed the subject. "I have a question for you."

"Yeah, what?"

"Why do you go by Caro?" asked Nichols, emphasizing the "o" at the end. "Isn't it usually Carol? Caro reminds me of the syrup my mom used when I was a kid. It was clear and called Caro syrup."

Shaw looked at Nichols with a squint in her eyes. "The syrup is Karo, with a K."

"Whatever," said Nichols. "Why Caro, with a C?"

"Not that it matters, but my father called me Caro for short when I was growing up. He always left off the L at the end. It caught on, and I came to like it as well."

"Okay," shrugged Nichols. "I thought maybe you didn't know how to spell Carol."

"If that was a joke, it wasn't funny," smirked Shaw.

Just then, Mary walked up with the drinks. "Do you two know what you'd like?"

"I will take the tuna melt, please," replied Shaw.

"And I will have the Spanish omelet with jalapenos. And please bring me two blueberry pancakes instead of the toast," said Nichols.

"Got it," replied Mary as she turned and walked away.

"You must be hungry," said Shaw.

"Well, we didn't get breakfast. And it's hard not to order the pancakes here."

Once their food was served, Shaw and Nichols continued to make small talk. Neither cared to talk of the dead body while eating.

Detective Caroline Shaw was a thirty-seven-year-old white female, five-foot-ten, with a slim build. She had medium-length dark blond, almost brown hair, which she pulled back and pinned in a French twist while at work. Her eyes were a bright blue, adding a touch of vibrancy to her overall look. Given her athletic nature, she possessed a toned physique with well-defined muscles. Her size and posture exuded confidence and poise. While growing up in Fort Wayne, Indiana, Shaw played basketball and softball in high school. She was talented enough at softball to play at the collegiate level at Indiana University. After graduating, Shaw moved out west for a change of scenery. She had always been interested in law enforcement, and when she found out the Boulder Police Department was hiring, she applied. They hired her at twenty-three years old.

Prior to becoming a detective, Shaw worked as a patrol officer. While working on patrol, she started dating a fellow patrol officer, Dan Milton, and after eight months, they married. They were happy for several years, but both seemed more dedicated to their work than each other. After six years together, they decided it would be better to divorce. It was soon after the divorce when Shaw was promoted to detective. She has been a detective for the last six years. For the first four years as a detective, Shaw worked on sexual assaults. After much success, Shaw transferred into aggravated assault and homicide. Several years after the divorce, her ex-husband, Dan Milton, was one of the first responders to Boulder's supermarket mass shooting that became national news. After the shooting, Milton struggled with post-traumatic stress and guilt over the death of one of the responding officers, who was also a close friend. He left the Boulder Police Department approximately eight months after the tragic shooting. He was now working as a realtor in Arvada, about 20 miles south of Boulder. Shaw still occasionally talked to him but hadn't seen him in over a year.

Detective Tom Nichols was a thirty-four-year-old white male, six feet tall and had a medium build. He sported shortcut brown hair that was combed to the right. His eyes were dark brown, and he had a tanned complexion, owing to his mother being Hispanic. Nichols typically wore short-sleeved polo shirts with either a sports jacket or a light windbreaker. On his left wrist, he always wore a shiny gold watch.

Nichols grew up in Denver and studied criminal justice for two years at Front Range Community College. After earning his associate degree, Nichols worked as a security guard for a local manufacturing company. While working, he put himself through the police academy at Arapahoe Community College. At twenty-four, the Boulder Police Department hired him. At twenty-five, he married his longtime girlfriend, Kristin, after she became pregnant with their son, Brian, who was now nine. Three years later, Tom and Kristin welcomed a baby girl into the family. They named her Lisa. Nichols had now been a detective for three years. Tom was currently assigned as a general detective, which meant he could be assigned to any type of case as needed. However, this was the first potential homicide he had ever been assigned to assist with.

After finishing their meal and paying, Shaw and Nichols left the coffee shop and drove back to the police department. They knew they had a lot of work ahead of them.

Chapter 3

Back at the station, Shaw and Nichols met with Detective Commander Greenberg and Sergeant Luca Martinez. They explained what little they knew about the deceased female and what they found at the scene.

"Are you assuming this was a suicide?" asked Sergeant Martinez.

"Not necessarily," responded Shaw. "There was only a small amount of blood near the cuts and no stains on her clothing."

"Wouldn't the water have washed the blood away?"

"Possibly, but the coroner found it unusual that all the blood would wash away."

"You said the body was not in great shape. Can you be more specific?"

"She looked emaciated and very pale. She could very well be one of our homeless. I also noticed some bruising, possibly from bouncing off the boulders in the creek."

"Did the coroner say when he would complete the autopsy?" asked Commander Greenberg.

"No, but I can call him and ask."

"All right, so all we can say is we found a deceased female in the creek at Eben G. Fine, and the cause of death is unknown. Is that correct?"

"That's correct," replied Shaw.

"Are you concerned this may be related to our dead body last fall?" continued Greenberg.

"There are some similarities, but the cause of death has not been determined to be a homicide."

"Yes, but it still worries me. Thank you, Caro. I'll brief the chief on what we know. Any calls you get from the media, you can forward to me."

"Will do."

After their meeting, Nichols asked Shaw what had happened to the victim referred to by the Commander.

"You don't remember it?"

"I remember the case, but I was on that auto theft detail with the county. I know it was never solved."

"No, it wasn't. There are some similarities to this case. Last fall, we found a woman along Boulder Creek near Central Park. She was dressed similarly to our current victim and wasn't in very good shape, health-wise."

"What was the cause of death?" asked Nichols.

"Undetermined. The coroner found some trauma to the body but didn't believe it was enough to kill her. He thought it might have been because of exposure to the elements. She only had on a shirt, shorts, and tennis shoes. It was the third week of September, and it was hot for that time of year. There was speculation she was cooling off in the creek and was overcome by the current."

"Cut marks on the wrists?"

Shaw laughed. "I don't think anyone would speculate she was just wading in the creek if her wrists were slashed."

"Yeah, right," said Nichols sheepishly. "It is puzzling."

"It is, and we have no evidence or witnesses."

"Is the case still open?"

"It's open but inactive for now. We don't even know that there was a crime."

"Kind of like this case," pondered Nichols. "Was she ever identified?"

"Yes. Her name was Aubrey Leaver. She was a white female, about five-seven, with long blond hair."

"I'm new to this homicide stuff," admitted Nichols. "But it sure seems strange to have two dead females of similar characteristics found along the creek within six months."

"It is," sighed Shaw. "But unless the coroner finds something, they may file this as a suicide. That's enough talk. I need to get these photos filed and sent to the coroner. We also need to get our reports done."

"On it," said Nichols as he headed toward his cubicle. Halfway through his report, Nichols received a call from dispatch. An officer had responded to a report of an assault from the previous day. The female victim believed she had been attacked by the killer of the woman found in Eben G. Fine Park. Nichols asked to have the woman brought to the detective bureau. He then walked over to Shaw's desk.

"Caro, we may have a lead."

"What is it?"

"Patrol is bringing in a woman who believes she was attacked by the killer of our dead female."

"We don't even know if she was murdered yet."

"Yeah, I know. But we need to interview this woman."

"I can't. I'm meeting with the coroner this afternoon to review the autopsy results."

"That's okay. I'll interview her myself."

"You're going to videotape it, right?"

"Of course."

"Let's meet later today to review what we both have," suggested Shaw.

"Sure. I'll see you later."

Nichols left to set up the interview room for the victim being brought in by patrol. He made sure the camera and recording equipment were set up and ready. Nichols retrieved two bottles of water and set them on the table for him and the victim. As he finished, the patrol officer walked in with the woman. Based on her manner of dress and disheveled look, Nichols assumed the woman was probably homeless.

"Tom, this is Ruby Ryan," announced the officer. "She was assaulted two days ago along Boulder Creek. I've taken an initial report."

"Dispatch told me the assault was yesterday," said Nichols.

"No, it was two days ago," said Ruby.

Ruby Ryan was a thirty-six-year-old white female with dirty brown curly hair and a thin build. Her skin had a tanned and leathery look. She wore a rainbow-colored knit hat and an opened red nylon winter jacket over a tie-dyed T-shirt. The jeans she was wearing were worn and soiled. She had pink tennis shoes on her feet. Ruby carried the scent of mildew about her.

"May I call you Ruby?" asked Nichols.

"Sure."

"This bottle of water is for you, Ruby."

"Thank you," replied Ruby as she opened the bottle and took several long drinks.

"Why don't you tell me what happened two days ago," continued Nichols.

"Like I told the officer, I was down by the creek when a man approached me and tried to rape me."

"Where at on the creek?"

"It was behind Boulder High School."

"Did you know this man?"

"I've seen him around some, but I don't know him."

"Okay, explain to me step by step what happened."

"It was in the morning, and I had just woken up. This guy comes up to me and acts nice. He asks me my name and other questions like where do I sleep and hang out. He then asks if I would like to have sex with him. I told him no. He tried to talk me into it. I kept saying no. Then he grabbed me, and I told him to go to hell and to leave me alone. He started screaming at me, telling me I was a no-good bitch. When he grabbed me again, I kicked him in the leg. He finally stopped and walked away."

"Were you hurt?"

"He grabbed me hard, but I'm okay."

"Where did he grab you?"

"He put one arm around me and pulled me close to him. Then he grabbed my left tit."

"He grabbed your breast?"

"Yes."

"What did you do?"

"That's when I kicked him in the leg."

"Did he touch you again after that?"

"No. He just kept calling me names and then walked away."

"Would you recognize this man if you saw him again?"

"Oh yeah. Like I said, I've seen him before."

"Where do you live, Ruby?"

"Here and there. I sometimes crash at the homeless shelter."

"You said you had just woken up. Were you camping along the creek?"

"Am I in trouble?"

"No, not at all. I just need to know all the details."

"Yes."

"Do you sleep there often?"

"It's a pleasant spot, but I sleep in different places."

"How long have you been homeless in Boulder?"

"I've been homeless most of my life. I've been to Seattle, Portland, Albuquerque, Denver, and other cities."

"But how long in Boulder?"

"I've been here two years now."

"All right. Have you seen the person who attacked you since it happened?"

"No, but when I heard about the woman found today, I figured that could have been me."

"You are right to report this. What did the man look like?"

"I already told the officer this."

"I haven't heard it yet. Please tell me."

"He was tall and had long brown hair."

"Was he a white male?"

"Yes."

"Thin or heavy build?"

"Thin."

"Did he have a beard or mustache?"

"He needed a shave but not a full beard."

"And what was he wearing?"

"A blue jacket and a baseball hat."

"Was there a team logo on the hat?"

"I don't know. It was red."

"Any other clothing you remember?"

"I think blue jeans."

"Great. We will alert our officers to be looking for someone fitting this description. If you see him, call nine-one-one right away."

"Okay, I will."

"It's a warm day today, so I have to ask. Why are you wearing a winter coat?"

"It still gets cold at night, and if I leave my jacket somewhere, I'm afraid it will get ripped off."

"Makes sense. Where did you get the jacket?"

"The big church down on Pine. They hand out warm clothing."

"Very nice. I appreciate your help, Ruby."

After the interview, Nichols confirmed that dispatch had aired a description of the suspect to officers. He then returned to his desk. Shaw had not yet returned from the coroner's office. Sgt. Martinez saw Nichols at his desk and walked over.

"Tom, what did our victim have to say?"

"Some guy sexually assaulted her two days ago. He asked for sex, and when she refused, he grabbed her and fondled her breast. He might be a transient in the area preying on women."

"Do you think there is any connection to today's dead body?"

"If I had to guess, I would say no."

"Let me know when we get something back from the coroner."

"I will, Sergeant."

While working at his desk, Nichols received a call from patrol officer Becky Weston. "Tom, I think I know who your sex assault suspect is."

"Yeah? Who is it?"

"Based on the description, I believe I contacted him three days ago on the Pearl Street Mall. He was harassing people walking the mall. His name is Shane Phillips. He is a white male, twenty-six years old, six foot three, thin build, and long brown hair."

"Do you remember what he was wearing?"

"Yeah, a dark jacket and a red baseball cap."

"That sounds like him," replied Nichols. "I will have dispatch put out a BOLO (*be on the lookout*) to include his name, age, and height. Thank you, Becky."

This gave Nichols confidence that Shane Phillips was the person who attacked Ruby. With the additional information, it wouldn't be long before a patrol officer found Phillips, assuming he was still in town.

It was about 4:30 pm when Shaw returned from the coroner's office. She asked Nichols to join her in Sgt. Martinez's office for an update on the autopsy.

"Well, are we dealing with a homicide?" asked Martinez.

"Most likely," replied Shaw.

"What does that mean?" asked Nichols.

"It means Ron is not yet positive it is a homicide. He wants to do more tests on body tissue before making the final call. However, he believes she may have been slowly strangled or suffocated to death."

"How did she cut her wrists?" asked Nichols.

"She didn't. Ron is sure the wrists were cut after her death."

"I don't get it," said Nichols. "How could he know that?"

"Her body was still full of blood. She had only lost a small amount of blood, indicating her heart had stopped before her wrists were cut. Had her heart been beating, it would have pumped most of the blood out of her before she died."

"Okay, that makes sense," nodded Nichols.

Shaw continued. "He found small stress marks and minor bruising around her neck. He also found minor petechial hemorrhages around her eyes and under the eyelids. Ron said this may indicate strangulation as the cause of death."

"My god," exclaimed Nichols. "That sounds awful."

"Did Ron find any other injuries?" asked Martinez.

"He found some marks and bruising, again leading him to believe some abuse may have been involved. He also told me she suffered from malnutrition."

"Could that be from being homeless?" asked Martinez.

"Possibly. But given the other evidence, Ron thought she likely was with her killer for some time and may have been abused somehow."

"Explain to me again what pectio...hemorrhages are," asked Nichols. "It's been a long time since the academy."

Shaw explained. "They are called petechial hemorrhages. When someone is strangled or suffocated, the tiny capillaries around the face, particularly around the eyes and under the eyelids, will often burst, causing pinpoints of red to show on the skin. Other things can cause it, such as sickness, but given the other evidence, Dr. Larsen believes she was strangled."

"Makes sense," replied Nichols.

"When does Ron believe he'll know?" asked Martinez.

"He thinks he'll have an answer by late tomorrow."

"Did he swab for DNA?" asked Martinez.

"Yes. He swabbed areas where someone may have grabbed her. He also took vaginal swabs and scrapings from under her fingernails."

"Any distinguishing marks?"

"Yes. She had tattoos on her upper right arm and a tattoo of an angel on the back of her right shoulder."

"Do we have anything else?" asked Martinez.

"Yes," interrupted Nichols. "I believe we know who attacked the woman along the creek two days ago. His name is Shane Phillips, a twenty-six-year-old white male, six foot three, thin build, with long brown hair. He is wearing a blue jacket and a red baseball cap. I had dispatch put out a BOLO."

"Good work," replied Martinez. "Let me know when we find him."

"We will, Sergeant."

Chapter 4

Della woke up, and the room was still pitch black. She did not know what time of day it was. All she knew was that she had to urinate. Not able to see, Della slowly got off the cot and stood up. She shuffled her bare feet along the cold concrete floor toward her bathroom bucket, holding her arms out to feel her way. As she shuffled along, Della's left foot tapped the bucket. She stopped and touched the wall with her hands. Della turned around, pulled her pants down, and squatted over the bucket. Knowing whether she was centered over the bucket was difficult, but she wasn't about to touch it with her hands. She began to pee and heard the splashing as her urine hit the contents inside. She breathed a sigh of relief that she didn't miss the bucket. Once finished, she shuffled back to the cot and sat on its edge. Della wrapped the blanket around her shoulders to keep warm.

After several minutes had passed, the light hanging above flashed on, temporarily blinding Della. "Good morning," said the man up above. "It's time for your music lesson."

"No, please, not again. I have a headache already," pleaded Della.

"It's part of the program, Della."

He placed a large black speaker on the grate and pointed it directly into the room. "How does Guns and Roses sound for today?" he asked.

"Nothing sounds good today," cried Della. "Please let me out of here. What do you want from me?"

Seconds later, the speaker exploded in sound. The Guns and Roses song, "You Could Be Mine," roared into Della's dungeon. The sound was so loud that she covered her ears and could feel the vibration in her bones. Della curled up and grabbed the pillow to further muffle the sound. She knew from previous times it would be several hours before the music stopped. Della would be in this position for the entire time, trying to protect her hearing and throbbing head. She cried at the thought.

How can no one hear this music outside? thought Della. *I need to get out of here, or I will die here.*

The music of Guns and Roses continued to pound into Della's cell. A series of six songs continued over and over. Della was a fan of Guns and Roses, but the man above played the music much too loud to enjoy. The sound reverberated off each wall. Della screamed for it to stop, but it was no use. For Della, the music continued for what seemed like all day when it had only been four hours. Finally, the music stopped. However, the ringing in Della's ears continued.

The disorientation Della experienced during the music seemed to intensify once it stopped. It was as though all her senses were still in shock and were now trying to recover. This increased disorientation gave Della the feeling of dizziness, and she could feel herself getting nauseous. She sat on the side of the bed and took a couple of deep breaths to relieve the nausea. She could feel her body shaking as though she had a fever. Taking deep breaths did not work. Della quickly got up and rushed to the bucket. She bent over, held her shoulder-length blond hair back, gagged twice, then vomited into the bucket. Not much came out as she hadn't eaten since the day before. Most of it was stomach acid that burned her throat. Della sat down on the hard, cold concrete and began to cry.

Della realized her only hope was to somehow escape. She had previously tried to fight off the man wearing the white hoodie, but he always carried a taser gun. Having been shocked multiple times, Della gave up the idea of overpowering him. Still, she had to find a way. Della stood up and climbed on top of the cot. Using her fingernails, she attempted to get a grip on the wooden wall. She thought if only she could get to the grate, maybe she could open it. Della dug her fingernails into the crack between two timbers. She attempted to pull herself up while bracing her opposite foot on the side wall to push. She raised her other foot off the cot as she pulled and pushed. As she did so, she lost her grip on the timbers and fell sideways onto the cot, hitting her left hip on the metal frame. Della immediately felt a sharp pain in her hip as she flipped over and fell on her back, hitting the floor. Her head snapped back against the hard concrete. Della screamed out in pain.

Della lay on the floor for several minutes, rubbing the back of her head. She could feel a lump growing on her scalp, and her headache throbbed more than before. Della's hip was badly bruised but not broken. She slowly rolled over and pulled herself up to her hands and knees. Her next task was to see if she could stand up. Della pulled her good right leg up first and used it to push herself off the floor. Carefully, she stood with most of her weight on her right leg, with just enough on her left leg to keep her balance. She took a couple of small steps toward the cot and fell back onto the mattress. Della could feel pain in several tips of her fingers. She looked at them and saw two nails broken back on her right hand and one nail broken on her left hand. Two other nails had slivers of wood jammed between the nail and the skin.

Della looked directly at the camera, raised both hands and defiantly flipped her middle fingers, holding them for several seconds. Della's body was getting worn down. Both her body and spirit were slowly draining away. She felt like she was losing her mind. Della had lost track of the days and hadn't seen herself in a mirror since being locked in her dungeon. *I must look horrible,* she thought. Even as a runaway, Della always tried to look her best. She knew she was good-looking and used it to her advantage. She rarely had trouble finding a place to stay, especially with men.

Della was well-proportioned at five-foot-nine with a captivating figure. Before her captivity, her golden hair flowed to her shoulders in soft waves, shining like golden strands in sunlight. Her facial features were delicately shaped with high cheekbones. Sparkling blue eyes and long lashes captivated others while enhancing her natural beauty. Her skin radiated a healthy glow. At least, that's how she used to look. Now, looking at her hands and skin and unable to care for her hair and face, Della knew her looks had changed.

As Della was resting, the grate up above opened. She looked up and saw the man in the white hoodie and white lab coat looking down at her.

"It's time for your lunch, Della. A treat today. I made you a chicken salad sandwich, and I'm including an extra bottle of water."

Della did not respond. She watched as a metal bucket, attached by a metal clip onto a cable, was lowered into her "dungeon." The bucket clanged to the floor. Della reached in and pulled out the half sandwich wrapped in cellophane and two bottles of water.

"Now hook up your potty bucket, and I will clean it out for you."

Della limped over to the waste bucket and carried it to the cable. She unclipped the food bucket and attached her waste bucket to the clip. "Are you going to give me another waste bucket?" Della asked.

"Use the one I just gave you," said the man as he raised the waste bucket.

Della gagged at the thought of the same buckets being used to deliver her food. At least the sandwich had been wrapped, and the bottles were unopened. It didn't matter; Della was so hungry and thirsty that she was ready to eat anything. She unwrapped the half sandwich and savored it with each bite. It was nice to have something other than peanut butter. She was thankful for the extra water as well. She drank one entire bottle with her sandwich.

After eating, Della lay back down on the cot to relax and try to relieve her pounding headache. She covered herself with the blanket to keep warm and tried to think of past times with her family. Della had not been a happy teenager. She often fought with her mother and believed she was too strict. As punishment, her mother would ground her, often for things her friends got away with. Della thought it was unfair that her mother was not allowing her to do everyday teenage activities. Now, she would give anything to be home and in her mother's arms.

After about 15 minutes, Della felt strange, as though she was intoxicated. *Maybe I have a concussion,* she thought. The sensation grew more intense as the minutes passed, and the room started spinning. *What is happening?* As more time passed, Della felt warmer, and the room appeared more prominent and colorful. *I think he drugged me.*

The metal door opposite the cot opened with a squeak, and the man in the white lab coat, dark slacks, and white hoodie stepped in. Della saw he had the same shoes on as always: suede derby-style beige with darker round oxford shoelaces. The toe on the right shoe had a scuff mark on it. The man shut the door behind him. "Hello, Amy."

As usual, Della was confused. "My name is Della."

"Your real name is Amy," he responded. "You suffer from delusions and false memories."

Della tried to keep her focus. "What did you give me?"

"I didn't give you anything. You are hallucinating. I am here to help you."

Della struggled to follow what he was telling her. The hallucinations were getting more intense.

"Della is a false personality. Your real name is Amy, and you were brought to us for help. You made up stories of being from Erie, Pennsylvania. You've never lived in Erie, Amy. You were orphaned when you were three years old and lived in multiple homes. You've created a fake family and personality to compensate."

"Huh? I, I don't know what......you are talking about."

"Who are you?" he asked.

"I'm..... I'm Della."

ZAP!

"EEEooowwww!" screamed Della as she jumped. "Why did you tase me?"

"It's called shock therapy, Amy. When you give me a wrong answer, you get shocked by this taser. It will help in getting your mind straight again."

Della could hardly focus on what he was telling her. The room kept expanding and contracting. She saw colors on the wall.

"What is your name?"

Della mumbled, "my name is Della."

ZAP!

"AAAAgghh! Stop it!" shouted Della.

"What is your name? Say it. Your name is Amy. Say it, or I will shock you until you do."

"AMY!" shouted Della. "Now leave me alone!"

"Again. What is your name?"

"AMY!"

"Excellent, Amy. I will leave you now to enjoy your hallucinations but return for further treatment later. Oh, and don't try to climb the wall again. The grate is locked, and you took a nasty fall. You need to be careful."

Della wasn't in a state of mind to fully comprehend what he had said. When the man opened the metal door to leave, Della saw different colors of light coming through the door. She couldn't tell if they were real or if she was hallucinating, but she was happy to be alone again. For the moment, Della no longer felt the pain from her nasty fall. She lay back on the cot in a mental daze, staring at the ceiling. The name Amy kept running through her mind. *Is my name Amy?*

Chapter 5

The following day, Detective Nichols was sitting at his desk when Shaw approached him. "Did you watch the news last night?"

"Yeah, Kristin had it on and was switching from channel to channel."

"I didn't like how they tried to tie yesterday's death to the death last November. We haven't confirmed that either one was a homicide."

"I didn't pick up on that."

"You said you watched the news."

"I only gave it half my attention. I was getting the kids ready for bed."

"How are your kids, by the way?"

"Doing well. Brian is playing soccer again this spring, and I think he is one of the better players. Lisa is more into dancing."

"Brian is your oldest, right?"

"Yes. He's nine, and Lisa is six."

"Those are wonderful ages. I have two nieces, a five-year-old and an eight-year-old."

"You have a sister?"

"No. I have a younger brother who is married with kids."

"Was he a star athlete as well?"

Caro smiled. "He played sports, but I was the one with more natural talent."

"Shaw!" shouted Greenberg in her raspy voice.

"Yes, ma'am."

"Patrol found Shane Phillips. They are bringing him in now. I want you and Nichols to interview him."

"Will do."

"I'm going to watch on the monitor," said Greenberg.

Shaw and Nichols quickly grabbed their notes and prepared for Phillips' arrival. When they were ready, a patrol officer escorted Phillips into the interview room.

The room was approximately 12 x 12 feet with a rectangular solid wood table sitting in the middle. The room was painted an off-white color with nothing on the walls. A video camera hung from the far corner, pointing at the chair reserved for those being interviewed. Phillips was as described by Ruby. He was tall and thin, with long brown stringy hair, and it was apparent he had not shaved for several days. Nichols noticed Phillips was not wearing a blue jacket. He only wore a long-sleeved beige knit shirt with three buttons at the top and dirty blue jeans. He did, however, have on a red baseball cap.

"Good morning, Mr. Phillips," said Shaw softly. "Do you mind if we call you Shane?"

Phillips nodded his head. "That's fine."

"Shane, do you know why you were brought here today?"

"The officer said something about an assault. I haven't assaulted anyone."

"Except Ruby Ryan, you mean?" interrupted Nichols.

Shaw gave Nichols a sideways glance and shook her head, trying to signal to him it was too early for that question.

Phillips laughed. "I haven't assaulted anyone."

"Let's back up a bit," suggested Shaw. "How long have you been in Boulder?"

"I don't know. A few weeks, I guess."

"And where are you from?"

"Nowhere."

Shaw sensed Phillips was not in the mood to be cooperative. "Where were you just before coming to Boulder?"

"Why?"

"We are investigating an assault and trying to determine if you are involved."

"I already told you. I didn't assault anyone."

"Then let's clear you from suspicion. Where were you before coming to Boulder?"

Phillips frowned and looked directly at Shaw. "I was in Denver."

"Thank you. And you came to Boulder a few weeks ago?"

"Yes."

"Was it four? Three?"

"I'm not sure."

"Okay. Can we say you've been in Boulder for at least two weeks?"

Again, Phillips looked at Shaw, then glanced at Nichols. "Why don't you let him ask me the questions?"

"Do you not like women?" continued Shaw.

Phillips raised both hands to his face and rubbed his unshaven cheeks. Shaw could tell he was uncomfortable with the question.

"Shane, do you have a problem with women?"

"No. I like women. But I don't like cops."

"Well, the sooner you answer our questions, the sooner you can get out of here. Can I continue?"

Phillips glared at Shaw but nodded his head yes. Nichols was enjoying the back and forth. He did not have Shaw's experience in interviewing suspects, especially those who might be suspected of homicide.

"Is it true to say that you've been in Boulder for at least two weeks?"

"Yeah."

"Good. Thank you."

"Where have you been staying?"

"I sleep in my van."

"And where is that?"

Phillips grunted. "Wherever I park it."

"Along Boulder Creek?"

"What difference does it make where I park it?"

"We're just gathering information. We would appreciate your co-operation."

Just then, there was a knock at the door. Nichols walked over to answer it. A records clerk had a file in her hand. "Here is the information you requested," she said.

"Thank you," said Nichols. He then walked back to his chair while looking at the file. Sitting down, he pulled out a booking photo dated three weeks earlier. Nichols handed the photo to Shaw.

"Hmmm," said Shaw. "It looks like you have been in Boulder for at least three weeks. This is a picture of you after being arrested for assault on the Pearl Street Mall." Shaw slid the picture toward Phillips. "That's you, right?"

Phillips stared at the picture but did not answer.

"It says here you were arrested for harassment and assault on another male. Do you want to tell me what happened?"

"The cops in Boulder suck. I was assaulted, yet they arrested me because I'm homeless! I've been harassed multiple times by your cops."

"I'm reading the report, and it says here you were begging for money, then harassing those who ignored you. A man named Walker told you to stop. You exchanged words, then you punched him in the face."

"He attacked me. Then I got arrested. The stupid cops don't believe anything a homeless person tells them."

"There are multiple witnesses listed here, Shane."

Phillips just shook his head.

"Tell me about Ruby Ryan," continued Shaw.

"Who?"

"The woman you wanted to have sex with three days ago."

"I want to have sex with a lot of women, Detective. You look like you could use a good time."

Shaw ignored the comment. "Just tell me about Ruby, the woman you met along the creek behind Boulder High School."

As Shaw talked, Nichols stared intently at Phillips.

"I don't know a Ruby," answered Phillips.

"She described you perfectly. Currently, all we have is her story to go by. Now is the time to tell us your version of what happened."

"Never met a Ruby. And what the hell are you staring at?" shouted Phillips as he looked at Nichols.

"I'm staring at a sexual predator."

"Shane," continued Shaw, "we have your DNA, and Ruby will identify you through this photograph. Now tell us what happened."

"I don't know a Ruby."

Shaw leaned over and whispered into Nichol's ear. "We'll be right back," said Shaw as they both got up and left the room. Phillips squirmed in his chair as he waited. After about five minutes, both detectives returned.

"Shane, why do you refuse to tell your side of what happened?" asked Nichols.

"Because nothing happened."

"I'll tell you what happened. You found Ruby near the creek behind Boulder High School. After some small talk, you asked her to have sex with you. When she refused, you forcefully grabbed her and pulled her close. You then molested her by grabbing one of her breasts. You only stopped when she continued to fight you off. This fits right in with the homicide we suspect you of."

"Homicide! What are you talking about?"

"You were going to do to Ruby what you did with the woman at Eben G. Fine Park."

"I don't know what you are talking about!"

"The dead woman found in the park. This is how you operate. If they don't have sex with you, you assault them. Only you went too far yesterday. That woman is now dead! Pretty slick of you to slice her wrists to make it look like a suicide."

Phillips was stunned to be accused of homicide. He was silent for several seconds. "I swear I did not kill anyone."

"Then you best be truthful about this incident with Ruby. Because things look grim for you right now."

For the first time, Phillips looked nervous. Shaw detected a quiver in his lower lip.

"Look, I never killed anyone."

"If you want us to believe that, you must be honest about Ruby."

"I don't know a Ruby, but I met a woman along the creek a few days ago. We had a friendly chat, and yes, I asked if she wanted to have sex. That's all."

"Was this along the creek behind Boulder High School?"

"Yes."

"When she told you she didn't want to have sex, what did you do?"

"Nothing. I said fine, and I left."

"But first, you pulled her close and tried to sweet-talk her into it, correct?"

"No."

"When she tried to push you off, you pulled her closer and grabbed her breast. We have your DNA."

"No, no, no. I did not grab that woman. I only asked her for sex."

"Well, you have a temper."

"Huh?"

"I'm talking about the fight on the mall."

"See, you are just like all of them. I told you, I was the one assaulted."

"All right. Can you describe Ruby to me?"

"I don't know. All I remember is that she had a red jacket and, I believe, dark hair."

"Okay, Shane. That's all I need."

"Am I under arrest?"

"No. Not right now," answered Shaw. "We still have some investigation to do, but we appreciate your help."

Shaw arranged for an officer to pick up Phillips and drive him to wherever he wanted to be dropped off. Shaw and Nichols then met with Commander Greenberg.

"I watched on the video feed," said Greenberg. "That was a good tag team approach. I didn't know you had his DNA."

"We don't," replied Shaw. "It was just a bluff. Once Ruby identifies him, we can collect his DNA to compare to the other cases."

"Well, but I don't consider him smart enough to make a homicide look like a suicide," replied Greenberg.

"I agree," responded Shaw. "He's too unsophisticated to pull something like that off. But at least we got him to admit he was with Ruby."

"Yeah, I liked how you scared him straight," laughed Greenberg. "You need to find Ruby to make a positive ID now, right?"

"Yes," answered Nichols. "Now that we know who he is, I will meet with Ruby and show her a photo line-up, and hopefully, she can pick him out."

"You can probably still get a warrant based on what you have, but I agree, getting a positive ID will tighten things up."

Nichols and Shaw left Greenberg's office and sat in the conference room to discuss the interview.

"Your idea of me going hard after him on the homicide really worked," admitted Nichols. "But you seemed disturbed when I jumped in early."

"Yeah, it's not a good technique to go after a suspect immediately during an interrogation," explained Shaw. "You need to ease into things to build up their willingness to talk. Once I had him talking, I thought it would be a good time for you to step in with the hard accusations. Sometimes, when you accuse someone of something much worse than they've done, they will confess to the less serious offense."

"Well, it worked," agreed Nichols.

At two o'clock that afternoon, Shaw called the Coroner, Dr. Ron Larsen, to check the status of his findings.

"I haven't received any DNA results back yet," advised Larsen. "I usually don't get them back before forty-eight hours."

"Any other findings you can divulge?"

"I've done more analysis of the tissue samples, and I'm almost certain our victim died from strangulation. It looks like this will be classified as a homicide. Cutting the wrists was an attempt to disguise the actual cause of death."

"But you can't yet call it a homicide?"

"I could, but I want one of my colleagues to check my findings first. I should have a solid answer by tomorrow."

"Thank you, Doctor."

There was not much more to be done other than paperwork. By four o'clock, Shaw was tired and ready to go home. "I'll see you tomorrow, Tom."

"You leaving?" asked Nichols.

"Yeah, I got here early, and it's been a long day."

"Any plans for tonight?"

"A hot bath and some wine are in my near future. How about you?"

"I need to leave by five-thirty to pick up Brian from soccer practice. And then from there, it's home for the night."

"See you tomorrow," said Shaw as she walked out.

Nichols finished his paperwork and was out by five-fifteen. He drove to Brian's school and arrived in time to see the last ten minutes of practice. The coach had the boys practicing passes to the forwards, breaking toward the goal. A goalie stood guard, trying to stop the shots from going in. Brian was in the group of players passing the ball. After practice, Brian excitedly told his father how much fun practice had been.

When they arrived home in the small town of Superior, just outside Boulder, Kristin told Tom she'd had a busy day and did not get home in time to fix dinner. Therefore, she told him they needed a night out. They all ended up at Superior's Tequila Mezchal, one of their favorite Mexican restaurants. As usual, six-year-old Lisa ordered chicken nuggets and fries. Nine-year-old Brian loved the street tacos, while Tom and Kristin each ordered a dinner of fajitas.

"Dad," asked Brian, "why do you and Mom always order fajitas?"

"It's because we both like them, Brian."

"I wouldn't want to give up eating tacos," said Brian.

"You might not eat the same things when you get older."

Brian didn't respond but went on to his next question. "Was that lady killed by someone?"

Nichols looked at his wife, Kristin.

"He heard you talking about it," Kristin said.

"We don't know what happened yet, Brian. That's what we're trying to find out." Nichols then changed the subject.

"I thought you looked terrific kicking that soccer ball today."

"Thanks. We practice that a lot."

The family continued to talk and enjoy their meal, and Brian didn't ask any further questions about the deceased woman. After dinner,

Nichols took his family to a local Dairy Queen for small blizzards. For a few hours, Nichols allowed himself to forget about work.

45

Chapter 6

It was Thursday afternoon when Shaw received the call from the coroner's office. It was Dr. Ron Larsen calling with the autopsy reports.

"Hello, Caro Shaw speaking."

"Caro, it's Ron Larsen. I've completed my work, and I'm ruling the death a homicide."

"Not really much of a surprise. Once you told me about the wrists being cut after death, I didn't know what else it could be."

"Yes, but I had to be sure. Further analysis of the tissue around the neck confirmed my suspicions. There was enough damage to conclude our victim was strangled to death. In my opinion, the victim was slowly strangled until she could no longer breathe."

"I get the sense there is more to it," replied Shaw.

"There is. Again, it's my opinion there was abuse prior to death. The victim was emaciated, and I found no food in her stomach or intestines. She had not eaten for days. There were also marks around her wrists, indicative of some type of restraint being used. She also had an unusual number of bruises about the body."

"That's interesting. It's almost as though you are describing torture."

"Certainly abuse. I doubt it was self-inflicted. I also found some trauma to the back of her head behind the lower right ear. I'm unsure what caused it, but it looked like she had been punctured or stabbed with a small, sharp object."

"Hmmm. That's weird. What about the DNA?"

"I won't have results from the state lab until next week."

"We have a murderer running around. You can't get the results sooner?"

Larsen sighed, "Caro, the state deals with multiple murders and sex assaults every week. We have to wait our turn."

"Yeah, but it sucks. What about vaginal trauma?"

"None."

"Huh? You believe she was physically abused but found no vaginal trauma?"

"I'll be honest. I was surprised as well. I found no evidence of sexual assault."

"Hmmm."

"One other thing. While scraping the nails for DNA, I found what appeared to be a tiny splinter of wood under one nail. I've arranged for the state lab to examine it to see if they can identify it."

"Do you believe it's connected?"

"I don't know. Let's wait and see if it can be identified."

"Thank you, Ron. Talk to you later."

"Okay, bye."

Shaw sat at her desk for several minutes, reviewing in her mind what Dr. Larsen had just told her. At the moment, she couldn't come up with a plausible explanation. She texted Nichols and Sergeant Martinez to meet her in the Commander's office in fifteen minutes.

It was 2:30 pm when all but Sergeant Martinez gathered in Commander Greenberg's office. Martinez was meeting with the DA's sexual assault team and thus unavailable for the meeting.

"What have you got, Caro?" asked Greenberg.

"We have ourselves a homicide. Larsen just gave me an update on his findings. He confirmed the cause of death was strangulation. And he believes our victim was abused or tortured in some manner prior to her death."

"Whoa," exclaimed Nichols. "She was tortured to death?"

"The cause of death was the strangulation, but in his opinion, our victim was also abused. He believes the strangulation was done slowly."

Nichols pursed his lips, looked down and shook his head.

"Damn. What about DNA?" asked Greenberg.

"He took samples but won't have results until next week."

"We need to get her photo out to the public," suggested Nichols.

"Where are we going to get a photo?" Greenberg asked.

"We have her body," said Nichols.

"The coroner will not release a photograph of the victim in that condition. The best we can do is get our sketch artist to do a drawing for release."

"I didn't know we had a sketch artist!" chirped Nichols.

"Not in the department. We have a local artist we use when we need a sketch."

"Oh. I guess I learn something new every day. We don't use sketch artists for auto thefts."

The commander just smiled.

"I'll arrange that," offered Shaw.

"You do that," agreed Greenberg. "I'll brief the chief on the news and then prepare an update to release to the press. This will create a windstorm of attention, but it may help us get some tips."

As they were walking back to their desks, Nichols turned to Shaw. "I feel stupid."

"Why?"

"I should have known about the sketch artist."

"This is your first homicide. I never used an artist before working homicides, either. Where were you earlier?"

"I was looking for Ruby. We need her to identify Phillips in my photo lineup. Once I get that, I can make the arrest."

"You can't find her?"

"No. I was on the mall and in Central Park asking our locals if they'd seen her. No one has, not even any of our officers. It's like she disappeared."

"She'll show up. There are many spots to hide out in this town. She might be afraid of Phillips finding her."

"Yeah, maybe."

Shaw arranged for the sketch artist to meet with the coroner on Friday morning. Commander Greenberg updated the chief and then released a new press release, formally announcing the case as a homicide. As expected, the press immediately began referencing the previous Boulder Creek death to the latest one.

Sgt. Martinez returned from the DA's office and approached Shaw. "I just heard our case is now a homicide."

"Yep, choked to death after being physically abused."

"I'm not surprised. Do we have any leads?"

"Not a single one."

"Maybe the publicity will bring in some tips."

"We can only hope."

It was 5:20 pm when Police Chief Ken Atkins knocked on the open door to Commander Greenberg's office. Upon the previous chief's retirement two years prior, Atkins was appointed the new police chief. Atkins had been with the department for thirty-eight years, working his way up the ladder through various positions and assignments. During his time as a homicide detective, Atkins worked on some of Boulder's most famous cases, including the JonBenet Ramsey case in 1996. Atkins was a large man standing at six-foot-three and a solid two-hundred-thirty pounds. A ring of white hair encircled his head from ear to ear, creating a visual contrast with the bare skin on top of the head. He wore gold wire-rimmed glasses that rested on his high cheekbones. Atkins had fair skin and a solid square jawline. His powerful baritone voice projected a commanding presence. Atkins often wore a dark business suit, a starched dress shirt, and a matching tie. On special occasions, he would wear his police uniform with three gold stars on each side of the collar. Today, he wore a gray suit, a light gray dress shirt, and a red and gray tie.

"Hello, Chief. Come on in," gestured Greenberg. "What's up?"

"Ever since the press release, our press officer has been getting calls about this homicide. Reporters want to know if this one is related to last fall's dead body."

"We don't know, Chief. The coroner is still unsure of the cause of death on last fall's victim."

"What do you believe?"

"If I had to say, I think they are related. Both victims were young, blond, good-looking women. And we found both along Boulder Creek, dressed in a similar manner."

"I agree," the Chief said. "We need to re-energize around that first case. Until we prove otherwise, investigate it as a murder."

"We will. But if the coroner continues to call it an unknown death, it will make things difficult."

"I'm going to meet with him tomorrow to discuss it."

"I like that."

"You have a good night, Stella. Get some rest."

"I will. Thank you, Chief."

Chapter 7

It was mid-morning on Friday, May 12th, when Chief Ken Atkins arrived at the coroner's office for their planned meeting. One of the lab technicians working in the office led the chief to a conference room and offered him some coffee. He politely refused. He only waited several minutes before Coroner Ron Larsen walked in. Larsen was wearing a white lab coat over a dark blue polo shirt.

"Good morning, Chief. How are you today?"

"I'm doing well, thank you. And you?"

"Busy, but otherwise good. I understand you want to talk about the dead woman, Aubrey Leaver, from last fall?"

"Yes. You've left the finding as undetermined, and I'd like you to look at it again. Because the circumstances between this week's victim and last fall's look very similar."

"You want me to rule it as a homicide?"

"I want you to re-examine the evidence. We haven't found two dead bodies along the creek within six months my entire career, let alone two young females with blond hair. Doesn't that raise your suspicion that these are connected?"

"I'm concerned as well," admitted Larsen. "And it's not just two bodies."

The chief looked at Larsen with concern in his eyes. "There's another one?"

"Not exactly the same, but do you remember the county finding a dead young woman up the Canyon near Boulder Falls about three years ago?"

"Now that you mention it, I do," replied Atkins.

"She wasn't found in the creek, but she was found about thirty yards up from the creek behind some boulders. We never identified the body, but she was a young woman, probably in her early twenties, a thin white female with light blond hair. Very similar to your victims. If I remember correctly, she was wearing a red T-shirt and white underwear. No shoes or socks. The autopsy showed she had been severely beaten. There were also signs of strangulation. I find that too coincidental."

"Agreed. Does the sheriff's office have any leads?"

"No. It is still an open homicide investigation, and as far as I know, they don't have any suspects."

"This is not good, Ron."

Larsen grunted. "You can say that again."

"And you said their victim had blond hair?"

"Uhh, yeah, she did."

"Just like these last two," sighed the chief. "We may have a serial killer on our hands."

"Sorry, Chief."

"Not your fault, Ron. Wasn't the Leaver gal from out of town?"

"Yes. She was from California. I will look again at the evidence from Central Park and get back to you. I have a better understanding of what to look for now."

"Thank you, Ron. I will get my detectives working on it as well and have them share notes with the sheriff's department."

That afternoon, Detective Shaw had finished an interview with a potential sexual assault victim and was walking toward her desk when Sergeant Martinez approached her.

"Caro! Where have you been?" Martinez shouted.

Shaw looked surprised. "Patrol brought in a sexual assault victim. I had to do the interview. What's up?"

"Well, the commander told me we need to get with the sheriff's department ASAP. The dead woman found up Boulder Canyon three years ago may be related to our case. We may have three homicides of young blond women over the last three years."

"Yeah, I remember that case. Wasn't the body found up the mountain?"

"It was in the mountains near the creek. The body was hidden in some boulders but only about thirty yards from the creek. It was just west of Boulder Falls."

"Who worked the case?"

"Detective Owen Gates is the lead detective."

"Okay, I'll get with him this afternoon."

"Thank you, Caro. Where's Tom?"

"He went out looking for Ruby again. He needs her to identify Phillips to get an arrest warrant."

"Okay, but this takes priority."

"I know," nodded Shaw.

Shaw was frustrated. She had to complete her report on the interview she just finished, didn't know where Nichols was, and now had to arrange a meeting with Sheriff's Detective Owen Gates.

Shaw picked up the phone and called the sheriff's office. "Is Detective Gates in today?" asked Shaw.

"I'm sorry, he's off for the day. He will be back in on Monday."

"Will you please tell Owen that Detective Shaw called and needs to talk to him as soon as possible?"

"I will leave him a message."

"Thank you."

Shaw then attempted to call Nichols but got no answer. *Where is he?*

Shaw liked Nichols but believed he could be somewhat scatter-brained. He always seemed to juggle too many things at one time. Shaw had just finished her report when the phone rang.

"This is Detective Shaw."

"Caro, it's Owen. I got a message you needed to talk to me."

"Thanks for calling back, Owen. We believe our recent homicide may be related to yours from three years ago. And we might have one from last fall that is connected."

"I'd like to tell you we have a suspect, but we don't," responded Gates.

"Yeah, I know that. But we need to meet right away to compare notes."

"Do you have a suspect?"

"No."

"Then this can wait until Monday. I already have plans for this weekend."

"This is a big deal, Owen. Once the press makes the connection, they'll believe we have a serial killer on the loose."

"Sorry, Caro. Our case is three years old, and I'm busy all weekend. I'll be there if you want to come to the sheriff's office on Monday around ten."

Shaw couldn't believe it. This case could involve a serial killer and draw national attention. Shaw reluctantly agreed to meet with Owen on Monday. "Okay, see you Monday."

Shaw then tried calling Nichols again. No answer. "Damn! Where is he?" she shouted.

Sergeant Martinez walked over and asked Shaw if everything was okay.

"It's fine, Sergeant. We're going to meet Gates on Monday morning."

"Why not today?"

"He's too busy. Monday was the earliest he would meet."

Martinez frowned. "Hmmm. Okay, but we will need an update early on Monday afternoon."

"Yes, sir."

Several minutes later, Shaw's phone rang. It was Nichols calling.

"Where have you been? I've been trying to call you," said Shaw with a hint of anger.

"I've been looking for Ruby. I need to get her to ID Phillips."

"Why didn't you answer your phone?"

"Hang on."

Shaw waited for several seconds.

"Oh, I had my ringer turned off. Sorry. What's up?"

"Our case is getting bigger. The coroner and chief now believe the murder in the county three years ago is related to ours. Not only that, the coroner is taking a second look at the dead woman from last fall."

"Oh, wow."

"Now get in here, and we can review the case from last fall."

"On my way."

While waiting, Shaw pulled the case file to refresh her memory. The victim from the previous September was twenty-three-year-old Aubrey Leaver, a white female, five-foot-four, extremely thin, with long blond hair. The body had been unidentified for several weeks until an artist's sketch was released to the national press. Aubrey's mother, Emily Leaver of Walnut Creek, California, saw the story on FOX News and recognized the sketch as her missing daughter. According to Emily, Aubrey was living a transient lifestyle. Not one where she lived on the street but one where she would go to various cities and work and live for a short time. She wanted to experience different lifestyles before settling down. Three months before her body was found, Aubrey stopped calling. Emily could not reach her daughter, and after several weeks, she reported her daughter as missing to the Walnut Creek, California,

Police Department, where Aubrey lived prior to her travels. Boulder was the last place Aubrey visited before she died. According to Emily, Aubrey had only been in Boulder for a few weeks when she lost contact with her. The last she knew, Aubrey had found a job as a waitress in some bar in Boulder.

"I'm here," announced Nichols as he walked over and pulled up a chair next to Shaw, bumping her arm as he did so.

"Ouch!" moaned Shaw.

"Sorry," said Nichols. "What have you got?"

"Here is the case file on Aubrey Leaver. She had only been in Boulder for a few weeks when she went missing. What is strange is that according to Mom, Aubrey had been missing for at least three months before we found her body."

"Maybe she hooked up with some guy," suggested Nichols.

"According to the report, Aubrey and Mom talked often. I doubt she would stop calling her mom."

"You think she was dead for three months?"

Shaw chuckled. "No, she had only been deceased ten to sixteen hours when we found her."

"What then?"

Shaw thought for a moment. "Drugs, maybe. Or maybe she was held captive somewhere. We won't know until we unravel the mystery."

Nichols nodded. "Yeah."

Chapter 8

Della looked at the front of her dirty T-shirt. It was a Bolder Boulder shirt from a 10k race run several years prior. The Bolder Boulder is an annual community foot race run every Memorial weekend that draws thousands of people. Not being from Colorado, Della did not know what the Bolder Boulder was. *What does Bolder Boulder mean?* she thought to herself. Her blue cotton shorts fit loosely around her waist, held up by a cotton rope. Della hoped someone would soon bring her a change of clothing. She knew there were at least two men involved in her imprisonment. Della could often hear them talking together above the grate. One time, she even got a glimpse of the second man when he looked into the room from above. He looked to be a larger man. She couldn't see his face as he also wore a mask. Whenever Della heard them talking, she focused on the voices, trying to memorize them.

Della's thoughts were interrupted by the two voices above. It sounded like they were arguing. She listened intently. The one who seemed in charge (the one she thought was larger) was giving directions to the other man. She strained to hear what was being said. Della couldn't make out everything, but it sounded like the larger man wanted the other one to speed up the process. *What process are they talking about?* The conversation ended when the larger man shouted, "You only have four weeks left. Get it done or get rid of her."

"Get rid of her?" Della whispered to herself. *What does that mean?* Della's worst fears took over her thoughts. *What does he have to get done?* Della heard the door opening and jumped off the cot to a standing position. When it fully opened, Della saw it was the smaller man wearing the same beige derby-style shoes. She gazed into his dark brown eyes.

"Don't look at me like that!" the man barked. "Get in the chair!"

"No, please," begged Della.

"Amy, get in the chair."

"No, I'm not letting you strap me down again."

The man reached into his right pocket, pulling out his taser.

"Please," begged Della. "Just tell me what you want."

Della looked into the man's eyes. They were very dark and cold-looking. It gave her chills.

"Where are you from?" he asked.

"Huh? I've already told you. You won't believe me."

"Where?"

"Erie, Pennsylvania."

"No, you are from Denver, Amy. We need to get your false memories removed from your head."

"Okay! I'm from Denver, and my name is Amy."

"Now I know you are faking it. Get into the chair. Now."

The man stepped toward Della with his taser in his right hand. Della backed up and sat in the chair.

"Now fasten the straps around your ankles," he said.

"Please, no. Just tell me what you want."

The man stepped forward and jammed the taser into her left thigh. Della let out a loud scream. "Now fasten the straps!" he shouted.

Della leaned over and strapped her ankles against the legs of the wooden chair.

"Now, put your arms on the armrests."

Tears ran down Della's cheeks as she did as instructed. The man stepped forward and strapped her arms to the chair. He cinched on the leather straps, creating pressure and pain in her wrists. Della could feel some numbness settling into her hands.

"You are mentally ill, Amy. That is why you are here. Once you fully submit to the truth, you will be free."

The man stepped behind Della. He took a long piece of blue cloth out of his back pocket. He folded the fabric into a strap approximately two inches wide. He then lowered the cloth in front of Della's face and pulled it around her neck.

"What are you doing?" cried Della.

The cloth was placed on the front of Della's neck and then pulled tightly, yanking her head back against the wooden headboard. He bound the cloth tightly around her neck, preventing her from moving and making it difficult to breathe or talk.

The man then pulled several long stainless-steel needles from his white lab coat pocket. The light from the 60-watt bulb glistened off the needles. The needles were approximately six inches long, with a sharp point on one end and an end cap on the other. It looked like a very long thumb tack.

"This will be painful, Amy, but we must increase your therapy. You have been more difficult than I expected."

Della could feel her heart rate accelerating, pounding inside her chest while her breathing became rapid and shallow. Beads of sweat formed on her forehead in anticipation of what was to come. Her body shook uncontrollably, and she found it difficult to swallow.

The man placed his left hand on top of Della's head and clenched it firmly. In the other hand, he held one of the stainless-steel needles. He bent her head slightly forward and to the left. With his right hand, he placed the needle against the skin of Della's head, just behind her right ear lobe.

"I need to find the space behind your ear to insert this needle," he told her. "This will enable me to disrupt your false memories."

Della's eyes grew wide in fear as she tried to escape from her restraints. It was no use. She was strapped tightly to the chair. The tight cloth around her neck made it challenging to scream, but she made as much noise as possible. Della felt excruciating pain as the man pushed the needle through the skin. She could feel him probing with the needle, looking for a gap in the skull. She continued to wail as he probed. Several seconds later, Della felt an explosive pain shoot through her head and down her spine. It was the last thing she remembered.

Four hours later, Della awoke to the blaring sound of "Learn to Fly" by the Foo Fighters. As before, the sound was ear-splitting, so loud it was difficult to understand the words. Della was lying flat on her back on the thin mattress cot. The back of her head was throbbing in pain, and her vision was blurry. Della's underwear and shorts were soaked in liquid. She attempted to pull herself to a sitting position, but the pain in her neck forced her to lie back down. She reached down with her left hand to feel her wet pants. Della brought her hand back up to smell it. Yep, she had urinated in her pants.

Della was confused and unaware of her surroundings. *What is wrong with me?* The pulsating music sent shock waves through her aching head and neck. Della raised her arms to cover her ears and felt a sharp pain emanating from the right side of her neck down through the back of her shoulder. She struggled through the pain to get her right ear covered. Della closed her eyes and waited for the music to stop. Unfortunately, the music continued for three more hours.

By the time the music stopped, Della was totally exhausted, with a throbbing headache, neck ache, and general weakness. Every time she tried to turn her head, the pain from behind her right ear caused her to stop. She felt hopeless as she lay in bed. *How long have I been lying here?* After what seemed like another hour, the metal door creaked open.

"Good morning," said the man wearing the beige suede shoes and white hoodie. Della did not respond.

"Sit up."

It was still too painful for Della to move.

"I said sit up."

"I can't," muttered Della.

"Sure you can," said the man as he grabbed Della by her shoulders and pulled her into a sitting position. Della screamed out in pain.

"Stop! You're hurting me."

"You're fine. But I need to know, what is your name?"

Della sat on the edge of the bed with her head hanging forward and toward her right shoulder. It helped lessen the pain. Della thought for a moment. "Amy."

"Excellent. We are making progress. And where are you from?"

Della thought again, then said, "Denver."

"And where are your parents?"

"They are both dead," responded Della with dry emotion.

"Excellent, Amy. You are on your way to being free from your psychological demons."

"What did you do to my neck?" asked Della.

"We did therapeutic acupuncture to help restore your memory. Stimulating the nerves closest to the brain often resets the memory."

"It hurts like hell," mumbled Della. "I can't even lift my head. Where am I?"

"This is a psychological therapy facility."

"How did I get here?"

"You were in a nightclub having a psychological meltdown. The police took you into custody on a forty-eight-hour hold and eventually placed you in our care for treatment."

"I don't remember any of that."

"Of course, you don't. You were in crisis."

"What happened to the other woman?" asked Della.

"What other woman?"

"I heard another woman screaming. It was more than once."

"That was all in your head, Amy. You are the only one here."

Della wasn't going to argue. She knew challenging him would only lead to more abuse. Her ears were still ringing from the loud music.

"Why the loud music? It hurts my ears and gives me headaches."

"Just part of the therapy."

Della shook her head. "You're going to kill me."

"Why do you say that?"

Della raised her voice. "Because you have me locked up like an animal! You barely feed me, make me pee myself, and torture me. What else am I supposed to think?"

Della could see out of the corner of her eye that the man was displeased by her response.

Several seconds passed before he said, "Get back in the chair."

"No, please. I'm sorry. I'll do whatever you want."

"I thought we were beyond this stage, Amy. Get back in the chair before I tase you."

Della cried. The man grabbed her by the shoulders and dragged her to the chair. Della was too weak to resist. He sat her in the chair in a slumped position, then strapped her legs and arms to the wooden supports.

"Please, no," begged Della.

He then pulled out the stainless-steel needles. Della closed her eyes in anticipation of more excruciating pain. She could feel him probing with the tip of a needle near the inside of her right kneecap. It felt like tiny pinpricks as he looked for a suitable insertion point. Della's leg flinched with each touch of the needle. Then, without further warning, she could feel an immediate flash of pain shoot through her knee and up the inside of her right leg. Della let out a blood-curdling scream. He continued to apply pressure, pushing the needle deeply into the muscle, tendons and nerves under her kneecap. Della continued to scream until she once again blacked out.

The next time Della opened her eyes, she was back on the cot. Only this time, there was silence, and the room was pitch black. Della was now dealing with pain in her neck and right knee. She reached down to feel her knee, ensuring she still had a right leg. She could feel the swelling around her knee. Della wanted to cry but was drained of emotion, and dehydration made it difficult to create tears. She drifted off into thoughts of her mother. *I'm so sorry I ran away, Mom. I take back all the horrible things I said to you. I need you now. Please come find me.*

Chapter 9

Monday morning, May 15th

Nichols walked into the detective bureau carrying a box of donuts. "Good morning, everyone," he announced. "I picked up donuts." He set the box on the coffee counter. Several detectives immediately rose from their desks to get a donut.

When Nichols arrived at his desk with a chocolate-covered, cream-filled Long John, Shaw gave him a look of disgust. "That is not a healthy breakfast."

"It's Monday, Caro. Someone usually brings in donuts to start the week. It was my turn. Those who don't eat leave more for everyone else."

Shaw shook her head. "We meet with Detective Gates this morning at ten."

"I thought you were meeting with him?"

"I set it up, but we should both be there."

"All right, I'll look for Ruby this afternoon."

"You still haven't found her?"

"No. I'm worried about her. I hope Phillips didn't do something to her."

"No one on patrol has seen her?"

"Not that I know of."

"The commander wants to meet with us at eight-thirty."

"Okay, I'll be there."

At 8:30 am, Shaw, Nichols, and Sgt. Martinez met with Commander Greenberg in her office. Greenberg looked at Nichols and brushed two fingers across her upper right lip.

"What?" asked Nichols.

"I think you have chocolate on your upper lip," responded Greenberg.

"Oh," said Nichols as he wiped off the chocolate with his fingers. "Sorry."

"This will be short," said the commander. "I'm not aware of any new information from the weekend. Any of you?"

"No," answered Shaw. Martinez and Nichols simply shook their heads no.

"All right then," continued the commander. "You are meeting with Sheriff's Detective Owen Gates at ten. Is that correct?"

Shaw answered, "Yes," while Nichols shook his head.

"Plan to give me an update today at two o'clock. I want to know if these cases are related. Then I will meet with the chief."

"Got it," said Shaw.

"Okay, see you then," said the commander as she waved them out the door.

Shaw and Nichols arrived at the sheriff's department at 9:55 am. The receptionist asked them to wait in the lobby for Detective Gates. After ten minutes, Owen Gates walked into the lobby to greet them.

"Good morning. How's everyone doing today?" Gates asked.

"Well. Thank you," responded Shaw.

"I've got my file here," said Gates as he patted a brown accordion-type file approximately four inches thick tucked under his arm. "Let's use the conference room."

Fifty-two-year-old Gates was short and stocky with thinning dark hair. A bald circle sat at the back of his head. He had a tanned complexion and a rounded jaw. His eyes were dark, and a thick mustache draped over his upper lip. Gates wore a light blue button-down shirt, red tie, and blue jeans over squared-off cowboy boots. He looked half detective and half rancher. His voice was deep and raspy, making him sound gruffer than he really was.

Shaw and Nichols followed Gates through a security door, down a fifty-foot hallway, then right into a second hallway. The conference room was twenty feet further on the left. The room was rectangular, with light beige walls and fluorescent lighting across the ceiling. A large oval-shaped gray-speckled formica table filled the room. Ten black, fake leather swivel chairs were evenly arranged around the table.

"Take a seat wherever," said Gates.

They all settled in seats adjacent to each other at the near end of the table.

Gates started the discussion. "So, I understand you have a case similar to ours?"

"We have two cases. One from last September and one from last week," explained Shaw. "From what we know about your three-year-old case, we believe they may be related."

"From what you've told me and what I've seen on the news, you may be right," agreed Gates.

"What can you tell us about your case?" asked Shaw.

"Well, let's see. It's labeled as a Jane Doe case. We've not been able to identify the body. The woman was a young white female, college age, about five-foot-eight, with long blond hair. She was skinny. Here are some photos of the crime scene. As you can see, she had a red T-shirt on and white underwear. No shoes or socks."

Shaw and Nichols studied the photos. The body had been found behind two large boulders high along the creek bed. Her arms and legs were tucked under the body as though someone intentionally hid the body behind the boulders. Close-up photos revealed bruising on the victim's arms and legs.

"Where exactly is this?" asked Shaw.

"A little west of Boulder Falls, about ten miles into the canyon."

"When was the body found?"

Gates looked at his report. "June thirteenth, three years ago."

"Who found the body?"

"A young kid about twelve years old. He and his family were enjoying a day of picnicking in the mountains along the creek. He was doing some rock climbing when he stumbled upon it."

"Must have been a real shock for the kid," said Nichols.

"How long had the body been there?" asked Shaw.

"The coroner estimated around seventy-two hours."

"Any cuts on the wrists?".

"No."

"What was the cause of death?"

"According to the coroner's report, she was strangled to death. He also said her body was in poor shape. She had been beaten and stabbed with a sharp object."

"Stabbed?" asked Shaw.

"Not with a knife, but with something similar to a needle. He found several puncture wounds on the body."

"Where?"

"Let me look." Gates flipped through several pages of the coroner's report. "Here it is. He found small puncture wounds on the right knee and lower back area. Here are the photos."

Shaw and Nichols looked them over. "Damn, whoever is killing these women must be a monster," suggested Nichols.

"Agreed," nodded Gates.

"What about sexual assault?" asked Shaw.

"No evidence of it."

"Did you send bulletins out across the country?"

Gates frowned. "Of course. We had a few inquiries from other departments with missing person cases, but nothing panned out."

"What about DNA?"

"Her DNA is not in the database. Some foreign DNA was found under the fingernails, but nothing came back as a match."

"Have you found anyone who remembered seeing this woman around town?"

"Nothing local. A few people have called thinking they knew her, but when we interviewed them, it never panned out."

"No suspects at all?"

"We interviewed locals, transients, sex offenders, checked bars, everything. We're no closer to solving this than we were three years ago. We even went into Nederland to interview known druggies and hippies living there. Nothing."

Shaw shook her head. "We have a serial killer somewhere in Boulder."

"I don't think you can say that," said Gates.

"You don't think three bodies in three years qualify?"

"Qualifies as a serial killer, but not necessarily in Boulder. Boulder may just be the dumping ground for the bodies. Whoever is doing this is very smart. He leaves very little evidence behind. For all we know, it could be someone from Longmont, Fort Collins, Denver, who knows?"

"You're right," agreed Shaw. "We can't assume anything. Thank you for meeting with us. Let's keep sharing information as we get it."

"Will do. Oh, and sorry I couldn't meet over the weekend."

"Don't worry about it. Thanks again."

As they were driving back to the police department, Nichols expressed concern over the complexity of the case. "This is a tough case for my first homicide."

"Well, you've got me and others to lean on. Just investigate as you would any other case. Be conscious of everything and don't make assumptions like I did."

"What assumption did you make?"

"I assumed we had a serial killer in Boulder. Owen corrected me. We don't know that the killings are taking place in Boulder."

Nichols nodded in agreement. "I suppose you're right."

Back at the police department, Shaw and Nichols met with Greenberg and Martinez.

"What did you find out?" asked Greenberg.

"It's obvious to me we have a serial killer out there somewhere," stated Shaw. "All three cases are very similar, and all three victims are young blond females."

The room was silent for several seconds. Greenberg broke the silence. "I was afraid of that. This won't play out well for Boulder, and it will create even more fear in the community."

"Especially for young blond women," added Shaw.

"I'll have our chief talk to Sheriff Higgins about making this a joint investigation," said Greenberg. "We'll need all hands on deck for this one. Luca, be sure all our detectives know they will assist whenever needed."

"Will do," replied Martinez.

"Will you be issuing anything to the media?" asked Shaw.

"When I talk to the chief, I'll see what he wants to do."

Shaw nodded, "Okay, thanks."

After the meeting, Shaw sat alone at her desk, trying to make sense of everything she had learned. She theorized what significance the puncture wounds had. She picked up her phone and called Dr. Larsen.

"Ron Larsen," he answered.

"Hey Ron, it's Caro at the PD. I have a question about the puncture wounds you've found on our victims."

"What is it?"

"On our recent victim, you found a puncture wound behind the right ear, and on the victim from three years ago, you found two puncture wounds, one on a knee and one on the lower back."

"Sounds right."

"What about Aubrey Leaver from last fall? Did you find any such wounds on her?"

"I'm about to review that autopsy for your chief right now, and I'm going back and looking at all the photos from all three victims. The types of wounds I'm talking about are not always obvious, especially given the condition of the bodies. Once I'm done with my reviews, I'll give you an update."

"That would be appreciated. Thank you, Ron."

An hour and a half later, Shaw received a call from Commander Greenberg. "The chief just informed me Larsen has now classified Aubrey Leaver's death a homicide. The chief believes we need to go public with what we know. A press conference is being arranged for four o'clock this afternoon. This will allow the media to have the information before the five o'clock news hour."

"Do you want me there?" asked Shaw.

"Yes. If any question comes up we don't have an answer for, we'll defer to you."

"Okay."

"We will hold it in the training room. Be there by three-thirty."

"Got it."

Shaw immediately notified Nichols.

"Which media do you think will be there?" asked Nichols.

"Once the word goes out that we are holding a press conference involving three related homicides, all the local media outlets will come. TV, radio, and newspaper reporters will be there."

"Will FOX and CNN be there?"

"I doubt it. This story hasn't gotten that type of attention yet. But, once the story gets out there, they might get interested. Sometimes it depends on what else is happening nationally."

Nichols sat silent as Shaw observed him take a deep breath while looking toward the floor.

"Are you okay?"

Nichols looked up. "Uh, yeah, I'm fine. It just seems a little overwhelming right now. I've never been involved in anything this big."

"Look, just do things the way you would always do them. Follow procedures and protocols. Don't allow the attention to change the way you do things. Chief Atkins gave me that advice. He survived more than one media circus during his time working on homicides. And then, of course, he had to deal with the supermarket shooting as the police chief."

"Yeah, that had to be tough," Nichols said.

"It was."

"I don't get it," said Nichols. "I understand it's news, but the media can sometimes be overwhelming."

"People are fascinated by unsolved or unusual cases. We see renewed stories all the time on old cases. Even when cases have been solved, you still see stories on whether the right person was convicted. I just watched a story a few weeks ago on the Lindbergh kidnapping. Some people still believe Bruno Hauptmann was innocent."

"You're right. I see stories like that as well. Should I be at the press conference?"

"Hell, yeah. It will be a good learning experience for when you have to do your own press conference."

Nichols laughed. "Not happening."

BPD PRESS CONFERENCE – MONDAY, MAY 15TH

By 3:55 pm, the press had arrived and set up in the training room. Shaw estimated that at least 12 news outlets were represented from Boulder, Denver, and Longmont. She recognized reporters from four Denver TV stations, the Boulder Daily Camera and the Longmont Times-Call. The others she didn't recognize. She counted six TV cameras set up in a semi-circle and pointed toward the raised podium at the front of the room. Bright lights were pointed at the stage from multiple angles. A buzz of conversation filled the room. On the stage, seated behind the podium, were the police chief, the county sheriff, and Commander Greenberg. Shaw and Nichols sat together a few rows behind the cameras. Shaw noticed Detective Gates seated with two other sheriff detectives on the other side of the room. Sgt. Martinez walked in just as the press conference started and sat behind Shaw.

Sheriff Alex Higgins was the first to speak. Sheriff Higgins had been sheriff of Boulder County for over eight years. He was sixty-two years old, of average height, around five-foot-ten, and had thinning gray hair and hazel eyes. He was not significantly overweight but had a pot belly extending beyond his belt. Higgins almost always wore his sheriff's uniform, including a brown cowboy hat. Today, he was not wearing the hat.

The sheriff opened the press conference by discussing the unidentified dead woman, Jane Doe, found in Boulder Canyon three years prior. He briefly described what efforts had been made to identify the woman and identify a suspect. A sketch and description of the woman were handed out to everyone at the press conference, and he asked for the public's help in solving the case. He pointed out that the sheriff's case was likely related to the two most recent cases in Boulder. He then introduced Boulder Police Chief Ken Atkins.

Chief Atkins was also wearing his police uniform. His six-foot-three frame towered over the sheriff. Atkins was wearing his police hat, and Shaw believed he looked impressive and had a command presence. The chief summarized the details of the two cases in Boulder. He also expressed his belief that all three cases were related. As the chief spoke, flyers with sketch drawings of both women were handed out by the department's press information officer. Chief Atkins then introduced Detective Commander Stella Greenberg.

Greenberg wore a dark woman's business suit with a beige blouse underneath. The blouse was buttoned up, covering her gold pendant necklace. Shaw noticed a fresh look to Greenberg's hair. It looked as though the commander had styled her hair for the occasion. Greenberg took her time in going over some details of all three cases, highlighting the similarities. Without being too graphic, Greenberg described some of the injuries sustained by all three victims. She ended by asking for the public's help in identifying the unknown victims and in finding the perpetrator. She then opened it up for questions.

Reporter #1: "Commander, why has it taken so long to realize these cases were related?"

"First, there was a significant time lapse between the first homicide in the county and the second homicide in Boulder. Second, the cause of death in our first case six months ago was not determined until recently."

Reporter #1 Again: "What took so long to determine Aubrey Leaver's death was a homicide? Based on what has been shared today, it seems obvious to me."

"It may seem obvious now, but not all the injuries were initially obvious. Once we had a second body found, we went back and reviewed the first case."

Reporter #2: "Commander, these victims have been found in public places, yet you have no witnesses. Dumping a body in the middle of Boulder can't be easy. How do you explain that?"

"First, the areas where the bodies have been found are hidden by trees and natural vegetation. We believe they were most likely transported and placed there during the early morning hours, a time when very few people would be walking along the creek."

Reporter #3: "Does Boulder have the resources to work on a case like this?"

"Yes, we do. However, we are not working on this case alone. As the chief and sheriff emphasized, our departments are working together. Second, we have engaged with the Colorado Bureau of Investigation to assist us in analyzing the evidence."

Reporter #4: "Why haven't you used DNA to identify the other two women?"

Greenberg chuckled. "It's not that simple. We've tried, but there have been no matches to the national or state databases."

Reporter #4 Again: "What about suspect DNA?"

"We only have foreign DNA from one victim. It does not match DNA in any of the databases. And let me stress, we don't know if the DNA even belongs to the perpetrator."

Reporter #5: "What do Boulder residents need to do to protect themselves from some monster roaming the streets?"

"First, we don't know these homicides are occurring in Boulder. Thus far, no one in this community has come forward and identified any of the victims. It is possible they are being murdered somewhere else and then brought to Boulder. It is not uncommon for killers to dispose of bodies in faraway locations. I would ask our community members to be watchful for anything suspicious and, as always, be aware of your surroundings. For young women, know whom you are going home with."

Reporter #5 Again: "That doesn't sound very reassuring."

"It's not. That's why we need help in finding the perpetrator."

Reporter #6: "How did you identify Aubrey Leaver?"

"Aubrey had been reported missing in California by her mother. When we released the sketch of Aubrey, her mother believed it looked like her daughter. She contacted us, and we confirmed the victim was Aubrey Leaver through DNA. We are hopeful the other two victims will also be recognized from their sketches."

Reporter #6 Again: "Do you think the other victims are from out of state?"

"As I mentioned earlier, given that no one has reported them missing in Boulder or come forward, we believe none of the victims are from Boulder, and probably not even from our county."

Reporter #7: "Other than being strangled and bruised, you have not been very descriptive of other injuries. There are rumors of torture. Can you address that?"

Shaw leaned over to Nichols. "Where did he hear that?" she whispered.

Nichols looked at her, raised his eyebrows and shrugged his shoulders. "Beats me."

Greenberg continued. "We don't have all the information. Some of what you hear is speculation. We will continue to investigate and provide any relevant information as we get it."

Chief Atkins stepped to the podium. "I'm sorry, but that's all we have for now. Thank you for coming. We will keep you as informed as we can without compromising our investigation. We appreciate your help."

Back in the office, Commander Greenberg asked, "How do you think it went?"

"Everyone did a great job," offered Martinez. "The presentation was professional and informative."

"I agree," said Shaw. "I thought you answered the questions in a straightforward manner. How do you think they got the information on the possibility of torture?"

"Too many people know between us and the sheriff's department," Greenberg answered. "Talk spreads quickly, and don't be surprised if other information gets leaked."

Greenberg then looked directly at Shaw. "Now, I need you and Tom to book a flight to California to interview Aubrey's mother. We need to know everything about Aubrey's last few months."

That night, over dinner, Nichols told Kristin he needed to fly to California on Wednesday to meet with Aubrey Leaver's mother.

"Tom, did you forget Brian has a soccer game on Wednesday?"

"No, but we need to get this interview done. You know how important this case is."

"I suppose. I just wish you could have arranged to go on Thursday."

"Greenberg wanted us to leave tomorrow. We couldn't get a decent flight, so Wednesday was the best we could do. I'll make his next game."

Kristin was silent for a moment. "What do you think is happening to these women?"

"I'm not sure. The coroner believes they may have been held hostage for some time before being murdered. But I find it odd that, besides Aubrey's mother, we haven't gotten any calls from people who knew the victims."

"Were they transients or runaways?" asked Kristin.

"Aubrey wasn't. We don't know about the other two."

"Well," sighed Kristin, "I understand why you have to go."

With a glass of cabernet in her hand, Shaw sat on the patio of her Longmont townhome, watching the sunset over the Colorado Rockies. Her thoughts slowly drifted from the details of each homicide to that of her ex-husband, Dan Milton. She hadn't talked to Dan in months and wondered how he was doing. Shaw grabbed her cell phone and dialed his number.

"Hello, Caro," answered Milton. "What's up?"

"Nothing much. I was just relaxing on the patio and wondered how you were doing."

"I'm doing well, thank you. In fact, I sold a house this past weekend for eight-hundred-thirty-thousand dollars."

"Good for you! I knew you would make a great realtor."

"I had no experience at all. How would you know that?"

"You have the personality for it, Dan. You've always been a people person. Kind of the opposite of me."

"Why do you say that? I always thought you were friendly enough."

"You were always our social director with friends and family. Now, I hardly go out with anyone. I do talk to my mom at least once a week."

Milton chuckled. "Are you still playing tennis?"

"When I can on weekends. Although I think my tennis time will be limited for a while."

"The homicides?" asked Milton.

"Yep. I think it will occupy most of my time."

"Well, if anyone can solve it, you can."

Shaw laughed. "I'm going to need a lot of help on this one. Have you kept up on it?"

"Some. I try not to get too engaged in police drama these days. It still brings back terrible memories."

"Yeah, I get it. I just wanted to check in with you."

"I'm glad you did. Let's get together for a drink when you have more time."

There was a pause. "Dan, I know our divorce was mostly my fault. I just get so involved in my work..."

"Stop," interrupted Milton. "It was both of us. I got just as involved in my work. It's tough being married to a police officer. It's double tough when both are police officers."

"I suppose," replied Shaw.

"I know you'll do everything possible to solve these murders, Caro. Just leave some time for yourself."

"Okay, I will. Have a good night, Dan."

Chapter 10

Shaw and Nichols landed at Oakland International Airport at 10:20 am. They rented a blue Ford Explorer from Hertz Rental Cars. Shaw navigated her way through the airport maze to the interstate that would take them to Walnut Creek. It was about an hour's drive from Oakland to the home of Emily Leaver.

Walnut Creek is in Contra Costa County, approximately 20 miles east of Oakland, CA. It lies west of the slopes of Mount Diablo with plenty of surrounding open space. In fact, it has more open space per capita than any other California city. Walnut Creek is a mix of rural and urban. Walnut Creek, for which the town is named, runs through downtown and has been routed into tunnels underneath the city. People are attracted to the downtown for its charming, bustling atmosphere. Temperatures in Walnut Creek typically range from 56 to 86 degrees, with lots of sunshine.

Emily Leaver lived in a contemporary two-bedroom condo nestled in the heart of Walnut Creek. Shaw and Nichols arrived at 11:45 am. Emily was a 52-year-old white female of average build and height. Her hair was dishwater blond, styled in a layered bob cut that hung just below her ears. Her skin appeared slightly tanned, and she wore a pastel green blouse and beige shorts. Emily welcomed the detectives into her home.

"May I get you something to drink?" asked Emily.

"A glass of water would be great," answered Nichols.

"How about you?" asked Emily as she looked at Shaw.

"Sure, I'll take a glass of water. Thank you."

The condo had an open-concept design that seamlessly combined the dining room, living room, and kitchen. The walls were painted in a neutral beige with white trim. A large living room window provided ample natural lighting. Shaw and Nichols sat on a three-cushioned fabric couch across from Emily, seated in a matching fabric chair.

"Thank you so much for coming to see me," said Emily. "I'm happy you are investigating my daughter's murder."

"We are both sorry for your daughter's death, Ms. Leaver." Shaw gently said.

"Thank you."

Shaw continued. "We know you talked to one of our detectives last fall before her death was ruled a homicide."

"Yes, but I knew she hadn't committed suicide."

"How did you know that?"

"Aubrey was a well-adjusted young woman. She had no reason to commit suicide. I talked to her two to three times a week while she was traveling. She was far from depressed."

"How long had Aubrey been living her transient lifestyle?"

"Probably about twenty months. She had been planning this for some time. Saved her money for the trip and then took odd jobs as she traveled. She said it was her big adventure before settling down."

"Do you know what city she visited before coming to Boulder?" asked Shaw.

"The last place she stayed for any length of time was Santa Fe. She really liked the lifestyle there. Similar in some ways to Boulder."

"How long was she there?"

"She stayed for about three months. She took a waitress job, as those are always easy to find. Everyone needs more help these days."

Nichols took notes as Emily talked.

Shaw continued. "Did Aubrey date anyone in Santa Fe?"

"She met a guy she worked with, and they hung around together, but it was nothing serious."

"Did this guy go to Boulder with her?"

"No. Aubrey went on her own, as she always did."

"When did Aubrey move to Boulder?"

"It was in early June of last year."

"I understand Aubrey found a job in Boulder, correct?"

"Yes. She got a job as a cocktail waitress in some bar."

"Do you remember the name of it?"

"Unfortunately, I don't."

"Do you know where it was in Boulder?"

"I think she mentioned one time it was on a street that was like a mall."

"Pearl Street Mall?"

"Yeah, that sounds familiar."

"That could be very helpful, Ms. Leaver. If we find where she worked, someone there might remember her."

Emily sighed. "I hope so."

"Did you give this information to the last detective who talked to you?"

"I told him she got a job as a cocktail waitress, but I didn't know where."

Shaw frowned. "Did he question you further about it?"

"Not that I remember."

"Did Aubrey mention meeting anyone in Boulder?"

"No. Just that she had found a place to stay and had gotten a job."

"A place to stay in Boulder?"

"Aubrey told me she couldn't afford Boulder. She found a place just outside Boulder. I can't remember where, but it was an apartment with several roommates."

"You don't remember any names of the people Audrey met or knew in Boulder?"

"I think she mentioned one of her roommates' name was Gail."

"Does Aubrey have a father?"

"Her father, my husband, died four years ago. Jack and Aubrey were very close. I think that's one reason she went on this adventure. She had to get away for some time on her own."

"That makes sense," said Shaw. "We will do everything possible to find out who murdered your daughter."

"I so appreciate that," responded Emily. "I knew she hadn't committed suicide, but your department told me it was suicide or accidental."

"I apologize for that. At the time, that's what we were told by the coroner. Newly discovered information and analysis lead us to now believe she was murdered."

"Thank you, Detective."

Shaw turned to Nichols. "Tom, can you think of anything else to ask?"

"Yes. Emily, why did you file a report with Walnut Creek? Did you think to call Boulder to file a report?"

"I didn't know if she was still in Boulder. I hadn't heard from her in weeks. I asked our police department, and they told me they would contact the Boulder Police. I didn't know she was found until I saw a sketch online that looked like her. That's when I called Boulder."

"You then went to Boulder to retrieve her body, correct?"

"By the time I saw the sketch and got to Boulder, she had already been cremated. All I got was a box of ashes. The coroner said they only hold unclaimed bodies for thirty days after the autopsy. He offered to show me a picture, but I wanted to remember Aubrey the way she was."

"How was the body identified?"

"Walnut Creek Police sent a sample of my DNA for comparison. From that, they could tell she was my daughter."

"One more thing," said Shaw. "May we have a good-quality photograph of Aubrey?"

"Yes, of course. I have just the picture."

Emily left the room and returned with a photograph in her hand. "This was taken when she was twenty-one. She had the same hairstyle in Boulder."

"How do you know she hadn't changed her hair?"

Emily grabbed her cell phone from a purse and pulled up a photo Aubrey had sent her. "This is the last selfie she sent me the week before she stopped calling."

Shaw and Nichols both looked at the picture.

"It looks like she is standing in a bar," stated Nichols.

"Do you know which bar?" asked Shaw.

"It looks familiar. Let me think about it some."

Shaw asked Emily, "Will you text this photo to my phone?"

"Yes, of course."

Shaw and Nichols continued to talk with Emily for another ten minutes about Aubrey's life. They could tell Emily enjoyed talking to someone about her daughter.

On the drive back to the airport for their 8:30 pm flight, Nichols asked Shaw what the next steps were.

"Based on what we know, Aubrey met some people in Boulder. She found a place to crash and got a job at a bar on the Pearl Street Mall. That means she met people in Boulder. I'm guessing no one realized the dead body was that of Aubrey. They probably hadn't gotten to know her well, knew she was moving from city to city, and didn't think anything of her not showing up."

"Wouldn't they have seen the news and the sketch?"

"Probably not. First, the people she met were probably young. Few young adults pay much attention to the news these days. They won't see it if it's not on Messenger, Facebook or TikTok. Second, remember the timeline. Emily stopped hearing from her daughter three months before her body was found. Aubrey either left Boulder and didn't want Mom to know, or she was being kept somewhere against her will. New friends may have thought it strange she disappeared, but after three months, they might assume she left Boulder. Once her body was found, even if they heard the news about it, I doubt they would equate it with Aubrey from three months prior."

"That makes sense. You've thought a lot about this."

"Part of being a detective is being analytical. I'm always thinking of different theories, even those that don't make sense. The worst thing a detective can do is to be close-minded."

"We need to find the bar she worked at," said Nichols.

"Yes, and I'd like to find out where and who she was staying with."

Thursday, May 18th

Shaw was at her desk adding Emily Leaver's information to the case file when her phone rang. It was Coroner Ron Larsen calling.

"Hello, Ron."

"Hi, Caro. I've got an update on Aubrey Leaver's autopsy. Reviewing all the photographs, I now believe there were two similar puncture marks on her body. Since I'm only looking at pictures, I can't be positive, but there appears to be a puncture-type wound behind the right ear. There also appears to be a similar wound to her lower right back near the spine."

"That's significant," exclaimed Shaw. "That strengthens the connection to all three victims. Could you testify the injuries were all similar?"

"Only going by pictures is more difficult, but I am ninety percent sure Aubrey had small puncture wounds."

"Thank you, Ron."

Shaw rushed to inform Nichols, Sergeant Martinez and Commander Greenberg. All were pleased to hear the update. Shaw then told Nichols they needed to talk with Detective Kevin Jordan.

"Wasn't he the lead detective on Aubrey Leaver's death?" asked Nichols.

"Yes. He had an interview this morning but said he could meet us in the small conference room at ten."

Nichols and Shaw were in the small conference room by 9:55 am. Detective Kevin Jordan walked in precisely at 10:00. Jordan was a 42-year-old slender African American. He stood at five-foot-nine inches and probably weighed no more than 155 pounds. His black hair was a close-cut fade with a tightly coiled nap on top.

"Good morning, Kevin," greeted Shaw.

"Hello," replied Jordan.

"Hi, Kevin," said Nichols.

"I understand you have some questions on the Leaver case?" asked Jordan.

"Yes," nodded Shaw. "We've read your reports and just have some follow-up questions."

"Sure, anything I can do to help."

"You talked to Aubrey's mom, correct?"

"Eventually. We didn't know who Aubrey was for several weeks. Her mom recognized a sketch we released."

"Did she tell you Aubrey had gotten a job in a bar on Pearl Street?"

"Yes."

"Were you able to locate the bar?"

"No, by then, the coroner had ruled the death a likely suicide or accidental. We put out a press release asking anyone who knew her to come forward. Nobody responded."

"You didn't think it was important to find someone she knew?"

"Sure, but at the time, we had no clear evidence it was a homicide. Obviously, now we know it is. And, like I said, we put out a press release, and no one responded. And if you recall, it was soon after that we had the case of the woman who was beaten and sexually assaulted in her apartment. I got assigned that case as well."

"Oh yes, I remember that one. Now that we know we probably have a serial killer on our hands, what do you think our next step should be?" asked Shaw.

"You need to find people who knew her and the other two victims. We know Leaver was in town, but we don't know if the other two victims were. And before you say anything, the commander already told me to help you with this case."

Shaw smiled. "Thank you. We can use the help. Tom and I will focus on finding out who she lived with for the short time she was here. Will you work the mall and try to find the bar she supposedly worked at?"

"Yes, I can do that."

"Show him the selfie of Aubrey in a bar," urged Nichols.

"Oh, yeah. I almost forgot. Look at this," said Shaw, holding up her cell phone. "Do you recognize this place?"

"No, I don't. But text me the picture."

"Done," responded Shaw.

"How are we going to find out who she stayed with?" asked Nichols. "Her mom didn't even know what city it was."

"It will be hard," admitted Shaw. "Now that this case has new widespread attention, another press release with a photograph of her might cause someone to come forward. The thought of a serial killer stalking the county gets people's attention."

"That it does," agreed Nichols.

"We will get with Owen to include all three victims in our release," said Shaw. "Someone out there knows these women. Tom, have you ever done a press release?"

"No."

"Time to learn. While I'm sharing information with Owen, you get started on a press release. Include as many details about these women as you can. And don't worry, we will edit it together. The commander will get any final edits."

"Okay," nodded Nichols.

"Any more questions?" asked Shaw.

Both detectives shook their heads no.

"Let's get going then."

Chapter 11

The following day, Shaw and Nichols presented their proposed press release to Commander Greenberg. The press release went into greater detail on the descriptions of each victim. With Aubrey Leaver, her last known whereabouts were included. The release described her working at a bar in downtown Boulder and moving in with several others in another town close to Boulder. The photograph from Aubrey's mom was included in the release.

"This is well done," agreed Greenberg. "Has the Sheriff's department approved this?"

"Yes," responded Shaw. "It just needs your approval."

"You've got it."

"Thank you, Commander."

It was noon when Shaw sent the release to all the news outlets in the Denver Metro Area. With the Commander's permission, Shaw even sent the releases to CNN, FOX News, and MSNBC.

"Are you hungry yet?" asked Shaw.

"Thought you'd never ask," replied Nichols.

"This is a good day," continued Shaw. "I will buy you lunch. Your choice."

"What!? You don't need to do that, Caro."

"I want to. Where would you like to go?"

"Hmmm. What iconic Boulder restaurant can I introduce you to today?"

"You DID NOT introduce me to the Village Coffee Shop," insisted Shaw. "I had eaten there before."

"How about the little diner on North Twenty-Eighth Street? Ever been there?"

"Yes, but it's been a long time. I occasionally ate breakfast there when I worked the dayshift on patrol."

"I love the meatloaf," said Nichols. "We need to hurry. They close at one-thirty."

"We've got plenty of time. Here, you drive."

"Oooooh. You're letting me drive?"

"Shut up. Do you want lunch or not?"

"Yes, let's go."

Shaw and Nichols arrived in plenty of time for lunch. The res- taurant is a throwback to old-time diners. Large windows face the street, and typical café style tables and chairs are inside. The diner even has a long breakfast/lunch bar lined with old-style round padded seats secured to the floor. The restaurant's "Good Times, Good Food" motto is painted on the window. Nichols picked a table near the window with a view of 28th Street.

"You do like the home-style restaurants, don't you?" asked Shaw.

"Yes. The food is usually good, and the portions are filling."

As planned, Nichols ordered the meatloaf lunch and an iced tea. Shaw ordered a chef salad and a Diet Coke. It didn't take long for their food to arrive.

"How do you eat so much?" asked Shaw.

"High energy level. Need to keep my strength up."

Shaw laughed. "If I ate like you, I'd be huge."

Nichols shrugged his shoulders. "Good genes, I guess. Besides, this food is good for the soul."

Nichols's plate contained a large slice of meatloaf made with ground turkey, a large portion of mashed potatoes and gravy, sauteed vegetables, and Texas toast. Shaw's chef salad came with a dinner roll and dill pickle.

Nichols looked up. "Are you going to eat your pickle?"

"You want my pickle?"

"Only if you don't want it."

Shaw couldn't help but smile. "Sure, go ahead."

Nichols reached over and swiped the pickle off her plate. He quickly took a bite out of it. "Mmm. Nice and crunchy."

"Do you believe our press release will create some leads?" asked Nichols.

"With an actual picture of Aubrey, I believe someone will recognize her. She had been in Boulder for two to three weeks before disappearing. Someone will remember her."

Several minutes of silence passed as both detectives focused on eating their food.

"Oh, it just came to me," exclaimed Nichols. "I think I know where the picture of Aubrey in a bar was taken."

"Yeah? Where?"

"There's a tequila bar on the Hill, 13th Street. I believe the mural in the picture is from that bar."

"What's the name?"

"Give me a minute. Ummm...."

"Is it the Maravilloso House?" asked Shaw.

"Yes! That's it. I responded there on multiple occasions while on patrol. I recognize the mural."

"Excellent memory, Tom."

"It was the meatloaf. It fueled my brain."

Shaw chuckled.

"Are you going to finish your soda?" asked Nichols.

Shaw sighed, "Seriously?"

Nichols broke out in laughter. "I knew that would rile you."

"Just finish eating. We need to go check out the Maravilloso."

Nichols finished his meatloaf, then used the last of his Texas toast to soak up the remaining gravy. Some of the gravy dribbled out of the left corner of his mouth.

"Oh my god," exclaimed Shaw. "You just dripped gravy on the front of your shirt."

Nichols looked down, and without saying a word, he grabbed his cloth napkin and wiped it off. He then dabbed a corner of the napkin in his iced tea and used it to further clean his shirt. Shaw watched in amusement.

"Good thing I wore a dark shirt today," said Nichols.

Shaw rolled her eyes. "Do you need to go back to the office to change?"

"Oh no, this will be fine. Once it dries, you won't even see it."

After they finished, Nichols drove to the area of town known as the Hill.

The Hill is a mixed neighborhood of business and residential properties located west of the University of Colorado. Broadway, a four-lane road, runs north and south between the university and the Hill. The business hub of the Hill is considered to be the intersection of 13th Street and College Avenue. It is a popular gathering spot for college students. The Maravilloso House sits on 13th Street.

Nichols parked on 13th Street, two blocks from The Maravilloso House. "Do you know what maravilloso means?" asked Nichols.

"I believe it means marvelous in Spanish," responded Shaw.

They walked two blocks to the bar, receiving glances from students milling around. The front of the bar had large glass windows looking out onto the street and a single metal framed glass door. A neon sign hung high above the windows. Nichols stopped and looked up before following Shaw through the door.

It was early afternoon, so the bar was not very busy. Shaw observed one waitress and a bartender. She walked over to the bar first, and Nichols followed. A dark brunette woman wearing a bright multi-colored blouse and orange shorts was working the bar. The bar was dimly lit, but sunlight from the windows brightened the room. Nichols looked around and saw the mural from Aubrey's selfie photo on the wall opposite the bar. The mural resembled a watercolor painting of a Mexican city on a hill overlooking the water. Palm trees lined the shoreline. It featured brightly colored buildings and a patchy blue sky. Nichols nudged Shaw on the shoulder.

"What?"

"There's the mural. I knew I had seen it here."

Shaw nodded, "Yeah, that's it."

Along the wall behind the bar was a row of multi-colored slushy machines, stirring concoctions of frozen margaritas and daiquiris. At the rear of the bar was a small stage and dance floor. A Yamaha drum set sat at the back of the stage. The smell of Mexican food drifted from the back kitchen. Shaw motioned to the bartender. She walked over.

"What can I get you?" she said as she placed two small napkins on the bar before Shaw and Nichols. Shaw flashed her badge.

"We would like to ask you a few questions."

The bartender looked confused.

"Don't worry. We are looking for someone who might have seen a woman here."

"Oh, okay," said the bartender.

Nichols pulled out his phone and showed the bartender the picture of Aubrey in the bar.

After several seconds, "I don't recognize her."

"How long have you worked here?" asked Nichols.

"At least a year."

"We know this woman was here. Are you sure you've never seen her?" continued Nichols.

"What night was she here?"

"It would have been about seven to eight months ago."

"Are you serious?" asked the bartender. "We get hundreds of people in here daily. How do you expect me to remember someone from that long ago?"

"Who else is working today?"

"Shelly is here, but she's only worked here for three months. Our assistant manager is in the back. Would you like me to get her?"

"Yes, please."

The bartender left and walked through a door leading into the back area.

"We are asking a lot," said Shaw. "It will be tough for anyone to remember her unless they got to know her."

A Hispanic woman of approximately thirty years old walked from the back and approached the detectives. "I'm the assistant manager. How can I help you?"

"We are trying to identify a woman who visited here sometime last fall," answered Nichols. "Were you working here last year?"

"Yes."

"Do you remember seeing this woman?"

The assistant manager looked at the phone. "She doesn't look familiar to me. What did she do?"

"Have you heard of the three women found dead in or near Boulder?"

"Yes."

"This woman was one of them, and we know she came here at least one time."

The assistant manager looked again at the picture. "I'm sorry. She does not look familiar to me."

"If we had posters made up, would you be willing to put one up in here?" asked Shaw.

"Yes, of course."

"All right, thank you."

After they'd left, Nichols told Shaw he thought the poster idea was good.

"When we get back," said Shaw, "I will have our print shop make us some posters. We need to do the same on our Jane Doe victim, and I will ask Gates if we can get one made on their victim."

"We don't have photos of the other victims," Nichols reminded her.

"No, but sketches are better than nothing. Someone out there knew these women."

Nichols nodded.

****

"Yeeeooow!" screamed Della as she lifted herself into a seated position. Her head behind the right ear still throbbed, and her knee was stiff and swollen. The knee was purple and reminded her of an egg-plant. She had drifted back asleep, not knowing how long she had been out. The light in her room was now on. She looked at the wooden chair and saw a new sandwich and two bottles of water. *Thank god, two waters.* Della slowly pushed herself into a stooped position, then shuffled her way to the chair while not putting much weight on her right leg. She carefully picked up the sandwich and waters, turned, and sat down hard on the chair. She gave a sigh of relief. Della removed the peanut butter sandwich from its wrapper and took a bite. The white bread was dry, and the peanut butter was thin, but Della was too hungry to care.

After two bites, Della took a heavy drink of water. She desperately wanted to pour water over her head and neck but needed to save it to quench her thirst. As she picked at her sandwich, Della's thoughts turned to how great it would be to soak in a hot lavender bubble bath. She closed her eyes and imagined the bubbles dancing on her skin with the scent of lavender all about her. Oh, and the hot water warming her body to the core. She continued to eat and drink with her eyes closed, preserving her pleasant thoughts. After finishing her sandwich, Della sat back in the chair, her eyes closed, trying to remember better times.

If only she could turn back the clock. Thinking of going back in time reminded Della of a song from the Beatles she liked called Yesterday. She hummed the tune, then began to softly croon the words. As she was singing to herself, Della heard the lock on the metal door turning. She drew her left leg up to her chest and wrapped her arms tightly around it while her lower lip trembled. *What now?* She thought.

The door creaked open, and the man wearing the white lab coat and hood walked in. Had the hood been pointed, he would have looked like a member of the Ku Klux Klan. She noticed he was wearing the same beige suede shoes.

"How are you today, Amy?"

Della remained silent. His cold, dark eyes stared back at her.

"You need to answer me, Amy."

"I'm fine," muttered Della.

"Good. More progress. Now tell me where you are from?"

"Denver," whispered Della.

"I couldn't hear you."

"Denver," said Della louder.

"Great. We'll review your history later, but you must clean up now. You look and smell horrible, Amy. I can hardly stand to be in the same room."

Of course, I smell, you asshole, thought Della. *You're the one keeping me locked in here like an animal.*

The man walked out the door, and Della heard some rustling noise. He returned, carrying two 5-gallon plastic buckets filled three-quarters full with water. He sat the buckets down in front of Della. The man walked back out, returning with a box containing soap, shampoo, a towel, a washcloth, and a change of clothes.

"Now, take your clothes off," he said.

"Excuse me?"

"You need to bathe yourself. I brought you clean clothes."

"You're going to watch me?"

The man laughed. "I've already seen you naked."

"When?" asked Della.

"When you arrived here. You were unconscious. I had to remove your old clothes and give you new clothes."

Della was horrified. "What did you do to me?"

"We had glorious sex for hours, Amy."

"WHAT?!" screamed Della.

He laughed again. "Calm down. Nothing happened. You were drugged and had to be changed. Don't worry, Amy, I've seen many naked bodies."

"Why was I drugged?"

"When the police brought you here, you were uncontrollable. We had to sedate you."

"I don't remember the police bringing me here."

"That's no surprise. You couldn't remember your real name or where you were from. Now get those clothes off, or I'll do it for you."

Della knew she risked being tased again, or worse, if she did not comply. She slowly removed her dirty T-shirt and shorts. She felt the man's gaze looking at her breasts.

"Now, the underwear."

Della moved slowly as the pain in her right knee still throbbed. She pushed the underwear down past her knees, then sat and used her left foot to work the underwear off her lower legs. The cool temperature and the steely look in his eyes made her shiver. Della crossed her legs and folded her arms across her breasts. The man walked over, picked up the dirty clothes and stuffed them into a white garbage bag. He then walked to the door, looked back at Della, and said, "Make yourself pretty again." He then walked out, locking the door behind him.

Della shuffled to the buckets, bent over, and stuck her left hand in one of them. She couldn't believe it. The water was warm. Della slowly kneeled down on her left knee while keeping her right leg straight out to the side. Her right knee was too swollen and sore to put pressure on. She slowly lowered her head into the first bucket, allowing her long blond hair to fall forward. The top of Della's head reached the water.

"Ahhhh," she said out loud. Della noticed a soothing, gentle sensation of warmth as it seeped into the pores of her scalp. It felt as though some of the tension had left her body. Old memories of childhood bubble baths embraced her mind. Della reached her right hand into the bucket to swirl the water. She then straightened to apply shampoo and massaged it into her hair. It felt so good that she closed her eyes as her fingers danced on her head. After a long scrub, Della bent back down to rinse her hair. Once finished, she wrapped her head in the towel. She slowly raised herself to a standing position, then moved each bucket to one side of the drain. Della first placed her right foot in one bucket, then her left foot in the other. She stood straddling the drain in the middle of the floor. Then, using the washcloth and bar of soap, she washed her body from one side to the other. Water ran down her back and across her buttocks. Della closed her eyes, and for a moment, she was in a luxurious spa getting the finest bath in the world.

Once Della dried herself and got into the fresh set of clothes, she fell back onto the cot. While her neck and knee still hurt, she was amazed at how much better she felt. Della gazed around the room assessing her small prison, when a glimmer from behind the chair caught her eye. Something was lying on the floor against the wall. She stared at it, trying to figure out what it might be. Slowly, she pulled herself up and shuffled to the chair. Looking behind it, Della observed one of the long needles used to punish her.

Della thought about picking it up but was aware of the camera mounted in the corner. She did not want him to know what she had found. Della shuffled back to the cot. *That may be my way out*, thought Della. *I could use it to stab him.* Della ran scenarios through her head, knowing none of them may work. She also did not want to die. She remembered what the larger man had said. "You only have four weeks left. Get it done or get rid of her." Della was not sure what that meant but assumed it wasn't good.

Della heard the metal door being unlocked. *I hope he didn't see me looking behind the chair.* The door opened, and in walked the man.

"You look much better," he said as he walked over and picked up the buckets. He carried the buckets and towel out and then returned.

"Time for our session, Amy. Get in the chair."

"Please, no."

"I need to assess your progress. Get in the chair."

Della shuffled to the chair and sat down. The man sat on the cot's edge, looking straight at Della.

"What is your name?"

"Amy," said Della softly.

"Where are you from?"

"Denver."

"Where are your parents?"

"My parents are dead."

"Why are you here, Amy?"

Della hesitated. "I'm suffering from mental illness?"

"Excellent, Amy. You are finally accepting reality. How did you get here?"

"I was having a mental breakdown, and the police brought me here for treatment."

"That's correct. Why do you want to harm yourself?"

Della looked up. "What do you mean?"

"You have tried to harm yourself in the past, Amy. Even once trying to commit suicide. You've even injured yourself while in our custody."

"I haven't tried to injure myself here," insisted Della.

"Look at your knee. How did that happen?"

Della was afraid to answer.

"Tell me. How did that happen?"

"You did this to me."

The man laughed. "Amy, you took a piece of wire from the cot and intentionally injured yourself. You did the same thing to the back of your ear."

"No. You tied me in this chair and pushed needles into me."

"That was your imagination at work, which is why you are here, Amy. You did this to yourself."

Della did not want to argue for fear of being tortured again.

"Before we can help you, you must accept your illness. We have this camera here to protect you."

"Is this a hospital?" asked Della.

"It's a special clinic."

"It feels like a dungeon."

"Amy, I need you to promise you will not try to harm yourself again."

Della was more confused than ever. *Have I been imagining things?*

The man reached into his right coat pocket and pulled out his taser. "Amy, I need you to promise."

"All right!" screamed Della. "I promise not to hurt myself."

"Good, because if you try something like that again, we will have to do more shock therapy."

"No, I won't do it again."

"That's the right answer. But you need to mean it."

"I won't. I promise."

The man stood up and opened the metal door. He reached around the outside corner and grabbed a tray off a small table. Della saw a plate of food and a bottled water on the tray.

"You've shown progress today, Amy. You've earned a full meal. I brought you ham, potato salad, baked beans, and a chocolate cupcake. When you are done, leave the tray by the door. I'll get it tomorrow."

"Why are you in a hood?"

The man hesitated. "It's just part of the program."

"What program?"

"You need to focus on the treatment, not on me. I want you to succeed, Amy. Not everyone does."

"When will I get out of here?"

"When you have forgotten all your fantasies and overcome your resistance to the truth. You must first realize how crazy you are. Once you've done that, you are on the road to getting out of here."

With that, the man left the room, locking the metal door behind him.

Della was famished. She quickly scarfed down her food. Once she had eaten, Della kept going back to what the man had said. *Maybe I am crazy.* Della crawled onto the cot and fell asleep.

When she later awoke, the light had been turned off, making the room pitch black. She lay in bed for several minutes thinking about her earlier interaction with the man. *Am I crazy? Did I do this to myself? Is the life Della led all a fantasy? No, I have memories I know are real. My mom is not a fantasy. I need to get out of here.*

Della remembered the needle behind the chair. Given the darkness, nothing could be seen through the camera. Now was the time to get that needle. Della carefully crawled out of bed onto the floor. She slowly crept toward the chair, feeling her way as she went. Putting pressure on her knee was painful, but Della was determined. Once she got to the chair, Della laid down on her side to reach behind the chair. She ran her left hand along the concrete floor to the wall. She slowly moved her fingers along the base of the wall until she could feel a thin metal object. Della grabbed it between her finger and thumb. She then crawled back to the cot, grimacing whenever she put pressure on her right knee. She lifted the cot and stuck the needle into the mattress, pushing it as far as it would go. Della then lay back down on her bed, pondering her next move

.

Chapter 12

Monday, May 22nd

"We got a hit!" shouted Shaw.

Nichols came over to Shaw's desk. "What do you mean?"

"Someone called in over the weekend who says she knew Aubrey! She saw the photograph on the news. Her name is Claire Cooper."

"How does she know her?"

"It says here Aubrey lived with her for about a week. I'm calling her now."

Shaw dials and waits for an answer. "Hello?"

"Hello. This is Detective Caroline Shaw with the Boulder Police Department. Is this Claire Cooper?"

"Yes, it is."

"I understand you knew one of our homicide victims, Aubrey Leaver?"

"Only for a short time. She lived with us for about a week and then just disappeared."

"I understand. Are you home right now?"

"Yes."

"May we come over for an interview?"

"Sure."

"I have your apartment address. It's off South Boulder Road, correct?"

"Yes."

"We will be there in twenty minutes."

Shaw and Nichols drove to Claire Cooper's apartment complex in Lafayette, Colorado, a few miles east of Boulder. The complex was a series of old, brown brick buildings. Cooper lived in building C, apartment 123. Cooper was a white female, 21 years old, with short dark hair. When Cooper answered the door, she was wearing a red T-shirt, white shorts, and sandals. Both detectives introduced themselves.

"Come on in," said Claire. "We can sit at the table."

The apartment was small, with a combined living room-dining room. The apartment was picked up and tidy, although Nichols noticed some marijuana paraphernalia on a shelf in the living room.

"Thank you for seeing us," stated Shaw. "How did you know Aubrey?"

"It was last summer when Aubrey answered an ad for a roommate. She came over, and my boyfriend and I really liked her. She moved in a day later."

"Do you know when that was?"

"It was in June of last year."

"When did Aubrey move in?"

"It was around the twentieth of June."

"Do you remember when she went missing?"

"Not the exact date, but she was only here for about a week, maybe eight or nine days."

"Did she say where she was going?"

"Nope. Aubrey just stopped coming back."

"Didn't you find that strange?"

"Somewhat. The only thing she took was her purse and whatever was in it. She left all her clothes behind."

"Did you try to call her?"

"Yes, several times. Aubrey never answered, so we figured she was off to another adventure. We knew she was living a traveling lifestyle."

"Did you know any of her friends or acquaintances?"

"I remember her talking to her mom on the phone. And once she was talking to a man. She said it was a friend she met in Santa Fe."

"May we see her belongings?"

"Sorry. It was mostly clothing and some personal hygiene items. After several months, we gave most of it to Goodwill, and the rest we tossed."

Shaw sighed. "Thank you, Claire. Detective Nichols has some questions now."

"Claire," said Nichols, "Did you know where Aubrey had gotten a job?"

"Yes. She found a waitressing job in Boulder. I remember she was excited about it."

"Do you know where in Boulder?"

"Yes. Aubrey told me it was downtown Boulder, near Pearl Street."

"Near Pearl Street or on Pearl Street?"

Claire thought for a moment. "I can't remember. I know she was happy to be near the Pearl Street Mall."

"You can't remember the name?"

"I'm sorry, Detective."

"Okay, thank you. Were you at all concerned that the dead woman found last September might have been Aubrey?"

Claire squirmed in her seat as she looked down. "I was not aware of it. I don't follow the news much. My boyfriend Derek saw her picture on the news yesterday and asked me if that was Aubrey. Once I saw it, I knew it was her."

"Would Derek know where she worked?"

"I doubt it. He pays less attention to that sort of thing than I do. But I will ask him when he gets home."

"Did Aubrey mention anyone she met or discuss being concerned about someone?"

"Not that I remember."

"Okay, thank you, Claire."

"Yes, thank you," agreed Shaw. "You've been helpful."

"Was Aubrey in the creek for all that time?" asked Claire.

"No. She hadn't been dead for long. That's why we're trying to find out where she was for three months."

"It's so sad," said Claire. "She seemed like a good person."

"I think she was. Thank you again, Claire."

Claire nodded.

"The timeline doesn't make sense," pondered Nichols on the ride back to Boulder. "It's like three months are missing from her life. Where could she have gone?"

"There could be several explanations," answered Shaw. "Maybe she shacked up with a new boyfriend. Maybe she wanted to disappear. Or maybe she was kidnapped."

Nichols stared out the passenger window.

"Hey, did you ever track down Ruby?" asked Shaw.

"Nope. I've got patrol looking for her."

"Where do you think she is?"

"I'm hoping she left town and isn't lying dead somewhere."

"You need to stay positive."

"How? We have three confirmed homicides, and my sexual assault victim is missing. She could be the fourth."

Shaw ignored the comment. "Let's check in with Kevin when we get back. Maybe he found where Aubrey was working."

"Stop at Starbucks on the way back. I need a coffee."

"You tired?"

"Yeah, I'm tired. We worked all day Saturday, and I barely slept over the weekend."

Shaw pulled into the Starbucks parking lot on Arapahoe Road, near the police department. Nichols ordered a caffe´ mocha, and Shaw ordered a medium roast coffee with half water.

"Half water?" asked Nichols.

"Yeah, I don't like too much caffeine. Let's go sit down."

"You don't want to get back to the PD?"

"No, we can afford to take a break occasionally."

Nichols smiled and sat at a table at the rear of the coffee shop.

"What did you do on your Sunday?" asked Shaw.

"Went to church, then took the kids to an indoor gymnastics place where they could burn some energy while Kristin shopped. She needed a break."

"You worked Saturday. Shouldn't you have been the one getting a break?"

Nichols shook his head. "No, Kristin worked all week and then had the kids alone on Saturday. If you had children, you would know how exhausting they can be."

Shaw laughed. "I suppose so."

"Did you and Dan ever consider children when you were married?"

"We talked about it, but we were so involved with our careers that we never had the chance."

"What about the future?"

"I've given up on that idea. I'm thirty-seven and not married."

"Does that bother you?"

"I think about it sometimes, but I've moved on. What's with all the personal questions?"

"Nothing. I'm just trying to get to know you better."

Shaw paused. "After our divorce, I focused all my attention on my career. I always wanted to be a detective, and here I am."

"Have you thought about getting promoted?"

"I thought about it, but I've found what I'm good at and enjoy it. I'm not sure I'd like being a supervisor. How about you?"

"Yeah," answered Nichols, "I'd like to be a Sergeant someday. Maybe even a commander."

"Well, it's great you're getting detective experience. You need a solid background to get promoted, and the competition is stiff."

"I've noticed that. I thought they would surely promote Martin to Sergeant last time. I was shocked that he didn't get it."

"I wasn't," said Shaw.

"He's a great cop. And he really knows his stuff," insisted Nichols.

"Yes, but you also need to relate to people. I don't think he does that very well."

Nichols nodded. "You said you talked to Dan recently. How is he doing?"

"He sounded great and seems to do well in real estate."

"I hated to see him leave," said Nichols.

"Me too. After the shooting, Dan just couldn't get over it. His entire attitude changed. And I wasn't very helpful."

"What do you mean?"

"I was hurting too, but I accepted it was part of the job, and we knew that coming in. I didn't handle Dan's mood swings and drinking very well."

"Is Dan an alcoholic?"

"No. In fact, he tells me he no longer drinks at all."

"That's good to hear. So, what do you do for fun?"

"Julie Reese and I hang out a lot. And when I don't have to work, I play in a rec basketball league on Saturdays."

"Julie's a good cop."

"Yes, that's one reason we get along so well. And I think that's enough with the questions. What do you do on weekends? Other than giving your wife a break from the kids?"

"We follow whatever sport our son is playing. Right now, it's soccer. We also try to do something as a family, like going to a park."

"Your daughter doesn't play?"

"Not yet. Kristin has her signed up for dance lessons."

"What about you?"

"With work and the kids, I don't have time for anything else."

"Tom, you need to find an outlet for yourself, or this job will consume you."

"I'm very content spending quality time with my family. That's my outlet right now. I enjoy it, Caro."

"Fair enough," said Shaw. "We should get back and check in with Kevin."

"Have you seen him today?" asked Nichols.

"No, I thought you saw him."

Nichols shook his head no.

"If you write up the interview with Claire Cooper, I'll track down Kevin," said Shaw.

"Got it," replied Nichols.

Back at the police department, Shaw looked for Detective Kevin Jordan. No one had seen him. She called his cell phone.

"Hello."

"Kevin, where are you?"

"I'm in the middle of an interview right now."

"For this case?"

"No, a sexual assault case. I can't talk right now."

"Don't you think our serial killer case is more important right now?" barked Shaw.

"First, you don't know it's a serial killer; second, my victim is alive and frightened. She deserves my attention right now. And I don't appreciate you talking to me that way," shouted Jordan. He then disconnected the call.

Shaw threw her cell phone onto her desk. "Damn it," she grumbled just as Sgt. Martinez was walking by. Martinez stopped.

"What's wrong?"

"Huh? Oh, nothing, Sarge."

"Must be something. You just tossed your phone and shouted damn it."

"Just frustration, sir. I want to get this monster off the street, and things are moving too slowly."

"Investigations take time, Caro. You should know that by now. We are much further along than we were just ten days ago."

"I suppose," said Shaw. "Sorry."

"No need to be sorry. Just remember that anger doesn't solve crime. Good police work solves crime."

After Martinez walked away, Nichols walked over. "What was that about?"

"Oh, I just got upset because Jordan is working on a sex assault right now."

Nichols shrugged his shoulders. "We still have to work on our other cases."

"Yeah! I get it. This one seems more urgent to me."

"If Jordan hasn't found the place Aubrey worked, we'll go out to find it this afternoon."

Shaw nodded, "Okay."

****

Della was awakened by voices coming through the grate above her. Her light was not on, but the light from above shone into the room. Della listened intently. She could hear two male voices. They were the same voices Della had heard before. One she recognized as the smaller man in the white hood who interacted with her daily. The second voice sounded like the larger man from before. He seemed to direct the man in the white hood.

"Yes, we are making progress," said the smaller man. "I'm not sure she believes everything yet, but she's giving me the right answers."

"She has to believe it," said the larger man. "And if it doesn't work, she has to be the last one. I assume you've been watching the news?"

"I have things under control," answered the smaller man.

The light in Della's dungeon flashed on, temporarily blinding her as the voices faded. Della shuffled over to the toilet bucket to urinate. The distraction of the conversation she overheard caused her to hit the side of the bucket, splashing urine onto her left ankle. She used some toilet paper to dry it off. After relieving herself, she sat in the wooden chair, waiting for the masked man to return.

While she waited, Della thought of ways to use the long needle to escape. She knew it wouldn't be easy, and if it didn't work, she would probably be tortured severely or even killed. Della thought of jamming the needle into one of her captor's eyes. She decided that would be too small of a target. Maybe the groin? The neck? The stomach? It had to be a way that would disable the man long enough for her to escape. Would she be strong enough? Della kept going back and forth on whether to even try. She knew the odds were against her.

Quickly, the metal door opened and in walked the hooded man wearing the same shoes. He stepped directly in front of Della and asked her the same series of questions about her name, where she lived, her dead parents, living in foster homes, etc. Della answered them as he had conditioned to answer.

When he asked Della who committed her to therapy, she stumbled. "I don't remember the police bringing me here."

The man reached down with his taser, shocking Della on her left thigh.

"EEEOOWW!" screamed Della as her entire body twitched. "Why did you do that?"

"To refresh your memory. Who brought you here?"

"The police!" she screamed.

Again, the man shocked Della in the left thigh. She screamed again.

"Why?"

"So that you don't forget from now on. Do you remember the police bringing you here?"

"YES!"

"They brought you here because you were a psychological mess. Once you erase your false memories, you will be on the road to recovery."

Della was crying. "Can I get outside for some fresh air? Just for a few minutes?"

"Not until I can trust you, Amy. By the way, it was a male police officer who brought you to us."

Della tried to remember what the officer looked like. As the man turned and walked out the door, he looked back and said, "I'll drop down some food soon, and then we'll have another session."

I must get out of here, thought Della. Again, she thought of ways to use the found needle. Was she strong enough to push the needle through his clothing? Through a lab coat and shirt? Once she got out of the room, would she be able to get out of whatever building she was in? Would there be security guards? There were so many questions with no answers. Ten minutes passed before the grate above opened, and the familiar bucket was lowered to the floor. In it, Della found a granola bar and a bottle of water.

"Really!" screamed Della as she looked up through the grate. "I'm already losing weight. This isn't enough to sustain me."

There was no response. At that moment, Della decided she had to attempt an escape. *Live or die, I need to get out of here.*

****

It wasn't until 3:30 pm that Detective Jordan returned to the police department. Jordan walked over to Shaw's desk and dropped a tri-folded brochure onto her desk. It looked like an advertisement for an Italian restaurant.

"What's this?" asked Shaw.

"That's where Aubrey Leaver worked before she went missing. The Mesa Pizza House."

"You found it!"

"Yes, and I talked with two people who remembered her."

"Let's go into the conference room," suggested Shaw. She waved at Nichols to follow them.

All three sat at one end of the white conference table surrounded by beige-painted walls. A large photograph of a Boulder Police car parked at Chautauqua Park hung on the wall. In the background stood the majestic, towering, flat sandstone slabs overlooking Boulder, known as the Flatirons.

The Mesa Pizza House is an Italian restaurant in the 1100 block of Walnut Street, one block from the Pearl Street Mall in downtown Boulder. It specializes in pizza but carries a full Italian menu. It caters to both the lunch and dinner crowds.

"What did you find out?" asked Nichols.

"Our victim worked there for approximately two weeks as a waitress in June of last year. The manager remembered her and said she seemed happy, but she stopped coming to work after two weeks. I only found one other employee who had any memory of her."

"Who did she hang out with?" asked Shaw.

"Nobody that I found. She was there for only a short time."

"Did the manager not recognize the sketch from last year?"

"He said he only vaguely remembered the case and didn't remember seeing the sketch. When I showed him Aubrey's photograph, he positively identified her as the person he hired. And before you ask, he didn't remember any boyfriends or customers who harassed her. The manager only remembered that Aubrey talked about how much she liked the Maravilloso House."

"Well, that's something," offered Nichols. "We have a picture of her at the Maravilloso House."

"It confirms the information provided by Claire Cooper and helps further establish a timeline," stated Shaw. "And Kevin, I'm sorry if I sounded bitchy earlier."

"It's okay. Forget about it. I've got a report to finish up. Are we done?"

"Yes. Thank you, Kevin," said Shaw.

"Now what?" asked Nichols.

"I will ask the commander to put out the information about the Maravilloso House. If she frequently went there, someone may remember her."

"Good idea."

Chapter 13

Tuesday, May 23rd, 3:30 am

The cell phone vibrated and rang on the bedside table. Nichols groaned, rolled over and reached for the phone. "Hello," he mumbled.

"This is Rachel in police dispatch. Is this Tom Nichols?"

"Yeah," responded Nichols while still half asleep.

"Sorry to bother you, Detective, but our night shift officers found the woman you were looking for. Her name is Ruby Ryan."

Nichols perked up. "Is she alive?"

"Yes. The officers are holding her, waiting to see if you want to interview her."

"Yes, I do. Have her taken to one of the interview rooms. I'll meet them there in about half an hour."

Nichols jumped out of bed.

"What is it?" asked Kristin.

"Officers found the victim I was looking for."

"Do you have to interview her now?"

"Yes. Ruby's not under arrest, so if I don't interview her immediately, she could disappear again."

Nichols quickly brushed his teeth, splashed water on his face, and combed his hair. He got dressed, grabbed his Smith and Wesson nine-millimeter handgun from the bedroom safe and strapped it to his waist.

He put his dark blue windbreaker on as he walked out of the bedroom, saying goodbye to Kristin.

"Be safe, Tom," yelled Kristin.

The drive to Boulder on U.S. 36 from Broomfield at that time in the morning was quiet. Morning rush hour traffic had not yet started. Nichols arrived at the police department at 4:07 am. Upon entering the interview room, Nichols observed a disheveled Ruby Ryan sitting at the table. Instead of the red nylon jacket, Ruby was wearing a dirty yellow University of Colorado sweatshirt. She still had the rainbow knit hat on her head and the pink tennis shoes on her feet. An officer was standing against a wall as far from Ruby as possible. When Nichols approached Ruby, a pungent, musky odor attacked his nose. He suppressed his desire to turn his head but now understood why the officer kept his distance. Nichols held a manila folder in his left hand that contained a photo line-up of six males. Nichols intended to have Ruby pick out her assailant for an arrest warrant.

Nichols turned to the officer. "Where did you find her?"

"She had a little campsite in Settler's Park near the mouth of the canyon."

"Well, thank you," said Nichols.

"Do you need me to stay?" asked the officer.

"No. I'll be fine."

Nichols sat across from Ruby, trying not to breathe too deeply.

"Where have you been, Ruby?"

"I've been lying low."

"Why?"

"Too much going on with all these homicides. Your cops are stopping and questioning all of us homeless. I don't need some overzealous cop dragging me in because I have an open bottle of Sutter Home Chardonnay. What am I doing here now?"

"Ruby, I need you to positively identify the man who assaulted you."

"Oh, I'm over that," grumbled Ruby.

"What do you mean?"

"I mean, I don't care anymore. I got hyped up over all the news and thought he might be the killer. Now I know he isn't. And I never said I wanted to press charges. I was just giving you information."

"How do you know he's not the killer?"

"He's new in town. He wasn't even here last fall."

"I put a lot of work into this, Ruby. And he could assault other women if we don't stop him."

"I don't think so," said Ruby. "Street people take care of things ourselves. Do you know Grizzly?"

"Yeah, I know Grizzly."

"Well, he took care of it."

"How did he take care of it?"

"I don't know. Griz just told me it won't happen again."

"Ruby, we need to charge this guy, and I need your help."

"Nope. I'm done. Are you going to arrest me?"

"No, I'm not going to arrest you. You were the victim."

"Then I have the right to leave?"

Nichols paused, holding his anger from showing. "You can leave, Ruby. But I'm concerned our suspect will continue to prey on vulnerable women."

"Can I leave now?"

"Yes, you can leave," snapped Nichols. "Do you want me to get you a ride?"

"Nope, I'll take care of myself."

Nichols walked Ruby through the police department to the front doors. As she walked out, Nichols said, "Ruby, you need to clean yourself up. You smell terrible."

"It's been too cold to bathe," snapped Ruby. "Don't worry about me."

"I won't," replied Nichols with a wave of his hand.

It was only 4:40 am. Shaw wouldn't be in for another three hours, and the detective bureau was eerily quiet. Nichols sat at his desk, looking through recent tip sheets for anything of importance. One tip stood out. A woman from Sheridan, Wyoming, called to report she knew the serial killer. How did she know this? Her dead grandmother came to her in a dream, telling her who the killer was. According to this woman, the killer was Boulder Mayor Asher Stone. Nichols laughed out loud over reading that one. He then had an idea. Nichols found a manila envelope and carefully sealed the tip inside. He then printed "For Detective Shaw Only" on the outside in black magic marker. Next, he wrote "Serial Killer Tip." Nichols then remembered the commander kept a red ink "confidential" stamp in her office. The commander's door was open. Nichols walked in and looked around. He saw the stamp and ink pad on a shelf behind the commander's desk. Taking the stamp and pad, Nichols stamped "confidential" diagonally across the top of the envelope. He then placed the envelope in the middle of Shaw's desk.

By 7:20 am, detectives slowly began arriving for work. Commander Greenberg arrived at 7:30 am. "Good morning, Tom," she said as she walked by Nichols and into her office.

"Good morning, Commander."

At 7:45 am, Detective Shaw walked in wearing a white blouse under a medium gray blazer. "Morning," she said to Nichols.

"Good morning," Nichols replied.

Once at her desk, Shaw removed her blazer and hung it on the back of her chair. She then saw the large manila envelope sitting on her desk.

"What's this?"

Nichols feigned ignorance. "Beats me. I saw it there when I got here." Nichols watched from the corner of his eye as Shaw opened the envelope. Shaw read the tip sheet and then tossed it onto her desk.

"Oh, my god," exclaimed Shaw. "Who put this nonsense on my desk?" Shaw scanned the detective bureau.

Nichols appeared surprised. "What is it, Caro?"

Shaw picked up the tip sheet and walked it over to Nichols. "Here, read this."

Nichols laughed out loud. "Is this for real?"

"Someone's making a joke," grumbled Shaw. "When I saw the envelope, I thought maybe we were catching a break. But no, we have a comedian in the building," shouted Shaw as she looked around the room. Several other detectives gave her a look of *what are you talking about?*

"Who's the smart ass!?" shouted Shaw across the room.

Everyone looked at Shaw like she was crazy.

"That's it, I'm going to see if the commander knows anything about this."

"I'm sure she's not involved," Nichols nervously replied.

"Probably not, but this looks like the confidential stamp she uses."

Nichols watched as Shaw entered the commander's office. After about a minute, Shaw returned to her desk.

"What did the commander say?" asked Nichols.

"She doesn't know anything about it."

"It could have been anyone, Caro. Maybe even a dispatcher."

"You think a dispatcher would use a stamp from the detective commander's office?"

"Caro, there are other confidential stamps in the department."

"I suppose," agreed Shaw.

"I have an update on Ruby Ryan," said Nichols.

"Yeah? What is it?"

"Patrol found her last night, so I came in to show her the photo line-up. She wouldn't even look at it."

"What?"

"She doesn't want to pursue charges. I tried to explain why it was important, but she wanted nothing to do with it. I think her homeless friends talked her out of it."

"Well, that's too bad. What time did you come in?"

"About ten after four."

"You're going to be tired today. Hey, did you see the envelope on my desk when you came in?"

"Yes. I already told you that."

"I'll figure it out, and then I'll get them back somehow."

Nichols just smiled.

Later that morning, Shaw received a call from Detective Gates with the Sheriff's Office. "Caro, the Sheriff thinks we need some help on this case. A psychiatrist in town has worked on criminal cases in the past. The Sheriff wants to call him in as a consultant to do a criminal profile."

"Who is this guy?"

"His name is Dr. Tony Lanaro. He has an office in Boulder and worked some cases in Colorado Springs."

"I've heard the name. Let me talk to my commander, and I'll get back to you."

"Sounds good," said Gates.

Shaw turned to Nichols. "Tom, have you ever heard of a Boulder psychiatrist named Tony Lanaro?"

"Nope, I've never needed one."

"Very funny. The sheriff wants to bring him on to help with the case. Would you mind doing some background on him? We can then approach the commander."

"Yeah, I can do that."

Nichols spent the next hour scouring the internet for information on Dr. Lanaro. He discovered Lanaro was fifty-three years old and a graduate of the University of Colorado. He practiced in Colorado Springs until approximately four years ago when he moved to Boulder and opened his recent office. While in Colorado Springs, Lanaro consulted with the Colorado Springs Police Department on two murder investigations and a kidnapping case. He provided criminal profiles in each case. According to a homicide detective in Colorado Springs, Lanaro's help aided the detectives in solving both homicides. Lanaro has given presentations on the criminal mind to police agencies and on college campuses. Much of his private practice involved helping college students struggling with emotional and stress-related issues.

Nichols also discovered that Lanaro's wife, Lilly, passed away six years earlier from an overdose of sleeping pills. According to news articles, Lanaro was out of town and came home to find his wife deceased. Nichols presented his findings to Greenberg and Shaw.

"He sounds credible," agreed Greenberg. "It can't hurt to bring him on. Any insight we can get into our murderer may be helpful. Let Gates know we're on board."

"Will do," replied Shaw.

Once back at her desk, Shaw phoned Gates to tell him the police department supported using Dr. Lanaro as a consultant.

"That's great," said Gates. "I'll call him and let you know what he says."

"Thank you, Owen."

That afternoon, Shaw and Nichols paid another visit to Maravilloso House on the Hill. They took the photograph of Aubrey Leaver with them. They showed the picture to everyone in the restaurant, then stood at the front door for two hours, showing customers the photograph. No one recognized Aubrey.

"We need to come back tonight to show people this picture," said Shaw. "Aubrey most likely partied here at night."

"I've been up since three-thirty," protested Nichols.

"Oh yeah, forgot about that. I can come back. We don't both need to be here."

"Thank you."

"It's already almost five o'clock. I'll take you back to the PD."

After dropping Nichols off, Shaw returned some phone calls regarding other cases she was working on and completed a few reports. It was 7:30 pm before Shaw finished. She wanted to be at Maravilloso House no later than 9:00 pm, so she put on her gray blazer and drove to Zodiac Subs on Arapahoe Avenue for something to eat. Shaw ordered the Caesar salad and seltzer water. She was finished by 8:10 pm and headed for Maravilloso House.

Shaw presented the picture of Aubrey Leaver to the night staff and all patrons who entered. A few patrons thought she looked familiar but couldn't provide details about when or where they might have seen Aubrey. Shaw knew that some of them may have seen the photo in the media, which may have been what they remembered.

At 10:35 pm, Shaw's portable radio crackled with activity. Patrol officers were in pursuit of a sexual assault suspect in the vicinity of Chautauqua Park. Chautauqua Park is a popular hiking area underneath the towering Flatirons south of the intersection of Baseline Road and Grant Place.

Shaw listened intently as officers updated details of the pursuit. From what she could gather, the suspect was a tall white male who had fled north across Baseline into the upper Hill neighborhood. Officers were with the victim at Chautauqua Park, requesting a detective response.

Shaw quickly keyed her handheld radio, "This is D twelve-twenty-six. Is the victim injured?"

"Some bruising," responded an officer on the scene.

"Was there penetration?" asked Shaw.

"Yes."

"Then have her transported to Community Hospital. I will meet you there."

"Roger that."

Shaw quickly rushed to her car and began driving to Boulder Community Hospital. While driving, she listened intently to the foot chase taking place. Officers had lost the suspect around 7th and Cascade.

"I think he's headed toward the foothills," said officer one.

"Where did you last see him?" asked officer two.

"Running west on Cascade. I'm not sure if he continued or ducked into a backyard."

"I'm west of your location," said officer three.

"I've got Sixth Street covered," replied officer four.

"Can someone cover north of us?" asked officer one.

"I see him!" shouted officer four. "He just crossed the street running east. I'm in foot pursuit!"

"Coming your way," replied officer three.

"He's now northbound on Seventh Street!" screamed officer four. "He's trying to climb a fence."

Shaw could hear the stress and heavy breathing in the officer's voice. The radio went silent for several seconds. It seemed like minutes to Shaw. *Come on, get him!* Several more seconds passed.

"We got him! He's in custody," announced officer four.

"I'm here with him," said officer three. "We are code four."

Hearing "code four" allowed Shaw to relax. It is Boulder's police code meaning everything is okay and no one is hurt.

Shaw beat the ambulance to Boulder Community Hospital. She waited in the emergency room for the victim to arrive. Within six minutes, the ambulance pulled up next to the double sliding glass doors to the emergency room. As a precaution, paramedics wheeled the victim in on a stretcher. She wore a gray sweatshirt, and a white blanket covered her from the waist down.

Officer Sheila Stenson walked in closely behind.

"What do we have?" asked Shaw.

"Our victim was walking in Chautauqua Park when our suspect approached her asking for sex. When she refused, he attacked her. She tried to fight him off, but he was large and much stronger. He ripped her shorts off and assaulted her. He threatened to kill her if she didn't stop screaming, but she wouldn't stop. Someone in the parking lot of Chautauqua heard the screams and called the police."

"Was there penetration?"

"She told me there was."

"What do we know about the victim?"

"She's a twenty-two-year-old white female, five-foot-four, thin, with brown hair. All she would say is that she lives in Boulder. I think she is homeless."

"Do you know her name?"

"Yeah, it's Catherine Rosario. She goes by Cat."

"Thank you, Sheila. I can take it from here."

Shaw entered the curtained-off exam room where Catherine Rosario was being treated. A nurse was already checking Catherine's body for injuries.

"Cat, I'm Detective Caro Shaw with the Boulder Police Department. I'm sorry this happened to you, but we will do all we can to see your attacker go to prison. How are you feeling right now?"

"Okay, I guess."

"I would like to interview you about what happened tonight. I know you probably don't want to talk about it right now, but the sooner we get all the details, the better it will be for the investigation and filing of charges. Is that okay with you?"

"Can I clean up first?" asked Cat.

"I'm afraid not, Cat. A nurse trained in sexual assault exams will be here shortly to conduct an exam and collect evidence vital to the case. Once she is done, you will be able to shower."

"Okay," responded Cat.

"Why don't you just explain to me what happened tonight?"

"I was just hangin' out at Chautauqua. It's one of my favorite places. This big man approaches me. I think he was hiding in the row of trees bordering the park because I didn't see him until he came up behind me. He asked me if I would have sex with him. I told him to get the hell away from me. I guess that made him angry because he grabbed me and dragged me into some tall bushes. And that's where he did it."

"I know it's hard, but you must be more specific, Cat."

"I tried to fight him off, but he was too big. I screamed."

"Then what happened?"

"He popped the button on my shorts. Somehow, he got my shorts off of me. I don't know if he ripped them or what."

"Where are your shorts now?"

"I think an officer has them."

"What happened after he got your shorts off?"

"I tried to kick him in the balls. After that, he choked me until I could hardly breathe."

"Then what happened?"

"He raped me!" shouted Cat with a look of anger in her eyes.

"It's all right, Cat. We can get more specific later. Have you ever seen this man before?"

"Yeah, but I don't know who he is."

"Where have you seen him?"

"I've seen him in the downtown park by the creek a few times. And I think I've seen him on the mall."

"Was it Central Park where you saw him?"

"No. It was the one closer to the mountains."

"Eben G. Fine?" asked Shaw.

"Yeah, that's it."

"When was the last time you saw him?"

"Last week sometime. He's been hanging out with the homeless crowd."

"But you don't know his name?"

"No."

Shaw was interrupted by a nurse. "We are ready for Ms. Rosario now."

"Okay," said Shaw. "Cat, they will now take you to an exam room to collect evidence. I want you to know our officers caught your attacker running from the scene, and he's been arrested."

"Thank you," replied Cat.

Shaw waited in the hallway for the exam nurse to bring her the collected specimens. They would include swabs for semen, saliva, blood, and hair combings. The exam nurse would also document and photograph any injuries. As she waited, Shaw called the Boulder County Jail to get the suspect's name. Shane Phillips.

Damn, thought Shaw. *Tom was right. He is going to be so pissed tomorrow morning.*

After forty-five minutes, the exam nurse came out and handed Shaw multiple sealed paper bags with labels identifying each item of evidence.

"She was definitely penetrated," said the nurse. "She had some internal bleeding, and we found semen in her vagina."

"Thank you," said Shaw as she gathered up the evidence. "What are you going to do with Cat?"

"We will admit her for the night for observation. If she seems okay in the morning, we will release her."

"Great, thank you again."

On her drive back to the police department, Shaw received a call from Commander Greenberg.

"I hear we may have caught our serial killer?" asked Greenberg.

"Um, I wouldn't say that," answered Shaw. "The M.O. doesn't fit. Our other victims were not sexually assaulted."

"No, but they were all strangled, and two were found near parks, so it's already being reported on the news."

"Yeah, it's possible, but I don't see it right now. I believe the other three victims were held captive somewhere."

"Well, suspects sometimes change and become more brazen. Keep an open mind."

"We will certainly look into it, Commander."

"Either way, great work, Caro."

"I only interviewed the victim. Our patrol officers did all the work in catching him."

"I heard. I will be sure to congratulate them. I'll see you tomorrow."

Shaw made it home at 2:30 am. She removed her Glock handgun from her waist and set the gun and her cell phone on the table beside her bed. She quickly brushed her teeth, then undressed, throwing her clothing onto a beige upholstered armchair in the bedroom's corner. Shaw slipped on an oversized sleep top before crawling under the covers of her queen-sized bed. She lay awake thinking about the night's events and how upset Nichols would be in the morning. She thought of calling Nichols but knew he had been up most of the night before. Shaw decided it was better to let him get some sleep. By 3:45 am, Shaw finally fell asleep.

Chapter 14

Della could not sleep. The room was pitch black and quiet, but her thoughts were on how she needed to escape from her captors. Della didn't know how much longer she could keep from going insane. She was already finding it hard to think clearly, and memories were becoming confused. Yesterday, she believed there had been an opportunity to use the needle to stab her captor. But she was too frightened it wouldn't work, and the torture would intensify. Suddenly, a light came on, shining through the grate. Della listened carefully and could hear two voices again. One was from the smaller man in the hood, and the other sounded like the larger man. The smaller man in the hood had a higher-pitched voice, while the larger man's voice was more profound and raspy. Della strained to hear what was being said.

"I believe so," said the smaller man. "She has not given me any trouble in three days."

"Where would you put her on the scale?" asked the larger man.

"I would put her around fifty-five," said the smaller man.

"Well, you need to get her closer to forty."

"Yeah, I know that."

"Don't screw this up like the last one."

"Trust me, I'll get her to break."

The voices then faded, and Della could no longer hear what was being discussed. *What scale?* Thought Della. *And break me? What does that mean?*

The metal door to the room swung open, and the light was turned on. There stood the man in the hood. "Are you ready for another session, Amy?"

"Yes, sir," replied Della.

"You sit in the chair."

"Why don't you sit next to me on the bed?"

Della could see the man's eyes squinting behind the mask.

"The chair is uncomfortable, and I trust you now. I know you are just trying to help me get better."

The man stood, saying nothing for several seconds.

"All right, let's give it a try," he said as he sat on the edge of the bed next to Della. He turned his knees and torso toward Della.

"Tell me, Amy, have you ever been sexually assaulted?"

"Oh yes, multiple times," answered Della, as she knew that was the answer he wanted.

"And who first assaulted you?"

"My father."

"Where are your parents now, Della?"

"Both are dead."

"When did you first start experiencing hallucinations?"

"When I was fourteen."

"Where are you from?"

"Denver."

"Tell me about the injury to your neck."

"I get episodes of depression, and sometimes I try to hurt myself."

"Is that how you got your neck injury?"

"Yes. I stabbed myself with a needle."

"Did you do the same to your knee?"

"Yes."

"You are making progress, Amy. The first step is recognizing your illness. Admitting to these things will help you overcome your illness."

"Am I close to being released?"

"No, not yet. But you are getting there. You just recently accepted being victimized by your father. You need to remember other things before we can release you."

"Why do I have to be locked in a dungeon-like room?"

"To completely isolate you from outside stimuli. We have found isolation to be ideal for this type of brain, uh, excuse me, this type of treatment."

"What were you going to say?"

"Forget it. I was thinking of something else. You are doing fine, Amy," said the man as he stood up. "I'm sorry, but I've got to turn the music on."

"Please, no. It gives me a migraine every time."

"That's a good thing, Amy. It means your brain is being stimulated."

Della fell back on the bed, knowing what was coming.

As he left, the man turned and said, "I will shut the music down when it is time for lunch."

Twenty seconds later, the speaker was placed on the grate, and the music of Michael Jackson blared into the room. Della covered her ears, trying to block out the pounding sound.

****

It was 6:40 am when Shaw's phone buzzed. She rolled over in bed and grabbed her cell phone. It was Nichols calling. "Hey, Tom. What's up?"

"Why didn't you call me last night?" asked Nichols. "I heard we arrested Phillips for rape!"

"It was late last night, and you hadn't slept much. I handled it."

"Did you interview him?"

"No. Patrol said he asked for an attorney."

"I knew it!" shouted Nichols. "If that bitch Ruby had simply pressed charges, we wouldn't have this!"

"Stop shouting at me. I had nothing to do with it."

"I'm sorry, I'm just upset. I knew this would happen."

"You did everything you could, Tom."

"Hang on," said Nichols. Shaw could hear muffled sounds over the phone.

"Sorry," said Nichols. "I was talking too loudly and woke up the kids. Kristin's not too happy with me right now. The news is saying this could be our serial killer."

"I don't think so," replied Shaw. "But we have to prove it, or they will continue speculating."

"When are you going in?"

"I was going to sleep in some, but now that you've woken me up, I might as well get ready for work."

"Yeah, sorry about that. Was the victim hurt?"

"Some bruising and penetration, but she will be okay physically. Mentally, who knows?"

"I'm going to get dressed and go in. I need to find Ruby."

"We have a solid case on Phillips. You need to focus on our serial killer."

"Yeah, I will, but I still need to find Ruby."

"Well, I'll see you when I get in."

"Okay. Bye, Caro."

Shaw rolled back in bed, took a deep breath and sighed. It was going to be a long day.

When Nichols arrived at work, Commander Greenberg was already in her office. Nichols walked in.

"I hear we caught a rapist last night."

"We did. The suspect you interviewed last week."

"I heard. I could have arrested him if the victim had cooperated."

"That's how it goes sometimes, Tom. It would be best if you let it go. You did all you could."

"Yes, but now another woman has been assaulted."

"It happens sometimes."

"I'm going to see if I can find Ruby. I now know she hangs out near Settler's Park."

"You know it's now called The People's Crossing, right?"

"Yeah, whatever," said Nichols with a wave of his hand. "I know it as Settler's Park."

Nichols returned to his desk and pulled up the reports from the sex assault. The description of the assault further angered Nichols. He grabbed his windbreaker and headed out. Nichols drove to the west end of Boulder at the mouth of the canyon, where Boulder Creek enters the city. Nichols hiked up the hill north of Canyon Boulevard and started walking the trail at The People's Crossing. Several encampments could be seen west of the path. Nichols walked toward the encampments, looking for Ruby. He found her behind a red rock outcropping. She was still snuggled in her brown sleeping bag.

Nichols kicked at the foot of the sleeping bag. "Ruby, wake up. It's Detective Nichols. I need to talk to you."

"Huh?"

"Ruby, get up. We need to talk."

Ruby slowly sat up. Her hair was matted. "What do you want?"

"Remember the guy who sexually assaulted you?"

"Yeah."

"Well, he just raped a woman last night. You could have stopped him."

"How could I have stopped him?"

"By cooperating and identifying him for me. I would have arrested him yesterday if you had helped me out."

Nichols pulled out the manila folder from inside his windbreaker. "I want you to look at this and point out who assaulted you." Nichols opened the folder and held it in front of Ruby's face. There were photographs of six men of a similar age and likeness. "Do you see the man who assaulted you?"

Ruby squinted her eyes and stared at the photo line-up.

"Come on, Ruby. Who is it?"

Ruby lifted her right hand and pointed to one photograph.

Nichols put his finger on the photograph. "Is that the man who assaulted you?"

Ruby nodded her head yes.

"I need you to say it, Ruby."

"Yes, that's the man."

"Well, that's Shane Phillips. He's the man who raped another woman last night. If you had cooperated, I could have prevented it from happening."

"He has friends," said Ruby while looking down.

"No one knows you talked to me, and if anyone bothers you, you just call me. I'll take care of it."

Ruby nodded.

"This will help us establish a pattern and shows he is not a first-time offender. He's probably done this many times before. Thank you, Ruby."

Ruby nodded again. Nichols hiked back to his car and returned to the police department. By the time he got back, Shaw was at her desk.

"Where have you been?" asked Shaw.

"I found Ruby and made her look at this line-up. She positively identified Phillips as the person who assaulted her. This will help establish a pattern."

"I hope you weren't too hard on her."

"No, I wasn't. I had cooled down by then. But I told her what happened."

Nichols' phone rang. It was Detective Owen Gates from the Sheriff's Department. "Hi, Owen. What's up?"

"Dr. Lanaro has agreed to help us out. He's coming in this afternoon."

"Uh, I think that would work. What time?" asked Nichols.

"He will be at the Sheriff's department at three o'clock."

"We will be there unless you hear otherwise," replied Nichols.

"What was that about?" asked Shaw.

"That was Owen. He shared the case file with Dr. Lanaro yesterday. Lanaro is coming in at three this afternoon to discuss the case."

"Works for me. Oh, I almost forgot. The commander wants to see us in her office."

"What about?"

"She was asking me about that bogus tip I got yesterday. She seemed irritated."

Nichols' throat tightened up. "What do you mean?"

"I mean, she seemed irritated that someone would make a joke out of a tip like that. Let's go find out."

Nichols was now concerned. He felt a churning in his stomach, and beads of sweat formed underneath his hair. Shaw and Nichols walked into the commander's office together.

"Sit down," said Greenberg.

Both detectives sat in chairs across from Greenberg's desk. The envelope stamped confidential rested on top of her desk.

"Caro, when did you receive this envelope?"

"When I came in yesterday morning. It was on my desk."

"Someone left it for you overnight?"

"Yes. I believe it was put there as a joke."

"Given how ridiculous the tip is, I agree. It concerns me that in the throes of maybe our biggest investigation ever, someone thinks it funny to leave a stupid tip on your desk, wasting your valuable time."

"I agree," nodded Shaw.

Nichols sat in fear. The beads of sweat grew more pronounced on the back of his neck, and his mouth was dry.

The commander turned to Nichols. "You were in very early yesterday. Did you see anyone around Caro's desk?"

Nichols hesitated. "Commander, I'm the one who put that tip on her desk," his voice shaking. "I found the tip ridiculous and thought it would be funny. I made a joke out of it, and I'm sorry."

Greenberg stared at Nichols for several seconds. Nichols swallowed hard.

"You came into my office and took my confidential stamp off my shelf?"

"Umm, yes, I did. Again, I'm sorry. I didn't realize it would be a big deal."

"You don't think a serial killer case is a big deal?"

"That's not what I meant, Commander," replied Nichols as he squirmed in his chair. Shaw could see how uncomfortable Nichols was.

"I know this is your first homicide, Tom, but I expect more from my detectives. You can spend the rest of the day packing up your desk. I'm transferring you back to Patrol."

"What!? I'm sorry, Commander. It will never happen again. In auto theft, we joked around a lot. I didn't realize....."

Shaw couldn't hold it any longer. She burst out laughing.

Nichols looked at her in astonishment. "This is not funny!"

"Yes, it is," laughed Shaw.

Nichols glanced at the commander and saw that she was also laughing. Nichols sat back in his chair. "What is going on here?"

"Got you back!" shouted Shaw.

A sense of relief flowed through Nichols' body. "How did you know?"

"It wasn't hard to figure out," replied Shaw. "Once I checked with patrol, records, and dispatch, I knew it had to be someone in the bureau. And the only one who came in early was you."

Nichols turned to Greenberg. "Commander, you scared the hell out of me."

Greenberg smiled. "Caro made me do it. I actually found the tip humorous myself. But just don't ever rifle through my desk. Okay?"

"No, no. I'd never do that. And don't worry, I won't be coming into your office again unless invited."

As Nichols and Shaw walked back to their desks, Nichols turned to Shaw. "Damn, Caro. You got me good."

Shaw laughed. "Just remember, what goes around comes around."

Both detectives spent the rest of the morning completing reports and reviewing tips. At 12:30, Nichols approached Shaw.

"I'm hungry," said Nichols. "I think I need a double cheeseburger to calm me down. You want to go?"

"No, I brought in a salad. I've got to finish up some reports from last night. Did you get through all those tips yet?"

"Can't work on an empty stomach, Caro. See ya."

Later that afternoon, Shaw and Nichols arrived at the Sheriff's Department to participate in the conversation with Dr. Anthony Lanaro. Present for the meeting were Sergeant Luca Martinez, Detective Owen Gates, Sheriff Commander Joel Clark, and Dr. Lanaro. Lanaro was a 53-year-old white male who stood approximately six-foot-two and a stocky 210 pounds. He had wavy dark brown hair with waves of gray mixed in. On his well-tanned face, he wore silver wire-rimmed glasses. He wore a long-sleeved light yellow collared dress shirt and gray polyester dress pants. On his feet were black slip-on penny loafers. Commander Clark made the introductions.

"Please, just call me Tony," said Lanaro.

Commander Clark started the meeting. "Tony, I understand you've reviewed each homicide and autopsy report, correct?"

"That's correct," responded Lanaro.

"Is there anything you can tell us, from the reports, that may give us some insight into who we are dealing with?"

"I believe so. I agree with the coroner's finding that each victim was probably tortured or abused in some manner. I also believe each murder was committed by the same individual."

Others in the room nodded in agreement.

"As you can imagine, the psychology of a serial killer is a complex and multifaceted subject that has been the subject of extensive research in the field of psychology. However, there are some common factors among all serial killers. Many lack empathy for others and have a diminished capacity for emotional connections. They often manipulate and deceive others to achieve their goals. We find that a significant number of serial killers have a history of childhood trauma, such as physical, sexual, or emotional abuse. These experiences can contribute to the development of psychopathic tendencies."

"Do you believe our killer suffered from sexual abuse?" asked Sgt. Martinez.

"In my assessment, no. You have found no evidence of sexual assault on any of the victims, correct?"

"That's correct," responded Martinez.

"Therefore, I believe you are looking for someone who suffered physical or emotional abuse. This individual would more likely seek power and control over his victims. By exerting dominance and taking someone's life, they gain a sense of superiority. This desire can be linked to deep-seated feelings of inadequacy and a need to exert authority."

"You're fairly certain that sex plays no role in these killings?" asked Shaw.

"Not necessarily," answered Lanaro. "I said it is my belief the person you are looking for was not sexually abused as a child. However, in seeking control over someone, sex can play a role. The act of killing may be intertwined with sexual arousal or gratification without ever sexually assaulting the victim. Since your victims have not been sexually assaulted, you can rule that out as motivation. But keep in mind the desire for power and authority over another could create sexual pleasure within the mind of the killer. These killers may create elaborate fantasies or narratives surrounding their acts. This may serve as a form of escapism from their own lives. These fantasies often involve dominance, control, and violence. You are also looking for someone with low empathy and impulsive behavior. Should a victim resist, the killer justifies applying torture and pain to his victims."

"In other words," stated Gates, "we are looking for a very deranged individual."

"Don't disregard the fact that a serial killer can act and look very ordinary in everyday life. Ted Bundy is an excellent example of this."

"You think we are dealing with a Ted Bundy-type killer?" asked Shaw.

"No. I was just pointing out an example of a serial killer who appeared normal to many around him. He could be friendly and charming. The difference is that Bundy did not keep his victims captive. He stalked them, and once he had them, he killed them quickly. Some may remember the sorority women Bundy attacked at Florida State University. He broke into their home and severely beat four women. Two of them died. There was no sex involved, but he probably experienced a sense of satisfaction similar to having sex."

"You're kind of freaking me out," said Shaw.

"It's not a pleasant subject," agreed Lanaro.

"What are we looking for, Tony?" asked Commander Clark.

"Eighty-two percent of serial killers are white males. Because we are in Boulder with primarily an all-white population, you can be reasonably sure your suspect is a white male. Second, I would put the age of your suspect between twenty and thirty. And he is probably someone who easily blends into the crowd. He is probably attractive, which helps in seducing his victims. An ugly fifty-year-old guy like me would have trouble saddling up to a twenty-year-old woman. It wouldn't surprise me if he drugs his victims, possibly in nightclubs. Forcefully grabbing and kidnapping a woman would be too noticeable in public."

"We know that one of our victims was at the Maravilloso House prior to her disappearance," offered Shaw.

"That may be where she met her killer," responded Lanaro.

Others in the room nodded in agreement.

"Anything else we should look for?" asked Martinez.

"I believe your killer is well-educated and sophisticated in how he tortures his victims. I base this on the autopsy reports. The injuries to the victims are very calculated and effective. He's not just beating them up. You're looking for an intelligent killer. If your belief that Aubrey Leaver was held captive for nearly three months is accurate, this person knows what he is doing. And he's doing it with no one else knowing. Since you haven't identified more than one victim, it tells me he selects those without local connections."

"I think you nailed it," agreed Commander Clark. "Are there any more questions?"

"I have one," said Shaw. "Why do you think our killer cut the wrists on our latest victim after she was dead?"

"My guess is to make it look like a suicide. I see it as a stupid mistake on his part. If he is intelligent like I believe, he should have known the blood would not all pump out once the heart had stopped beating."

"Thank you, Tony," said Commander Clark. "We appreciate your help."

"No problem. Call me if you have other questions."

"We will. Thank you."

Upon returning to the police department, Shaw, Nichols, and Martinez met with Commander Greenberg to give her the update.

"He sounds like an excellent resource," suggested Greenberg.

"Very informative," agreed Martinez. "He gave us a profile that may help us search for a suspect."

"Yeah, every twenty-something white male in Boulder," grumbled Nichols.

"It's better than nothing," responded Martinez. "He also said our suspect is probably intelligent and good-looking. He may also hang out at nightclubs. At least it's something."

"We clearly need a break. Someone out there knows our guy," said Shaw.

"Well, we better get it soon," said Greenberg. "City Council is concerned over the fear being expressed by the community. Women are afraid to go out at night anymore."

Chapter 15

It was 3:12 pm when Shaw's phone rang. Detective Gates was calling. "Hi, Owen. What's up?"

"We might have an ID on our victim from three years ago."

"Seriously?"

"Yes. We just finished interviewing a Thornton woman who thinks the composite drawing looks like a woman she knew as Jennifer Bryant. We are trying to locate the family now."

"That's great news. Who is the witness?"

"A young woman named Allison Adams. She was Jennifer Bryant's friend for about four months, and then she just disappeared."

"Did she report her friend as missing?"

"No. Allison said Jennifer was semi-homeless, hopping from one town to another, partying with whomever she met. Allison figured Jennifer just hit the road again."

"She wasn't concerned Jennifer disappeared without a word?"

"Well, somewhat. But after nothing came up in the news, she forgot about it. We are trying to locate Jennifer's family to get a DNA sample to compare to our victim."

"Do you know where the family is?"

"Yes. We ran the name through NCIC and found a missing person report filed in Little Rock, Arkansas, almost three years ago. I'll let you know what we find out."

"Thank you, Owen."

Shaw shared the news with Greenberg, Martinez, and Nichols.

"This is a significant development," stated Greenberg. "It will draw more interest in the case, and hopefully, more tips will come in."

"It seems strange to me that people don't call the police when their friends just disappear," pondered Nichols.

"Remember," said Martinez, "these are young adults, not from Boulder. They are free-wheeling partiers living a youthful lifestyle. It is not unusual to bounce from place to place."

"We don't know that about our recent victim," said Nichols.

"With all the publicity and the composite being released, if our victim was local, someone would have called us by now," insisted Martinez.

"He's right," agreed Shaw. "Our latest victim has to be from out of town."

"I've got an idea," suggested Greenberg. "Let's create a poster with all three victims' descriptions, photos or composites. We can then hang one in every bar, café, and restaurant in town. Put them where others may have met, worked with, or partied with these women."

"I can work on that," offered Shaw.

"In the meantime, keep visiting the bars in town. Show people our photos and sketches. Get Jordan to help," directed Greenberg.

There was a new sense of urgency among the detectives. With Dr. Lanaro's insights and the possible identification of another victim, the team was energized.

Shaw collaborated with the city's communications department to prepare posters while detectives Nichols and Jordan began visiting every bar and restaurant in downtown Boulder. By 7:00 pm, Shaw had newly printed posters in hand. She called Nichols.

"Tom, I've got two hundred freshly printed posters. Where are you guys?"

"We're up on the Hill. Meet us at The Sink."

"Be there soon."

The Sink is a famous iconic Boulder bar and restaurant known for its pizza and burgers. It has been in Boulder since 1923 and was once famously visited by President Barack Obama. Its walls are covered in photographs and signatures, many of which are of famous people who have visited. While people of all ages visit the sink during the day, in the evening it is quite popular with the college-aged crowd.

Shaw arrived at 7:20 pm. Shaw could not see Nichols in the dim lighting. She called him on her cell phone.

"Hello."

"I'm here. Where are you guys?"

"Keep walking toward the back. We are against the south wall."

Shaw found them seated at a table with four chairs. Three iced teas were on the table.

"What are we doing?" asked Shaw.

"We're getting something to eat," said Jordan. "We haven't eaten since lunch. Sit down. We got you an iced tea."

"We need to get these posters out."

"Relax, Caro," Jordan responded. "We've been interviewing people for four hours. Have you eaten?"

"No."

"Then sit down and join us for some dinner. We'll get back to it after we get some food."

"Would you like to share a pizza with us?" asked Nichols.

"Yeah, that's fine."

"Great. We ordered a large Slaughterhouse Five."

Shaw looked at them both with a frown. "Slaughterhouse Five?"

"You'll love it," said Nichols. "It comes with just about everything piled on. You only had a salad for lunch. You can afford to eat some pizza."

"You know we're working late tonight, right?"

"Yeah, we got it," interrupted Jordan. "That's why we need to fuel up."

After dinner, Shaw agreed the pizza was good. "You were right. The pizza hit the spot."

"I'm never wrong about food, Caro," bragged Nichols.

Shaw laughed. "Uh, I wouldn't go that far. Enough about food. Where do we go next?"

"The Maravilloso House."

It was the last week of school for college students. The bars on the Hill and the Pearl Street Mall were crowded that night. For some, it was the last night of partying before heading home. It was 8:05 pm, and a good-sized crowd was already drinking inside the Maravilloso House. Shaw handed Jordan and Nichols a poster.

"Let's split up," said Shaw. "Kevin, you take the back. Tom, you take the north side, and I'll work the bar side."

Each detective spoke with patrons and showed them the posters. After fifteen minutes, Nichols approached Shaw, grabbed her arm, and leaned close to her ear. "Follow me," he said. Shaw followed Nichols to the sidewalk outside the bar.

"What is it?" asked Shaw.

"I found a witness."

Shaw flashed a look of surprise.

"A woman named Jessica Daniels recognized the photo of Aubrey Leaver. She was acquainted with her from the bar. And get this. Jessica remembers Aubrey getting friendly with a guy just before she stopped coming to the bar."

"Are you kidding me?"

"Nope."

"We need to take her back to the PD right now."

"No, no. She won't go. This is her last night with some of her friends. I have all her information, and she promised to meet us at the station tomorrow morning at eleven."

"Tom, we must take her in and get a statement."

"You will just piss her off, Caro. She is cooperative and promised to be there tomorrow. I have all her information if she doesn't show up."

"There you are," said Jordan as he walked out the door. "What's going on?"

"I found a witness who saw Aubrey with a man just before she disappeared," responded Nichols. "She's going to come in tomorrow for an interview."

"That's terrific."

"All right," agreed Shaw. "We'll wait until tomorrow. Let's finish getting posters distributed on the Hill. How much of downtown did you cover?"

"We got all of Pearl Street. We were going to do Walnut next," advised Nichols.

"Okay. After we're done here, you two take the west end of Walnut, and I'll start at Fifteenth and work my way west."

By 10:30 pm, the three detectives had covered all the open restaurants and bars on Walnut and the side streets between Ninth and Fifteenth Street. No other witnesses were located.

"Tomorrow may be another long day," said Shaw. "I will leave the commander a note telling her we won't be in until nine. How does that sound?"

"That sounds great," smiled Jordan.

"I agree," said Nichols.

"Okay, guys. Good work. I'll see you in the morning."

"Good night, Caro," said Nichols.

The following day, around 9:30 am, Commander Greenberg called the team into her office.

"We are getting inundated with tips," advised Greenberg. "By last count, we have received thirty-five hundred tips. I've got three light-duty officers, two records clerks, and six citizen volunteers going through every tip. I've told them to forward it to Martinez if they see anything that could be legitimate. He will then pass them on to be followed up."

"Thirty-five hundred?" asked a surprised Nichols.

"That's what I've been told. Your work and the news releases have gotten people's attention. And the appearance of Dr. Lanaro on the news last night stirred things up."

"Lanaro was on the news?" asked Shaw.

"Didn't you see it?"

"No, we were out until well past the news."

"He gave the profile of the type of person we should look for."

"That should help," said Jordan.

"Did you know he was going to do that?" asked Martinez.

"No," responded Greenberg. "And the Chief didn't know either. But it will certainly generate more tips."

"Well, we might have found a witness last night," advised Shaw. "A woman is coming in at eleven who saw Aubrey at Maravilloso House talking to a man shortly before she disappeared."

"That's good work, detectives. Keep me updated on your progress."

It was 11:02 am, and Jessica Daniels hadn't shown up.

"Damn it, Tom, I told you we should have brought her in last night," scolded Shaw.

"Relax, will you? I can read people. She will be here."

"Well, she's not timely."

Nichols chuckled. "She's a college student. She will be here."

At 11:07 am, Nichols' phone rang. "Hello. Oh, good. I'll be right there." Nichols turned toward Shaw. "She's here. See, I told you."

Shaw rolled her eyes.

"I'm going to bring her up to interview room one. I'll see you there," said Nichols.

When Nichols brought Jessica Daniels into the interview room, Shaw was already seated at the rectangle table. Nichols pulled out the chair on the opposite side for Daniels to sit down. He then joined Shaw across from Daniels. Jessica Daniels was a white female, 21 years old, with long, dark hair. She wore her hair in a ponytail tied with a yellow ribbon. She wore a green tank top, white shorts, and white sandals.

"Thank you for coming today," said Nichols.

"Yes, thank you," agreed Shaw.

Nichols started by laying the photograph of Aubrey Leaver on the table in front of Daniels. "Is this the woman you knew as Aubrey Leaver?"

"I'm not sure of the last name, but that's definitely the Aubrey I knew. I can't believe she is dead."

"You have our condolences, Jessica. Can you please tell us how you knew Aubrey?"

"I first met Aubrey at the Dark Horse. I liked her right off. She was outgoing and friendly."

"How well did you get to know her?"

"We exchanged phone numbers. I told her about the Maravilloso House on the Hill. That's where I usually hang out. I would text her if I knew I was going to the House. Sometimes, she would meet me there."

"How often did you get together with Aubrey?"

"Hmmm. I'd say at least six times. She was fun to be with."

"Do you know where Aubrey worked?"

"The last time I saw her, she told me she had gotten a job at a restaurant downtown. I don't know the name of it."

"You told me she met a man at the Maravilloso House. Is that accurate?"

"Yes."

"Can you describe him?"

"Hm, white male, mid-twenties."

"Can you be more descriptive? How tall was he?"

"I'd say average height. I'm five-five, and he was probably three to four inches taller than me."

"That would make him five-nine. Does that sound about right?"

"Yeah."

"What about weight? Was he heavy, skinny, or what?"

"I'd say average. He was not heavy."

"What about hair color, eyes, and complexion?"

"He was clean cut. Lovely, dark wavy hair and dark eyes. I remember the eyes."

"What was his name, Jessica?"

"I've been trying to remember, but I just can't come up with it."

"Was it an unusual name?"

"I'm sorry, I just don't remember."

"Any tattoos or descriptive markings on him?"

"Not that I remember. He was good looking. I remember that."

"What about clothing?"

"Oh, he was a sharp dresser. He always wore nice shirts and pants, like he was going to a fancy restaurant."

"When you say nice shirts and pants, what do you mean?"

"He was always in a long-sleeved dress shirt and dress pants. He stood out from most of the other men. He could have been going to church."

"Thank you, Jessica. Detective Shaw has a few questions for you."

"Jessica," started Shaw, "can you describe this man's personality for us?"

"He seemed a bit shy and quiet."

"Did he concern you?"

"No. He wasn't outgoing, but he was polite. I remember him asking Aubrey questions about where she was from and where she was living."

"Can you be more specific, Jessica?"

"No. It was like seven months ago."

"How often does he come to Maravilloso House?"

"Oh, I haven't seen him since Aubrey stopped coming."

"Once Aubrey stopped coming, you no longer saw this man?"

"Not that I remember."

"The last time you saw Aubrey, did she leave the bar with this man?"

"I did not see them leave together, but I assumed so. I was probably talking with other friends when they left."

"Was Aubrey dating him?"

"No. She had just ended a relationship with a guy in Santa Fe and didn't want to get tied down again. Aubrey told me she was on an adventure of travel. Having a boyfriend was too difficult."

"Didn't you think it was strange that Aubrey just disappeared?"

"Somewhat, but she was traveling around. I figured she just left Colorado. It was nothing to call the police about."

"Would you recognize this man if you saw him again?"

"Yeah, I believe so."

"You said he had dark hair and dark eyes. Was he Hispanic?"

"I don't think he was Hispanic. He just had dark features."

"Will you be staying here for the summer?"

"No. I'm going back to Naperville, Illinois, for the summer. That's where I'm from. I'll be back in August for school."

"If we have more questions, is it okay to call you?"

"Yes, absolutely. Anything I can do to help. But I have a question myself."

"Go ahead; what's your question?" asked Shaw.

"Do you think this man from the bar had something to do with Aubrey's death?"

"We don't know, Jessica. That's what we need to find out."

After the interview, Nichols asked Shaw her opinion.

"I believe this is the first genuine lead on a possible suspect. It seems too coincidental to me that he disappears when Aubrey disappears."

"I agree," replied Nichols. "He may have gained Aubrey's trust to go with him."

"If he is our suspect, his M.O. is to gain women's trust. He is not a snatch'em and run type of offender."

"Should we put out the description we have to the public?" asked Nichols.

"It's a question for the commander. The description we have is not unique or detailed. Women will be calling in every dark-haired man they know. We could get bogged down with false leads."

"Very true," agreed Nichols.

Chapter 16

After the heart-pounding, jaw-rattling music had stopped, Della felt dazed and confused. The rapid beat of her heart was palpable, and sweat had soaked her T-shirt. She lay on the bed until her heartbeat and breathing returned to normal.

While lying there, thoughts of her parents consumed her mind. How did they die? When? At times, Della had memories of living in Erie, Pennsylvania. Then she would think she was from Denver. Della could not understand why the police would bring her to a place of isolation and trauma. She envisioned the night when the police dragged her away, handcuffed her, and brought her to the treatment facility. There were moments when Della believed everything the man in the hood was feeding her. The living conditions, abuse, mind games, and manipulation had confused Della to where she could not trust her memories. One memory Della had was of coming home from school to find her mother baking fresh chocolate chip cookies. The sweet aroma of freshly baked cookies would fill her nostrils as she entered the house. The first bite of a warm cookie with melted semi-sweet chocolate was something no one could forget. Della remembered her mom would often bake goodies for the family. She hoped this was an accurate memory, as it helped her cope with the stress and isolation.

Della was afraid that if the police put her in such an awful facility, they were people she could not trust for help. During moments of lucid thinking, Della did not believe the man would ever allow her to leave. If she were to get out, she would have to do it alone. She had previously thought about using the hidden needle as a tool for escape but had been too afraid to try. While it had become difficult to know her reality, Della knew she had to run from her captor. The needle was her only hope.

****

It was Friday morning, May 26th, when Shaw and Nichols were told by Commander Greenberg that the description of a possible suspect had been released to the media the previous night.

"You released the description?" asked Nichols.

"Didn't have much choice," said Greenberg. "I know it will apply to about twenty-five percent of American males, but if we didn't release it and someone else was killed....."

"I get it," said Shaw.

"We are going to get swamped with tips," responded Nichols.

"Sorry, guys. Just do the best you can," said Greenberg.

After the commander had left, Nichols asked Shaw if she had heard whether the Sheriff's department had confirmed their victim's identity.

"They will let us know. The DNA comparison with the family could take a few days."

It was 1:20 pm when one of the light-duty officers reviewing tips walked to Shaw's desk with a stack of thirty-three pages.

"What's this?" asked Shaw.

"We received over a hundred new tips overnight," said the officer. "We evaluated them all, and these are the ones we think someone should look at."

"Damn, that many?" asked Shaw.

"Yep."

Shaw shook her head. "Thank you, I guess."

Shaw divided the stack of tips into thirds. She kept a third and gave a third each to Nichols and Jordan.

"It will take a week to properly vet these tips," protested Jordan.

"Until we identify a suspect, what else do we have to do?" asked Shaw.

"You know we'll get more tomorrow, right?"

"Yes, Kevin. I know that. But again, what's our choice? Any one of these tips could be our guy."

Jordan sighed and walked away.

While she didn't show it, Shaw was just as concerned. She approached Sergeant Martinez. "Sarge, I'm not sure we can investigate all the tips coming in."

"You're not investigating all the tips. These are just the best ones."

"I know, but we got thirty-three just today."

"Well, the Sheriff's department is helping. The batch tomorrow will go to them. We will rotate the distribution of tips every other day. I've also reached out to Broomfield to see if they can assist us."

"That will help. Thank you, Sergeant."

The team spent most of the afternoon vetting the thirty-three tips of young white males with dark hair and eyes. When names were provided, database searches were used to check backgrounds, family history, and past criminal behavior. However, there was one tip received by Nichols that stood out. Athena Gibson, a woman living in Idaho Springs, Colorado, had called and reported someone had kidnapped her in Cripple Creek, Colorado and held her captive five years ago. The man who abducted Athena was a white male with dark brown eyes. She was released after seven weeks in captivity. Her abductor was never found. Nichols showed the tip to Shaw and Jordan.

"That," said Shaw, "looks promising. We need to get an interview with her. Can you set it up, Tom?"

"For when?"

"As soon as she is available."

Nichols called and talked briefly with Athena Gibson. He learned she was a twenty-six-year-old white female. Ms. Gibson told Nichols she was abducted from a casino in Cripple Creek, Colorado, when she was twenty-one.

"We would like to interview you in depth about your abduction," advised Nichols. "When are you available?"

"I work at the local library. Tomorrow, I get off at two o'clock."

"I can be at your home after you get off work."

"Okay. Can you meet me at two-thirty? I have plans at five o'clock."

"Yes, absolutely. Thank you for calling, Athena. I will see you to-morrow."

After he got off the phone, Nichols called out to Shaw. "I have an interview set up tomorrow at two-thirty with Athena Gibson. Do you want to go?"

"Yes. Are we meeting her in Idaho Springs?"

"Yes."

"Let's meet at the PD at twelve-thirty. That will give us plenty of time," suggested Shaw.

"Sounds good. I'll be here."

Nichols then asked Jordan if he was interested in coming along.

"Can't," said Jordan. "I already have three interviews set up tomor-row myself."

The following day, Saturday, Shaw and Nichols were on the road to Idaho Springs by 12:45 pm. Shaw allowed Nichols to drive. Their trip would take them south on Highway 93 from Boulder to Golden. From there, they would hop on I-70 and head west to Idaho Springs, approxi-mately 30 miles west of Denver.

Idaho Springs is a small mountain town of roughly 1,900 residents, once known for mining. It is now known for its hot springs and rafting on Clear Creek, which flows along I-70 and through the center of town.

Tourist shops and restaurants line the few blocks of downtown. The town sits at 7,526 feet above sea level.

"Where do you want to stop for lunch?" asked Nichols.

"Lunch? I ate before I came in."

"I know a good mountain restaurant in Idaho Springs," continued Nichols.

"Did you hear what I just said? Besides, we have no time for lunch."

"Give me a break, Caro. My daughter had swimming this morning, and my son had a soccer game. I didn't have time to eat. Besides, we have plenty of time. I can get us there in forty-five minutes, sixty minutes tops, if traffic is heavy."

"Well, we're not stopping at a nice restaurant for lunch. If you need to get something to eat, stop at a McDonald's or Seven-Eleven."

Nichols frowned. "Really?"

"YES! Really. I don't want us to be late."

"All right," sighed Nichols. "I know a Burger King along the way. I'll stop there. Haven't had a double whopper in ages."

Shaw rolled her eyes.

After driving through Golden, but before getting onto I-70, Nichols found a Burger King. He pulled into the parking lot.

"Just go through the drive-thru," said Shaw.

"We have time for me to sit and eat a burger. It won't take me long."

"What if we run into traffic? I'll drive, and you can eat."

"No, no. I hate eating in the car. Let me sit down for ten minutes and eat a sandwich."

Shaw shook her head. "You're never driving again."

Nichols laughed. "Would you like something to drink?"

"No, thanks."

After finishing the last bite of his double whopper, he wiped the ketchup from the right corner of his mouth.

"You missed some," observed Shaw.

Nichols dabbed the other side of his mouth and then wiped the napkin across his lips. "Did I get it?"

"No, doofus. You've got ketchup on your shirt."

"Where?"

"Left side. Below your chin."

Nichols looked down, squeezing his chin against his upper chest. "Damn. Let me go wash this off."

Shaw watched Nichols walk toward the bathroom with a look of amusement. Several minutes later, he returned with a wet baseball-sized spot where the ketchup had been. "I should have worn a darker shirt today."

"Let's go," responded Shaw.

Nichols refused to give up the keys. They arrived in Idaho Springs at 2:15 pm. By 2:22 pm, they were parked in front of the six-unit apartment building where Athena Gibson lived. The dark brown brick building was two-story, with three units below and three above. White painted wood framed windows looked out onto the street from each apartment. Athena Gibson lived on the first floor in unit #3.

As the detectives approached the white front door, it opened. "You must be the detectives," said Athena.

"Yes. I'm Detective Caro Shaw, and this is Detective Tom Nichols. Are you Athena Gibson?"

"Yes. Come on in."

The apartment was a small one-bedroom unit, and the main area comprised a living room and dining area. The kitchen was off the dining room, and everything looked clean and tidy. Walls in the living room were covered in bygone pastel floral wallpaper. Two brown cushioned lounge chairs sat in the living room with a table between them and a flat-screen TV sitting on a cabinet opposite the chairs.

"Why don't we sit at the kitchen table?" suggested Athena.

Shaw and Nichols sat at the table. Athena sat across from them. Shaw estimated Athena Gibson was approximately five-foot-three and 160 pounds. She had light brown hair down to the top of her shoulders. Her eyes looked hazel. Gibson's face was round and beautiful.

"Do you mind if we record the interview?" asked Nichols.

"Not at all."

Nichols placed a small digital recorder on the table in front of Athena.

Shaw began the questioning. "Athena, we are talking to you to determine if you may have been kidnapped by the same person we are looking for. I understand they never caught your kidnapper?"

"That's correct," replied Athena.

"Why don't you just tell us your story? We will follow up with questions we have."

"It is still hard to talk about, but I'll do my best."

"We understand," replied Shaw.

"It happened five years ago when I was twenty-one and living in Colorado Springs. I had gone to Cripple Creek, where they have all the casinos, to do some partying with a few friends. I'm ashamed to say I got pretty wasted. All my friends did. We had a room, so we didn't have to drive anywhere. I don't remember much about the rest of the night, but I do remember talking to a man at the casino. I remember he had dark hair and dark eyes."

"Was he a white male?" asked Nichols.

"Yes."

"About what age?"

"He was young. About my age."

"Do you remember his name?"

"No, I don't. Sorry."

"Continue with your story, Athena," said Shaw.

"I don't know what happened the rest of that night. However, the next memory I have is of waking up locked in a white room with no windows. All I had in the room was a twin bed, a chair, and a bucket. It was horrible. I was so scared. I remember screaming for what seemed like an hour. I had to pee so badly, but there was no bathroom. I just peed my pants."

"That sounds terrifying," said Shaw.

"It was. Many of my memories came after months of psychiatric care. That's why the police said my situation was difficult to investigate. Much of what I told them came from therapy. The police told me my memory would be challenged in court, even if they found a suspect."

"Just tell us what you remember," urged Shaw.

"I remember being beaten for peeing in my pants. This man comes into the room with a rubber hose and beats me for wetting myself. I told him I couldn't hold it. That's when I learned the bucket was to be used to relieve myself."

The memory caused Athena to begin crying.

"It's okay, Athena. Take your time."

"I was in that hellhole for a long time. Each day, I was subject to being tortured in some manner. There were these large speakers hanging in opposite corners of the room. Sometimes, he would play music so loud I thought I would lose my hearing. In fact, I did lose some of my hearing. Someday, I will probably need hearing aids. Denial of food and light was another form of abuse. And that chair. Sometimes he would strap me in that chair and use the rubber hose on me. Other times, he would stick needles into me. He always said it was therapy. Many details of my time in that room are gone or fuzzy. But I remember his eyes. He had the darkest eyes I've ever seen. Maybe it was because he was evil, but his eyes were dark."

"And this man was the same one you met at the casino?" asked Shaw.

"I don't know. He always wore a mask."

"He wore a mask?" asked Nichols.

"Yes. It was like a ski mask with the eyes and mouth cut out. I never saw his face. But those eyes. I could see his eyes."

"Can you describe the ski mask?" asked Nichols.

"It was a dark-knit ski mask. That's all I remember."

"How was he dressed otherwise?"

"He wore what looked like a lab coat. It was white."

"A lab coat?" asked Shaw.

"Yeah. He would have looked like a doctor if he hadn't been wearing that ski mask. He always wore nice slacks and shoes."

"Did he say he was a doctor?"

"He told me he was my therapist."

"You're therapist?" asked Shaw.

"Yeah. He said they brought me to the facility for treatment and diagnosed me with a mental illness."

"Did he say who brought you in for treatment?"

"The police."

"You were told the police brought you in?"

"Yes."

"Is that true?"

"At the time, I believed it. Now I know it wasn't true."

"Athena, how did you escape?" continued Shaw.

"I didn't. He let me go."

"He let you go?"

"My time with him got easier the longer I stayed. I'm not sure why. One day, he comes in and tells me I'm ready to return to my life. I remember being driven to downtown Colorado Springs and released. I didn't know where I was or even who I was. I mean, I thought I knew who I was, but it wasn't who I really was."

"Okay, you just lost me," interjected Nichols. "What do you mean by that?"

"I thought my name was Jackie Renaud."

"Why did you think that?"

"I was brainwashed. According to my psychiatrist, my assailant used pain, sensory deprivation, and brainwashing to make me believe I was someone else. Even my memories were confused. It took two years of intensive treatment to get me back to where I am today. I still suffer from PTSD."

"We are so sorry you had to go through that," empathized Shaw. "It sounds horrible."

"The police never found your kidnapper?" asked Nichols.

"Because of my confused memory of everything, they couldn't even investigate it. They thought I was nuts. And, truth be told, I was. I was afraid of the police. The man had convinced me it was the police who put me in that god-awful place. He said I had a psychological breakdown, so they brought me in for treatment. Once I was convinced of that, I wanted nothing to do with the police. For a long time, I would only talk to them with my therapist present."

"Why do you think your case is related to our serial killer case?" asked Shaw.

"I don't know that it is. However, the description you put out fits the man who kept me in that room for several months. It also matched the man I met in the casino."

"I thought you only saw his eyes?" asked Nichols.

"I did. But your description emphasized dark brown eyes. I've read everything about this case. Your victims had been missing for many weeks before being found. They had all been abused. They were dressed in T-shirts and shorts. That's what he gave me to wear after I peed my pants. And if the man I met in the casino is the same person who kidnapped me, he also has dark brown hair."

"You are a courageous and astute woman, Athena," replied Shaw. "And you may be right."

"I feel fortunate I was able to get out alive."

"Is there anything else you can remember?"

"I forgot to tell you that at least two people were involved."

"Two people?"

"Yes. I never saw anyone else, but I remember hearing voices talking outside the room."

"How many voices?"

"Only two at a time. I think there was only one other man, but I'm not positive."

"You never saw him?"

"No. Only the man in the ski mask."

"Did the man who kidnapped you ever sexually assault you?" asked Nichols.

"No. I was afraid he would, but he never did. He abused me physically and psychologically, but never sexually."

"That seems to fit," replied Nichols.

"Do you remember anything about how you were kidnapped?" asked Shaw.

"My last memory is being with the man I described. I believe he drugged me because the next thing I can remember is being in that locked room."

"Did the police ever find the room you were locked in?"

"No. I couldn't help them. As I said earlier, they didn't investigate much. To them, I was just a crazy young woman with hallucinations."

"Did anyone ever report you as missing?" asked Shaw.

"The two friends I was with at the casino reported me missing after four days."

"Why did they wait four days?"

"They thought I had hooked up with someone. After four days of no contact, they got worried."

"Do you think your friends could give us a better description?"

Athena laughed. "No. The police tried, but they were more wasted than I was. They didn't even remember me being with someone."

"And your family?"

"I'm from Texas. After high school, I left home to see the world. I had only been in Colorado Springs for three months. My parents called the police after not hearing from me for two weeks."

"I'm going to ask you a sensitive question now, Athena," warned Shaw.

"Okay, what is it?" asked Athena.

"Your body type and hair differ from the three victims we know about. Our suspect seems to target thin blond women. Were you aware of that?"

"Yes, and it's another reason I called. I used to be like those other women. I was thin and shapely before my captivity. And my hair was blond five years ago. When I was released, I only weighed one hundred and nine pounds. He only fed me once a day. After being released, I ate to quell my anxiety. I've put on over forty pounds since then. As for my hair, I now dye it light brown. Psychologically, it makes me feel safer."

"That makes sense, Athena. Thank you for sharing that. Tom, do you have any further questions?"

"Not right now, but I assume we can call you if more comes to mind?"

"Yes. I want whoever is doing this to be stopped."

"Thank you for your time, Athena," said Shaw. "And we are sorry for what your kidnapper put you through."

"I appreciate that. Just find the bastard."

"We will do our best."

With that, the detectives said their goodbyes and left. Nichols drove as he still refused to give up the keys. During the drive back to Boulder, the detectives discussed the interview.

"She had a compelling story," said Nichols.

"I agree," replied Shaw. "It was disturbing. But I'm not fully convinced her case relates to our homicides."

"I was thinking the same. Our victims were murdered."

Upon returning to the police department, Nichols downloaded the digital recording of their interview with Athena Gibson.

"I'm looking forward to a couple days off," said Nichols.

"Couple days?"

"Yeah, Monday is Memorial Day."

"Oh, yeah. I forgot. Unless something more happens over the weekend."

"If it does, I'll be in the doghouse," said Nichols.

"Why's that?"

"Kristin is none too happy about all the hours I've been putting in. She needs help with the kids, and on Monday, we plan to go to Denver's parade."

"Goes with the job, Tom."

"Yeah, I know that, Caro. But it doesn't make it easy."

"That's one reason I never had kids."

"What are you saying? We shouldn't have had kids?"

"No. I'm saying that's why I didn't have kids. They get in the way of police work. Don't be so sensitive. Go home. I'll see you on Tuesday."

Nichols wanted to respond again but dropped the subject. "Yeah, I'll see you on Tuesday."

When Nichols arrived home, it was 5:25 pm. Kristin met him at the door.

"How did it go?" asked Kristin.

"It was an interesting interview. If the woman was telling the truth, she endured great suffering over many weeks."

"Is this related to your homicides?"

"We don't know. Could be."

"Did you get something to eat?"

"I stopped at a Burger King along the way but haven't had anything since then. I'm starving."

"I'll heat you up some spaghetti."

"Caro was in a strange mood today."

"Why do you say that?"

"Ah, just how she gave me a hard time about needing to stop for lunch and then about the kids."

"What about the kids?"

"I had mentioned how I haven't been around much for the kids recently, and she insinuated we shouldn't have had kids."

"Caro told you we shouldn't have had kids?" questioned Kristin.

"No, no. She just said that was why she hadn't had kids. It was more how she said it."

"It's none of her damn business," said Kristin.

"Calm down, Kristin. I think Caro was just tired, like all of us. We are under a lot of pressure. It's no big deal, and I shouldn't have mentioned it."

"You've given up more than your share of family time for this case. She has no right to criticize how we feel."

Nichols was sorry he had mentioned anything about the kids. "It's okay, Kristin. She was referring to herself, not you or me. By the way, where are the kids?"

"They are upstairs playing a game."

"I'm going to go say hi to them."

Shaw arrived home in Longmont at 5:45 pm, exhausted from the long week. She showered, then put on a pair of pale green yoga pants and a T-shirt. Her dark blond hair now hung down to her shoulders. Shaw opened her refrigerator looking for something to eat. She grabbed a leftover half of a spicy Italian sub sandwich from Subway. She then poured herself a glass of Chardonnay, reached for the TV remote, and plopped herself on the living room couch. Shaw turned on the local six o'clock news.

Unsurprisingly, the leading story was about the search for a serial killer in Boulder. A video of Commander Greenberg's statements from the previous night was aired. The next segment featured Anthony Lanaro, a psychiatrist, in a live interview. Shaw nearly jumped off the couch. *Why is he on TV again?*

Dr. Lanaro generally talked about the characteristics of a serial killer. The reporter then asked follow-up questions. "You've talked about the need for serial killers to have power and control, correct?"

"Yes," said Lanaro. "Serial killers have a desire to exert dominance over another person's life. This gives them a sense of superiority. This desire for control often comes from deep-seated feelings of inadequacy and a need to exert authority. Some of this may stem from being mistreated or abused by an adult during childhood."

"Interesting," said the reporter. "You've also talked about how serial killers may live out their fantasies. Could fantasies be driving this madman to kill?"

"Quite possible. Some serial killers create elaborate fantasies surrounding their acts of violence. This allows them to live out their darkest desires."

"Thank you for your comments, Dr. Lanaro. We appreciate your willingness to talk to us. Again, police are looking for a young white male with dark hair and dark eyes, possibly in his early to mid-twenties. If you know anyone fitting this description and exhibiting any of the characteristics described by Dr. Lanaro, please call the Boulder Police Department or Boulder County Sheriff's Department."

Good Lord, thought Shaw. *Lanaro sure likes the bright lights of the media's attention. I guess it's good advertising for him. I'm sure we will have a hundred more tips on Tuesday morning.*

Chapter 17

On Tuesday, May 30th, Nichols arrived at the police department at 7:45 am. He walked down the hall to the large room housing the detective bureau. Shaw was already at her desk.

"Good morning."

"Hi. Did you have a good Memorial Day?" asked Shaw.

"Yeah, it was good. Went to the parade and then a farmer's market in Broomfield. Spent the rest of the day relaxing with family. What about you?"

"I cleaned the house and did some laundry."

"You didn't do anything for fun?"

"Well, I went to a movie."

"By yourself?"

"No." There was a long pause.

"Well, with whom?"

"Nick and I had dinner together and then went to a movie."

"Nick Collier from patrol?"

"Yes. It wasn't a date or anything. We're just good friends, and neither of us had anything to do, so we went to dinner."

"Sounds like a date."

"It wasn't a date."

"Sure sounds like a date to me."

"Stop acting like a teenager and go through those tips I left on your desk."

Nichols laughed as he walked to his desk. There were dozens of new tips lying on top. "What did you do? Give me all the tips?" grumbled Nichols.

"Nope. That's a third of them. Our Dr. Lanaro was on the news over the weekend."

"Again? Wasn't he on last week?"

"Yes, he was. I think he likes the attention."

Nichols began the tedious task of reviewing the tips from over the weekend while Shaw reviewed the police reports from Cripple Creek on Gibson's abduction. According to the reports, Gibson was missing for 16 weeks. She was eventually found ambling directionless in a Colorado Springs park. She gave her name as Jackie Renaud. It took the Colorado Springs police eight days to determine her true identity as Athena Gibson.

On the day of her abduction, Gibson's two friends could only provide minimal information. They admitted to being heavily intoxicated but remembered Gibson latched on to a man she met at the casino. Gibson never showed up in the room that night. Both friends figured Gibson had spent the night with the man she met. They returned to Colorado Springs the next day. After several days of not hearing from Gibson, they called the Colorado Springs Police Department. Since she was last seen in Cripple Creek, the case was forwarded to the Cripple Creek police. The primary detective on the case was Anna Horton. Shaw called the Cripple Creek Police Department and was connected to Sgt. Anna Horton.

"Hello, this is Sergeant Horton."

"Sergeant, this is Detective Caro Shaw with the Boulder Police Department. I am currently working on a series of murders, and I understand you were a detective on the Athena Gibson abduction five years ago."

"Yes, I've seen the news reports on your serial killer situation. I'm very sorry to hear that. How can I help?"

"In the reports I received, you are listed as the investigating detective."

"Yes, I was the lead detective. I've since been promoted to sergeant, and I'm currently assigned to patrol."

"We recently interviewed Athena Gibson after she called to tell us the person who kidnapped her might fit our limited description of a suspect. What can you tell me about your investigation?"

"We never solved the case. Athena was in an awful state of mind immediately after being released, making it difficult to make sense of what she told us. In fact, it took several months and psychiatric help before we could get much out of her."

"Did you ever develop any suspects?"

"Unfortunately, no. Athena could not provide us with enough information. Her abductor wore a mask the entire time she was in captivity."

"Were you able to collect DNA or any other evidence from Athena?"

"No. She was originally found in a Colorado Springs park in an incoherent state of mind. Officers put her on a forty-eight-hour mental health hold. It was days before the case came to us."

"Are you still actively investigating the case?"

"No. It hasn't been closed, but we've had no leads or suspects. You might try calling Detective Dan Benson in Colorado Springs. I remember they had a case of a suspicious male trying to pick up women around the same time."

"Thank you, Sergeant."

Shaw immediately called the Colorado Springs Police Department. She was forwarded to Detective Benson.

"Benson here."

"Detective, this is Detective Caro Shaw with the Boulder Police Department. We have a series of homicides in Boulder...."

"Yes, I've seen the news," interrupted Benson. "How can I help you?"

"Have you seen the description of our suspect we've sent out to departments?"

"How could I not? It's been all over the news."

"I was told by Sergeant Anna Horton of the Cripple Creek Police Department that you investigated a suspicious male trying to solicit women approximately five years ago. Does that ring a bell?"

"Yeah. It was around the time of their kidnapping. We thought the reports might have been connected."

"Who did you investigate?"

"We never came up with a suspect."

"Did the description you had come close to what we have?"

"Now that you mention it, yes."

"What was the description you were given?"

"From memory, we had two reports of a young white male trying to solicit women at two different bars. Both women thought he was creepy. All we had was that he was young, of average height and weight, with dark hair."

"Did you ever identify anyone?"

"No. We had patrol officers checking local bars for weeks, but nothing resulted from it. There are a lot of young males with dark hair."

"Tell me about it," agreed Shaw. "Thank you for your time."

"Hang on. I've just pulled up the report on my computer. Yep, I knew there was something. One woman reported the man had a one-inch scar above his right eyebrow."

"That's something," said Shaw. "But thinking your suspicious person from five years ago is our murderer might be a stretch."

"Agreed. Good luck to you, Detective."

"Thank you."

After much thought, Della decided to attempt an escape. She believed it was the only way she could leave her dungeon. Della's plan to escape had changed numerous times over the last ten days. The most recent shock treatment, as her tormentor called it, pushed Della to make a decision. She would use the long needle to stab her captor in either the stomach or throat. The throat would be more damaging, while the stomach was a bigger, softer target. Della knew she would have to be close to the man to pull it off. She wasn't confident she was strong enough, but Della believed it was her only hope. After stabbing him, Della planned to run out the unlocked door and hoped there was a way to escape from the building. She knew if it didn't work, he would likely kill her.

The most serious injury to her right knee had healed enough to allow her to stand and move freely about the room. Della decided the next time the man entered, she would make her move. However, she had to get him to sit close to her for any chance of success. In preparation, Della retrieved the long, sharp needle from the mattress. She was careful to shield the retrieval of the needle from the ever-present camera. Della then lay on the bed and covered herself with the thin blanket. She then slowly worked the needle inside the right leg of her shorts. It had been some time since the man visited her inside the room. Della was guessing it was almost time for him to visit again.

****

"Martinez!" shouted Commander Greenberg. "Round up the team. I've got some news."

Sgt. Martinez and Detectives Shaw, Nichols, and Jordan met with the Commander in her office.

"What is it?" asked Martinez.

"I just got a call from the Sheriff. They positively identified their victim from three years ago. As expected, DNA testing confirmed she was Jennifer Bryant."

"How old was she?" asked Shaw.

"She was only eighteen when she died."

"That's horrible," said Martinez as he shook his head.

"Any suspects?" asked Jordan.

"No," responded Greenberg. "But now the Sheriff can put out a new release positively identifying her. Maybe more friends will come forward."

"Whoever this monster is, someone knows him," offered Shaw. "We just need the right person to come forward."

"What do they know about Jennifer Bryant?" asked Nichols.

"Not much," said Greenberg. "We know she was from Little Rock, Arkansas."

"None of our victims have been from Boulder or even from Colorado," noted Martinez.

"How are the tip follow-ups coming?" asked Greenberg.

"Slowly. We don't have the time to follow up on all of them," responded Nichols.

"I know," agreed Greenberg. "Do the best you can. Go on, get back to work."

"Commander, I've got the preliminary hearing this afternoon on Shane Phillips," advised Shaw.

"Why isn't Tom going?"

"I was there and interviewed the victim that night," explained Shaw.

"Ah, yes. I forgot. Let me know how it goes."

"I will."

Back at his desk, Nichols called Sheriff's Detective Owen Gates.

"Any more information we should know about your victim?"

"Yes," replied Gates. "She left home after high school graduation from Little Rock, Arkansas. Her parents kept track of her from Arkansas to Dallas to Denver. After that, they lost contact."

"It sounds similar to Aubrey Leaver."

"We're looking for the same killer, Tom."

"I believe you're right," agreed Nichols.

After talking with Gates, Nichols sat at his desk reviewing autopsy photos of their most recent victim from Eben G. Fine Park. He studied the tattoos on the victim's upper right arm and shoulder. And then it hit him. They hadn't released photographs of the tattoos. A sketch drawing was often hard to identify, but those who knew the victim would remember a distinguishing tattoo, such as the angel. Nichols picked up the phone and dialed the coroner's office. Ron Larsen answered the phone.

"Ron, I don't remember seeing photographs of our victim's tattoos in any press releases."

"That's because they weren't included."

"Why not?"

"I don't believe we've ever released actual photographs of dead bodies. That's why we use sketches."

"Yes, but this isn't your usual case. We need to identify our victim, and I'm sure there are people out there who would remember the tattoo of an angel on her right shoulder."

"Hmmm. I don't know."

"Why don't you send it to me and let us release it? That way, you can still say you've never released a photo of a dead body. We really need to identify our third victim."

"Don't you already have the photo?"

"Just a printed copy. I need an original photo."

"Yeah, I can do that. I'll send you a photo in the next hour. You can then use it however you want."

"Thank you, Ron."

Meanwhile, Detective Shaw met with the prosecutor prior to the preliminary hearing for Shane Phillips. They reviewed the testimony Shaw would give about her interview with the victim, Catherine Rosario. The only other person testifying for the prosecution was one of the arresting officers. Documents supporting the injuries suffered by Rosario would be submitted as evidence, including photographs.

When Shaw entered the courtroom, she saw Shane Phillips sitting at the defense table. Phillips had his head bowed, looking at the table. His long hair hung down the sides of his face, covering his cheeks. Shaw wanted to look him in the eye, but Phillips refused to look at her.

The arresting officer testified about the initial call, the response of officers, and the chase that eventually captured Phillips. It was then Shaw's turn to testify. She told the court how she responded to the hospital to interview Rosario. Shaw described what Rosario had told her and read some direct statements made by the victim from her report.

After all testimony and evidence had been presented, the judge ruled there was probable cause to believe the crime of First Degree Sexual Assault had been committed, and there was reasonable suspicion Phillips had committed the crime. The case was bound over for trial. As he was led from the courtroom, Phillips finally looked back at Shaw. He squinted his eyes, and his upper lip curled in anger. Shaw stared back at him until he looked away.

Once Nichols received the photo of the victim's tattoos, he showed it to Commander Greenberg. "I believe we should release this tattoo to the media," said Nichols. "It is the best identifying feature we have."

"Wasn't this in the original release of our victim's description?"

"No. The coroner has never released photos of dead victims."

"Then why is he releasing this one?"

"He's not. We are. If you approve it."

Greenberg thought for a moment, then smiled. "Yeah, I approve of releasing it."

"Thank you," said Nichols as he turned to walk away.

"Tom."

Nichols turned back toward the commander.

"I'm glad you thought of that. Good work. Have Martinez look it over before you release it."

Nichols nodded and smiled before returning to his desk to prepare a new press release.

When Shaw returned to the detective bureau, Nichols asked her about the preliminary hearing.

"It went well. He was easily bound over for trial on a class three felony sexual assault. He faces up to sixteen years in prison."

"I'm sure he's done this before. Ruby wasn't his first attempt."

"With his DNA now in the system, we may soon find out," said Shaw. "What are you working on?"

"The commander approved the release of this photograph from the coroner's office. Our victim has a distinctive tattoo of an angel on her right shoulder."

"Wasn't that described in the first release?"

"Just mentioned near the end of the release. But no photographs have been released until now."

"The news will eat this up," predicted Shaw.

After preparing the press release, Nichols gave it to Sergeant Martinez for approval. "This looks great, Tom. I'll send it out right now. It will be in time for the four o'clock early news."

Nichols returned to his desk to continue going over the tips. As he sat there, Detective Kevin Jordan walked over with a tip sheet in hand.

"What is it?" asked Nichols.

"Read this tip we received over the weekend."

Nichols quickly read the notes written by the volunteer who received the tip. It read: *His daughter has been missing for approximately four months. He saw on the news our victim had tattoos on her right arm and shoulder. If the right shoulder tattoo is of an angel in blue and pink ink with a golden halo trimmed in blue, he believes our victim may be his daughter.* The tipster who called was Robert Quinn of Wichita, Kansas.

Nichols immediately grabbed the tattoo photograph. The angel tattoo was just as the caller described. "Look at this."

"It looks just like what the man described," said Jordan.

Nichols picked up his phone and called the number provided.

"Hello?"

"Hello, this is Detective Tom Nichols with the Boulder, Colorado Police Department. Am I talking to Robert Quinn?"

"Yes, this is Robert Quinn."

"Sir, I just saw the tip you called in over the weekend. I don't know if our victim is your daughter, but I have a photograph of the tattoo on our victim. Would you mind if I texted you a picture of the tattoo?"

"Yes, we would like to know one way or another."

"I must warn you, the photograph is of our victim's upper right arm and shoulder. Are you sure you want to see it?"

"Yes. We need to find our daughter."

"Okay, you'll get it soon."

Nichols used his cell phone to take a photo of the tattoo photograph. It was the best he could do on short notice. He sent the cell phone photo to Robert Quinn. "Now, all we have to do is wait."

Thirty minutes passed, and nothing.

"What do you think?" asked Jordan.

"I don't know. I hope he calls either way. I'll call him back if I don't hear in another thirty minutes."

"Let me know what you find out," said Jordan.

"Yeah, I will."

Shaw walked over to Nichols' desk. "Your photograph is the top story on the four o'clock news."

"Well, I'm waiting on a call from a man who believes our Jane Doe is his daughter. He called on Saturday."

"And we just heard about it?"

"It was in the pile of tips on Kevin's desk."

"Well, let me know."

After another ten minutes, Nichols' phone rang. "Detective Nichols here."

"Detective, this is Robert Quinn," he said, his voice cracking. Nichols could hear it in the man's voice before he even told him.

"You have our daughter."

"Are you sure?"

"Yes. All the tattoos are the same. We even," he paused. "We even recognize her shoulder. That's our Melanie," he cried.

"I'm so very sorry, Mr. Quinn."

"Thank you," Quinn sobbed. "Is her body still available for a proper funeral?"

"Yes. You can make the arrangements with our coroner's office. When you can, we have some questions to ask that may help us find her killer. Let us know when you feel up to it."

"Okay. We are making plans to come to Boulder in a few days."

"How old was Melanie?"

"She was only twenty-two."

"Is her last name Quinn?"

"Yes," he sobbed.

"Okay, I'll talk to you later, Mr. Quinn. Again, I'm sorry for your loss." Nichols could hear more crying, and then the phone went dead.

Nichols asked the team to join him in the commander's office.

Once Greenberg, Martinez, Jordan, Shaw, and Nichols were all together, Nichols made the announcement. "Our victim has been identified by her parents. Her real name is Melanie Quinn. She was only twenty-two."

"Where was she living?" asked Shaw.

"I couldn't interview the father. He was too distraught. They will come to Boulder in a few days."

"Now that the tattoo photo is out, we may get someone calling in who knew her in Boulder," said Shaw.

"Should we release her name?" asked Nichols.

"I would wait," replied Greenberg. "Let's be absolutely sure our victim is Melanie Quinn. While it's not likely anyone else has the same tattoos, I don't want any embarrassing mistakes. I'll let the chief know we probably have our victim identified. It's been another long day, and we've made good progress. Everyone go home and get some rest. Tomorrow could be busy."

"Busier than we have been?" asked Nichols.

Greenberg laughed. "You never know."

Chapter 18

Nichols arrived at work on Wednesday, May 31st, at 8:35 am.

"Where have you been?" asked Shaw in a sarcastic voice.

"School is out, and Kristin had to be at work early today. I had to drop the kids off at daycare. So don't give me any crap."

"Well, have you seen social media today?"

"No, why?"

"Your tattoo photo did its job. The picture is everywhere. Facebook, Twitter, Snapchat, everything. And two women called last night, each saying they knew Melanie Quinn."

"Are you just yanking my chain again?"

"No. Here are the names. Alani Taylor and Trina Perez. Alani is coming in at ten-thirty, and we need to go see Trina. She is at work."

"Should we go now?" asked Nichols.

"Yes. We need to be there by nine. She is expecting us."

"Where does she work?"

"At the Clean Stop car wash in Broomfield."

"Let's go," said Nichols.

The detectives arrived at the car wash at 8:55 am. The car wash was a full-service station, providing a high-tech vehicle wash, a detail service, hand drying, and an attached convenience store. Trina Perez was busy wiping down a wet car when Shaw and Nichols approached, introducing themselves to Perez, an attractive 23-year-old Hispanic female with short black hair. She was wearing a blue employee smock provided by the car wash.

"Wait in the lounge," said Trina. "I will be there in a minute."

Shaw and Nichols went inside the lounge and sat down. The lounge was an open area inside the convenience store. Trina Perez walked in five minutes later.

"Is there somewhere else we can talk?" asked Shaw. "This is a public area and kind of noisy."

"Let me ask the manager if we can use her office."

After several minutes, Perez returned. "She said we could use it for about fifteen minutes."

The office was small, with only a desk and two chairs. "Go ahead and sit," said Nichols. "I'll stand."

Shaw pulled the chair from behind the desk to the side and sat down. Perez sat in the chair in front of the desk while Nichols stood off to the side. They could hear the sound of tumbling brushes and high-pressure water coming from behind the back wall.

"We understand you knew Melanie Quinn?" asked Shaw.

"Yes, but I hadn't seen her for like four months."

"How long did you know her?"

"It wasn't long. Maybe four or five weeks. We met at work."

"Melanie worked here?"

"Yes. She started around the first of the year. Melanie was easy to like. I couldn't believe it when I saw pictures of her tattoo. It's so sad."

"Why did she quit working here?"

"She just stopped coming to work. I tried calling Melanie every day for a week, and she never answered. I figured she went back home to Kansas."

"Did Melanie have a boyfriend?"

"No, but she met some guy at a bar in Boulder."

"How do you know this?"

"I was with her. This guy starts hitting on Melanie. She liked him, but I thought he was strange."

"Did Melanie stop coming to work after meeting this guy?"

"Not right away. It was about a week or two later when she stopped coming in."

"Did that worry you?"

"Yes, but she had just moved here from Kansas and was living in a hotel room. I thought she moved back home."

"Did Melanie start dating the guy she met in the bar?"

"I don't know for sure, but I think she either went out with him or planned to meet him somewhere."

"Why do you say that?"

"Alani and I often go bar hopping on Friday nights. After Melanie started working here, I invited her along. We all went out together two Friday nights in a row. This was in January. On the third Friday, Melanie said she was busy. I suspected she might have been going out with the guy she met, but she wouldn't tell me."

"Is that the last time you saw Melanie?"

"Yes."

Shaw looked at Nichols, who gave a puzzled look back.

"Didn't that concern you?" asked Nichols.

"Yes, and no. Melanie was not looking to put roots down here. She was going where the wind would take her. That, and she wasn't too happy with this job. She wanted something that paid more."

"Tell us about this man Melanie met," said Shaw.

"He was probably mid-twenties. He seemed friendly but was especially attracted to Melanie."

"Was she attracted to him?"

"Definitely. And you could tell he liked Melanie."

"What was his name?"

"His name was Steve. I didn't know his last name."

"Try to describe for us what he looked like."

"White male, dark complected, black hair."

"How tall was he?"

"He was about three inches taller than me, so probably around five-eight."

"Was he heavy, thin?"

"He was thin, but not skinny thin. He was a good-looking man."

"Any specific features that stood out?"

"He parted his hair on one side and slicked it back."

"Did he have long hair?"

"No, just a clean-looking cut. It wasn't over his ears."

"What about eye color?"

"He had dark brown eyes. I remember how sometimes it was like he could look right through you."

"Do you think he was Hispanic?"

"No. He wasn't Hispanic."

"Tom, do you have anything else to ask?" said Shaw.

"Yes. Trina, do you remember anything else about him, like tattoos or scars?"

Trina thought for several seconds. "No, I can't remember anything like that. Are we about done? I have to get back to work."

"Almost," said Nichols. "When was the last time you saw Melanie?"

"It was on a Friday at work. It was the same day Melanie told me she couldn't go out with us."

"Thank you, Trina. We'll let you get back to work now."

On the drive back to the PD, Nichols said, "We may finally have a suspect to look for."

"It's looking that way," answered Shaw. "Let's see what Alani Taylor has to say."

When they returned to the police department, Alani Taylor was already waiting in interview room number two. Alani was a 24-year-old white female with long brown hair held in a ponytail with an elastic band. As they introduced themselves, Nichols immediately noticed her bright brown eyes and friendly smile. Alani was dressed in a University of Colorado T-shirt and blue jeans.

"Thank you for calling us," said Shaw. "We are investigating the death of Melanie Quinn. I understand you knew her?"

"Yes. I met Melanie through Trina, who worked with her for a short time," answered Alani.

"You didn't work with Melanie?"

"No, I work as an assistant in a dental office."

"And where do you live?"

"I have an apartment here in Boulder."

"Okay. How did you know Trina?"

"We both went to the university and became good friends. We still like to get together, although we don't do it as much as we used to."

"And how did you get to know Melanie?"

"Trina met her at work, and they really hit it off. She invited her to go out with us one Friday night. Melanie was very nice."

"Trina told us about the man Melanie met when the three of you were going out together last January. Do you remember that?"

"Oh, yes. She met some guy at the bar we were at."

"Trina couldn't remember what bar it was. Do you?"

"It may have been the Dark Horse or one of the many bars in downtown Boulder. I'm not sure."

"Was it Maravilloso House on the Hill?"

"I don't believe so. It could have been The Sink."

"Do you remember his name?"

"I didn't until Trina reminded me his name was Steve."

"Okay, just tell us what you remember about the man Melanie met."

"He seemed shy but charming at the same time. I could tell Melanie seemed to connect with him. He became more interested in her when he learned she wasn't from Boulder. I remember thinking he was asking too many questions about her background."

"Were you concerned about him?"

"I wouldn't say concerned, but something about him turned me off. I can't explain it very well. Just a weirdness about him."

"Melanie wasn't concerned?"

"No. She liked the attention and the talk of travel."

"They talked of traveling together?"

"Yes. Melanie had left home to explore the world. When he found out, he talked about all the places he wanted to explore. I think this fascinated her."

"I understand he met with Melanie a second time?"

"Yes, we agreed to go out again the following Friday. It's my understanding Melanie called Steve and invited him."

Shaw paused and looked at Nichols. Nichols nodded back, letting her know he was thinking the same thing.

"Alani, do you happen to know what phone service Steve was using?" asked Shaw.

"No. Sorry."

"Do you have his phone number?"

"No."

"I didn't expect you to know that, but I had to ask. Were Steve and Melanie always with the two of you?"

"The first night, yes. But on the second Friday, they left us to sit alone at another table."

"Did Melanie leave with Steve that night?"

"No, she went home with us. On the ride home, Melanie told us she liked the guy and was thinking about going out with him."

"Did you go out with Melanie again?"

"No. That night was the last time I saw her. Trina saw her at work after that, but we never went out again. We both figured Melanie went off somewhere with Steve."

"You knew about Melanie's tattoos?"

"Yes. Melanie had shown us her tattoo. The angel is hard to forget."

"To the best of your ability, can you describe Steve for us?"

"Sure. White male. I'd say he was in his mid-twenties. He had black hair and dark brown eyes. I can't describe it, but looking into his eyes gave me a weird sense that he wasn't all there."

"How tall was he?"

"Five-eight, maybe five-nine."

"Any estimate of how much he weighed?"

"He wasn't heavy. I'd call him slender."

"Is there anything else distinguishing about him?"

"He was a good dresser. He always had on nice clothes and dress shoes."

"What about scars or tattoos?" asked Nichols.

"I don't think so."

"You never noticed a scar above his right eye?"

Alani thought for a moment. "Now that you mention it, there was a light line above his right eye."

Nichols looked at Shaw. Shaw looked back.

"Use your finger to show us where," said Nichols.

Alani raised her right forefinger, placed it above her right eye, then dragged it diagonally toward her temple.

"Thank you, Alani. I have no more questions."

"Neither do I," said Shaw. "Thank you so much for coming in today. You've given us something to look into."

"Anything I can do to catch this monster," replied Alani.

Nichols escorted Alani to the lobby and thanked her again for her help. He then quickly returned to the detective bureau, where Shaw was waiting.

"Can you believe it?" asked Nichols. "I think we have a suspect."

"We do," agreed Shaw. "It's that asshole from Colorado Springs. I'm going to call Gates at the Sheriff's Department right now. He needs to know this. You go tell the commander."

"On it," said Nichols as he headed towards the commander's office.

****

Della had waited two days for a chance to escape her abductor. He had entered the room the day before but never sat down. Della was afraid to attack him while the man stood with his ever-present taser in his coat pocket. Over the past two days, Della heard the same two distinct male voices talking about her. One voice always belonged to the man keeping her in the room. The other voice belonged to the man she'd never met, but she would never forget his voice. The second man's voice was of a lower tone than her captor's voice. She had trouble making out the conversation. However, at one point, Della thought she heard the lower voice say, "It has to work, or they can never find her."

Then again, Della wasn't always sure about what she really heard and what she imagined. She often thought she could hear her mother talking to her, which she knew was crazy. Della struggled to distinguish actual events from illusions in her mind. *I'm going crazy,* thought Della.

Della was startled from her thoughts when the light came on, and she heard the latch on the door being opened. The door slowly swung open, and there stood the same man, the only man she had seen for weeks, still wearing the same white hood, the same white lab coat, and the same derby-style brown suede shoes.

"How are we feeling today, Amy?" asked the man.

Della was nervous. She could feel beads of sweat forming on her scalp under her long blond hair. "I'm okay."

"Are you ready for another round of treatment?"

"If that's what you believe I need," said Della softly as she placed her right hand on her right hip. She wanted to be sure the needle was still there. She could feel it.

"Why don't you go sit in the chair?"

"I'd feel more comfortable sitting next to you."

"Not today, Amy. This is an intense therapy day. I need to ensure you are progressing on schedule."

Della's hopes fell into the pit of her stomach. She had been ready for this to be the day of her attempted escape. But with her seated in the wooden chair, it would be too risky. She trembled when he reached into his pocket and pulled out the taser.

"It's going to be an intense session today, Amy," said the man in a monotone voice.

"Please. I'm making progress. I've learned so much about myself from you," her voice cracking.

The man grabbed her left arm and strapped her wrist tightly to the arm of the chair. He then strapped her right wrist to the other arm of the chair. Della gently shut her eyes and cried.

"Now, stick out your right leg for me."

"Huh?"

"I said stick out your right leg!"

Chapter 19

After learning about the development of a suspect, Commander Greenberg was pleased. "Excellent work, Tom. Did you schedule either to meet with our sketch artist?"

"Uh, wow. Neither of us thought of that. Sorry," responded an embarrassed Nichols. "I guess we should have done that."

"I would suggest you get going on that. If we can release a sketch, a description, and the name he goes by, someone will know him."

When Nichols reached Shaw's desk, she was still on the phone with Detective Gates. He waited patiently for Shaw to finish.

"What is it?" asked Shaw after ending her call.

"The commander reminded me we should have scheduled one of our witnesses with our sketch artist."

"Damn! I should've thought of that," exclaimed Shaw. "I guess I was so excited about finally getting good information that I spaced it out."

"Do we call them both in?" asked Nichols.

"No. We might get two different sketches. Which one did you think had the best memory of this Steve character?"

"I thought Alani Taylor was more detailed in everything."

"I agree. You take care of getting that scheduled while I call Athena Gibson back. I have a few more questions for her."

"Got it," said Nichols as he walked away.

Shaw looked through her notes for Athena's phone number. After finding it, she dialed Athena's cell phone.

"Hello?"

"Athena, this is Detective Caro Shaw with the Boulder Police Department."

"Okay."

"I'm calling because we are making some progress, and I have a few more questions for you. Is that okay?"

"I'm at work right now," said Athena.

"This won't take long."

"Just a minute. Let me go into the office." After a brief pause, "All right, what are your questions?"

"Think back to the man in the casino. Does the name Steve bring back any memories for you?"

"Steve? Uh, no. I have a friend named Steve, but it wasn't him."

"Do you remember the man in the casino having a scar anywhere on his face?"

"I don't think so. I might have told more details to my therapist. Much of it I've erased from my mind."

"Would it be okay if I talked to your therapist?" asked Shaw.

"Yeah. I don't see him anymore, but you can talk to him."

"What is his name?"

"It was Dr. Lanaro."

"What?! Dr. Tony Lanaro?"

"Yeah, that's him. He helped me get through my trauma."

"You came to Boulder to see Dr. Lanaro?"

"No. He was in Colorado Springs."

Shaw then remembered they had been told Lanaro initially practiced in Colorado Springs but was stunned by the coincidence. "Do you have a printer and fax machine at the library?"

"Yes."

"I will email you a release form to allow Dr. Lanaro to share things you may have told him about your case. Would you be willing to sign and fax it back to me?"

"Yes, I can do that."

"Thank you, Athena. Maybe this will help us find the person who abducted you."

After the call, Shaw sat back in her chair and massaged the back of her neck with both hands. *This has to be the craziest, damnedest case I've ever worked on.*

After emailing the form to Athena, Shaw shouted to Nichols and Jordan. "Follow me. I've got an update." Nichols and Jordan followed Shaw into the commander's office.

"What's going on?" asked Commander Greenberg.

"You won't believe this," said Shaw. "I just got off the phone with Athena Gibson, the woman kidnapped in Cripple Creek five years ago."

"Okay, what's up?" asked Greenberg.

"The psychiatrist who helped Athena overcome her trauma was our own consultant, Dr. Tony Lanaro."

"Dr. Lanaro treated Athena?" asked Nichols.

"Yes, five years ago. Lanaro treated her for two years. He may have information she told him in therapy that could help us."

"Why wouldn't he have told you that?" asked Jordan.

"I don't think he knew we were talking with Athena," answered Shaw.

"Was he practicing in Colorado Springs back then?" asked Greenberg.

"I knew he had assisted Colorado Springs sometimes, but I assumed he practiced out of Boulder," answered Shaw.

"Can he share what Athena told him?" asked Nichols.

"He can if she signs the waiver I just sent her."

Greenberg nodded her approval. "Nice work, everyone. Where are we on getting a sketch of our suspect?"

"Trina will be in tomorrow morning to meet with our sketch artist," replied Nichols.

"Excellent," said Greenberg. "Our PIO is working on a press release with our suspect description to be released in time for the ten o'clock news. It's getting late. Go home and get some rest."

Shaw arrived home at 7:30 pm, plopping her body onto her living room sofa. Her body felt weathered and tired. She called her friend and fellow officer, Julie Reese.

"Hey, Caro. What's up? Haven't heard from you in a while."

"I'm sorry. It's been so busy at work that I haven't had the time."

"I understand. Patrol has been busy answering calls on suspicious men. Some of them don't even match the description of the suspect. Women are very frightened right now."

"I get it," said Shaw. "An updated description will be on the news tonight, and by tomorrow, we should have a sketch of our suspect."

"It sounds like you've made good progress."

"It's more than we had last week. I'm just afraid he will attack again before we catch him."

"Are you okay? You sound like you're depressed."

"Actually, I'm excited with the progress we've made the last two days. I'm just hungry and tired right now."

"Would you like me to pick up some food and come over?"

"Don't you have to work tonight?"

"No. Thursday is my day off. You know that."

"Yeah, I'm just losing track of the days. Sure, some takeout and company would be nice."

"I'll stop at Panda Express on my way over. The usual?"

"Yes," said Shaw. "The chow mein with fire-roasted chicken."

Forty minutes later, Julie Reese was at Shaw's door. "Come on in, Julie."

"What would you like to drink?" asked Shaw.

"Do you have Coors Light?"

"You know I do," said Shaw as she reached into the refrigerator and pulled out two ice-cold beers. "Here you go."

Reese sat across from Shaw at the oval dinner table. "So, tell me about this suspect."

"We're pretty sure he goes by Steve and has a one-inch scar above his right eye. He has dark hair and dark eyes. Probably five-eight to five-nine."

"You've made progress," said Reese. "How do you know his name?"

"Two friends of Melanie Quinn gave us a description and name of the last person they saw her with."

"Does he live in Boulder?"

"We don't know. We think he was in Colorado Springs and abducted a woman five years ago."

"So, between then and now, he's been kidnapping and killing women?"

"I don't know. Could be."

"That's horrible. Let's get your mind off it. I heard you went out with Nick last weekend."

"We got together, is all. We're good friends, like you and I."

"Uh-huh. What did you do?"

"Nothing. We went to dinner. No different from you and I getting take out tonight."

"And did you enjoy the movie?"

"Julie, did Tom tell you this?"

"No. Nick told me."

Shaw blushed. "We are just friends, Julie."

"With benefits?"

"Stop it. Do you want another beer?"

"Yes, please."

"Here," said Shaw as she handed Julie another beer. "FOX 31 News is about to come on."

Shaw and Reese settled in to watch the news. The lead story was an update on the "Boulder Creek Murders" and included the updated information on a suspect named Steve.

"Boulder Creek Murders," muttered Shaw. "They always have to be so dramatic."

"People are avoiding the creek path at night," said Reese. "I've never seen this town so on edge."

"We're all on edge," replied Shaw.

"Well, I'm happy to be here drinking beer with you and not working tonight," said Reese. "Patrol will receive a ton of calls tonight."

After the news, Shaw told Reese she needed to get some sleep. The following day would be a busy one.

It was 2:25 am when Nichol's cell phone rang. He picked it up off the bedside table. "Hello," he said, half asleep. It was a dispatcher calling.

"Detective, we need you to come in. Patrol has a suspect in custody who attempted to abduct a woman at Scott Carpenter Park."

That immediately woke Nichols up. "They've arrested someone"?

"Yes. The suspect is in a holding cell at the jail. The patrol sergeant has asked for you and Detective Shaw to respond."

"Okay. I'll be there as soon as possible. Does Detective Shaw know yet?"

"Yes. We've called her as well."

"What's wrong?" asked Kristin.

"I have to go into work. We may have our suspect in custody."

"Be careful."

"Always," said Nichols as he got dressed.

Nichols was the first to arrive at the Boulder County Jail. He was met by Sergeant Gomez.

"We had a report of a woman screaming at Scott Carpenter Park, close to the creek," explained Sgt. Gomez. "When officers arrived, our suspect was fighting with a young woman. She claimed he was trying to abduct her. The suspect ran, but our officers caught him. There was a struggle, and officers had to use a taser on him."

"You think he is our serial killer?" asked Nichols.

"We don't know, but he attacked a woman near the creek, and he has dark hair. We thought you would want to interview him."

"Yes, of course. Thank you, Sergeant. Do you know his name?"

"Logan Clark. A white male, twenty-two years old."

"Thank you. I'll wait for Caro to arrive before I talk with him."

Nichols looked through the small glass window into the holding cell. Clark was sitting on the metal bench along the west wall. Nichols watched for a few minutes. Clark's right leg was bouncing up and down like a nervous twitch. At one point, he saw Clark use the left sleeve of his black T-shirt to wipe his nose.

Logan Clark was a twenty-two-year-old white male who was short and overweight. His stomach protruded over his belt. His black hair was short and curly, and he wore a black T-shirt with a multi-colored logo on the front. He also had on a pair of blue jeans and Nike running shoes.

Shaw finally arrived several minutes later, and Nichols filled her in on what he already knew. Nichols noticed Shaw had bloodshot eyes, and her hair had not been combed.

"Are you okay?" asked Nichols.

"Yeah, I'm just exhausted. All I did was get dressed and drive straight here. Sorry if I don't look like a prom queen."

Nichols chuckled. "I never thought you looked like a prom queen."

Shaw glared back.

"Come on, let's talk to him," said Nichols.

Nichols grabbed two metal folding chairs from the booking area and took them into the holding cell. He set the chairs up across from Clark, who was still seated on the metal bench. Nichols introduced themselves and then asked Clark if he would be willing to talk.

"I wasn't going to hurt that girl."

"That's good to know," said Nichols. "But first, I need to give you your Miranda Rights." Nichols read Clark his rights from a card he kept in his badge wallet.

"Knowing these rights, are you willing to talk to us?" asked Nichols.

"Yes, sir," said Clark.

"Tell us what happened," said Nichols.

"I was just trying to scare her. I wasn't going to harm her."

"Why were you trying to scare her?"

Clark looked down at the floor. "I don't know. Just all this news about a killer running loose..... I guess I just thought it would be funny to scare people."

"Funny to scare women?" interrupted Shaw. "Maybe it would be funny for me to cut off your balls!"

Clark's eyes widened. Nichols looked at Shaw, hardly believing what she had just said. He bit his lip to keep from smiling.

"I didn't mean any harm. I'm not the killer," pleaded Clark.

"Regardless of what you intended, you attacked that woman. She was afraid for her life. She believes you were trying to abduct her," said Nichols.

"I would never do that."

"You just did."

"No, I wasn't trying to abduct her. Just scare her. Please believe me."

"You were going to sexually assault her, right?" asked Nichols.

"No."

"Did you know any of the three women found dead along Boulder Creek?" asked Nichols.

"No."

"Where do you keep the women after kidnapping them?" asked Shaw.

"Huh? I've never kidnapped anyone."

"You better be telling us the truth, Logan," warned Nichols. "We will collect your fingerprints, DNA, and a photograph. We will show that photograph to all our witnesses. You better hope no one identifies you as the killer."

Nichols could see beads of sweat along the top of Clark's forehead and his right leg moved faster. "I screwed up," said Clark.

"You will be charged with harassment, attempted assault, and re-sisting arrest. And if we find evidence you are involved in our killings, you will also be charged with homicide. Are you sure your DNA won't show up on our victims?"

"Yes. I haven't killed anyone."

Nichols and Shaw left the room. "I don't believe he is our killer," said Nichols.

"No, he's not," agreed Shaw. "He's too heavy, nervous, clumsy, and doesn't match our description. Did you notice his eyes?"

"I sure did. Hazel."

"We'll show his picture around, but it's not him," said Shaw.

"Are you going back home?" asked Nichols.

"No. It's already four-thirty. I've got stuff at the PD. I can shower and fix myself up there."

"You look like you need sleep," said Nichols.

"And you don't?"

Nichols just smiled. "See you at the office."

At 11:00 am, all personnel assigned to the serial killer case met with Police Chief Ken Atkins. He had scheduled the meeting for an update on the investigation. Officers and non-sworn personnel working on the phones for tips were included in the meeting. Detective Owen Gates from the Sheriff's Department was also present. The meeting began with Commander Greenberg providing everyone with a synopsis of the investigation. Her update included a more detailed description of the suspect, known only as Steve.

"What about last night's arrest?" asked Chief Atkins.

"We're looking into it, but he doesn't match the description of who we believe is our suspect," responded Greenberg.

"Where are we on getting a sketch of this suspect?" asked the chief.

"Alani Taylor, one of our witnesses, is with our artist now, Chief. We hope to have it for the media this afternoon."

"You said someone was meeting again with Dr. Lanaro?"

"Yes, sir," responded Greenberg. "Detectives Shaw and Nichols have a meeting with him this afternoon."

"Thank you," said the chief. "We all appreciate the good work everyone is doing."

After the meeting, Nichols approached Shaw. "Are you hungry?"

"I'm starving. All I've had was a muffin from the vending machine."

"Let's go. We need to eat before meeting with Dr. Lanaro."

"Where are we going?"

"Moe's Bar-B-Que."

"At 30th and Baseline?"

"Yeah. Have you eaten there?"

"No. I try not to eat sloppy food while I'm working."

"You'll love the food."

"Wherever we go, you always say that."

Nichols looked at Shaw. "It's because I only eat at the good places, Caro. Why waste your time and money eating bad food?"

Shaw shook her head.

Nichols drove to Moe's and parked out front. The lunch crowd had not yet gathered. Large glass windows faced the parking lot. As they walked in, Shaw could smell the aroma of smoked meat and barbeque sauce.

"I love the brisket," said Nichols. "But I think you'd like the pulled pork."

Nichols ordered the brisket with baked beans, potato salad, and cornbread. Shaw ordered the smoked turkey with a side of marinated slaw.

"Smoked turkey?" asked Nichols. "I just told you how good the pulled pork was."

"Yeah, and I prefer the turkey. I love smoked turkey."

Once the food came, neither detective talked much. Both were more focused on enjoying the food. Nichols slathered his brisket with a spicy bar-b-que sauce. The brisket practically melted in his mouth. He ate slowly, savoring each bite.

Once she finished her smoked turkey, Shaw looked up and saw BBQ sauce on the sleeve of Nichols' shirt. "Uh, you have sauce on the sleeve of your nice shirt."

"What?" Nichols looked down and saw a dime-sized dark red spot on the left long sleeve of his light blue shirt. "Crap. I need to go wash this off."

Nichols returned to the table with a pink wet spot where the bar-b-que had been.

"Don't say anything," said Nichols. "Let's just go."

Shaw ignored his request. "This is the third time you've dripped on yourself in the last three weeks. I think you need to carry a bib."

"Funny. Three times in twenty-one days is not bad."

"We haven't eaten lunch together all those days. We've probably had lunch together nine times in the last three weeks. That's a thirty-three percent drip rate."

"What the hell? You're analyzing the rate at which I drip on myself?"

"I find it entertaining," smirked Shaw. "Are you a slob at home as well?"

"Accidental drippage does not make me a slob."

"Uh huh."

"Whatever. Just tell me where the doctor's office is."

"He lives and has an office on 11th Street up on the Hill. Here's the address."

"I didn't realize he was on the Hill," said Nichols.

"I just found out today myself," said Shaw.

Nichols drove to the address on 11th Street. "Looks like a house."

"It is a house. He told me he lives in one half and has his office in the other half. If you look, you can see it is divided. He has a sign outside on the right next to the door. See how the porch is divided? There are two entrances."

"Yeah, I see it."

The Hill Neighborhood is one of the oldest in Boulder, built around the turn of the twentieth century. Dr. Anthony Lanaro lived and practiced in a two-story Victorian-style home built in 1907. There was a front porch that extended around the northeast corner. There were two entry doors, one on the north side of the porch and one on the south side. A white colonial-style wood railing surrounded the porch, with a matching barrier splitting the porch into two sides. The north side had a brown sign hanging above the door with Dr. Lanaro's name and "counseling and psychiatric services" under his name, all printed in white.

The plank wood siding, popular at the time of build, was painted a medium gray with bright white trim. Bay windows adorned both the front and sides of the first floor. On the northeast corner, a Queen Anne-style round tower rose toward the sky to the second-story roof. Windows were in both the first and second levels of the tower. The building was topped off with a steep gabled roof. The immaculately groomed front lawn was highlighted with brightly colored marigolds surrounding the front porch.

"That's one large home," said Nichols.

"That's what money will get you in Boulder," replied Shaw.

The detectives walked up the stairs leading to the north door, the one with the sign hanging above it. The door opened before either detective could ring the doorbell.

"Come on in, Detectives. I saw you pull up."

Shaw and Nichols marveled at the condition of the office. The room had a high ceiling with a large, intricate chandelier hanging in the middle. The wooden oak floor sparkled, and a hallway led to a second room. A staircase to the right of the hallway led up to the second floor. Dr. Lanaro's oak desk sat facing into the room from the round corner created by the Queen Anne-style tower. A shaded lamp sat on one corner of the desk. Facing the desk were two high-backed brown leather chairs with a small round marble table between the two chairs.

"You have a beautiful office, Docter," said Shaw.

"Thank you," replied Lanaro.

"Is this where you see your patients?"

"No. This is where I do my consulting work. Down that hall is another office where I work with my patients. There's also a bathroom down there if you need it."

"And what is upstairs?"

"Two bedrooms and a bathroom. They were part of the original build."

"And on the other side is where you live?"

"Yes. I had the house remodeled so that I could both work and live here. On the phone, you said you had some more questions about the case?"

"Yes, sorry," said Shaw. "I understand you practiced in Colorado Springs?"

"Yes. That is where I had my first office."

"And sometimes you assisted the police department?"

"Occasionally. They called me in on a few cases."

"When did you relocate to Boulder?"

"Approximately four years ago."

"If you don't mind me asking, why did you quit your practice in Colorado Springs?"

"After my wife died, it was hard to stay in the Springs. Too many memories."

"I'm sorry to hear that. When did she die?"

"About six years ago."

"Before moving to Boulder, did you treat a patient by the name of Athena Gibson?"

"I'm sorry. I can't disclose that type of information."

Shaw handed Dr. Lanaro the release form signed by Athena Gibson. "This is your copy of the release form signed by Athena. It releases you from confidentiality and protects you from whatever you tell us."

Lanaro read over the document. "May I ask, why are you interested in Athena Gibson?"

"We believe she may have been a victim of kidnapping and abuse by our murder suspect," explained Shaw.

"Hmmm, Okay. Yes, I treated Athena for severe psychosis."

"What were her symptoms?" continued Shaw.

"She was extremely disturbed. Her sense of reality was completely distorted. As I recall, some of her symptoms included hallucinations and feeling sensations or remembering sensations that were not real. Athena suffered from hallucinations and false realities. As I recall, she didn't even know her real name."

"Did you ever determine what caused this?"

"Some of Athena's psychosis started when she was younger. I believe the trauma of her ordeal only made it worse."

"Did Athena tell you what happened to her?"

"According to the police, Athena was kidnapped and held captive. However, it's possible she ran off and made up the entire story. It was hard for her to distinguish reality from false realities. It took me a long time to sift through her hallucinations and false memories. As I recall, this also made it difficult for the police."

"You don't believe Athena was held captive?"

"I didn't say that. I'm saying I couldn't believe everything Athena told me."

"Why hadn't you told us about her before?"

"First, I didn't have a release, and second, why would I?"

"Because we are working on a serial killer case, and Athena was held captive for weeks."

"Maybe she was held captive. Regardless, your case involves a serial killer. Athena was not murdered."

"But we have evidence our victims were held captive and abused before being killed. You don't see some parallels?"

"Detective, I've studied many cases. All cases like this have some parallels. If Athena was kidnapped and held captive it was over five years ago. It simply didn't cross my mind."

"The suspect Athena described to us matches the description of a male some witnesses have seen our victims with just before their disappearance," continued Shaw.

"Did Athena tell you this before they aired the description on every TV news show?"

Shaw thought for a moment. "No."

Dr. Lanaro removed his silver wire-rimmed glasses and sighed. "There you go, Detective. I told you Athena had difficulty distinguishing reality from false reality. Those news reports triggered something in Athena. I would not rely on what she told you. A defense attorney would eat her alive."

Shaw and Nichols looked at each other.

"Is there anything else?" asked an irritated Dr. Lanaro.

Shaw looked at Nichols again. He shook his head no.

"No, that's all we have, Doctor. Thank you for your time."

Dr. Lanaro stood and walked the detectives to the door.

As Shaw and Nichols walked onto the porch, Dr. Lanaro said, "One more thing, Detective Shaw."

Shaw turned. "Yes?"

"I'm willing to help any way I can, but don't ever question my expertise again."

"I wasn't...."

Dr. Lanaro held up his hand. "Yes, you did."

"I'm sorry," said Shaw. "I didn't mean to."

Dr. Lanaro turned and shut the door.

"You sure pissed him off," said Nichols as they approached the car.

"What did I ask that was challenging to him?"

"Well, you did kind of challenge him. Then you insinuated he should have told us about Athena."

Shaw shrugged her shoulders. "Maybe."

"You'll probably be in the Chief's office later this afternoon."

"Shut up," said Shaw.

Later that afternoon, Shaw sat at her desk, trying to keep her eyelids from closing as she worked on her report. Nichols walked over and placed a sketch of the suspect, known as Steve, on top of Shaw's desk. Shaw looked it over.

"That's an excellent sketch," said Shaw.

"I thought so, too," replied Nichols.

"Caro!" shouted Commander Greenberg. "I need to see you now."

"Uh, oh," said Nichols.

Shaw stood up and walked over to Greenberg's office. "What is it, Commander?"

"Did you challenge Dr. Lanaro's expertise today?" said an obviously irritated Commander Greenberg.

"No. I only asked him why he hadn't told us about Athena Gibson's case."

"It had to be more than that," replied Greenberg. "I just got off the phone with the chief. Dr. Lanaro was not happy with your line of questioning."

"I'm sorry, Commander. I did not intend to offend the doctor. But I got the impression he still believes Athena is delusional. She wasn't delusional when we talked to her."

"Well, it's okay. Some experts we work with can be pretentious sometimes. Learn to ask your questions respectfully."

"I thought I did, Commander. I'm sorry."

"You look exhausted. Haven't you been in since four this morning?"

"More like three-thirty."

"You and Tom have been here long enough. Go home and get some rest."

"Thank you, Commander. I have a follow-up call to make, then I'll go home."

Shaw's follow-up call was to Colorado Springs Detective Dan Benson. "Benson speaking."

"Dan, this is Caro Shaw from the Boulder Police Department."

"Yes, I remember you calling earlier this week. What can I do for you?"

"I just have a few follow-up questions. I talked to Dr. Lanaro earlier today, and he made it sound like Athena Gibson was still delusional. Did she ever fully recover from her experience?"

"Athena was undoubtedly delusional when we first found her. Frankly, it hindered our investigation. However, she eventually got better. I thought she was doing well the last time I talked to her."

"When was that?"

"Probably two years ago."

"I take it you didn't have any concerns about Dr. Lanaro's opinions of Athena?"

"Not really. He told us we shouldn't rely on Athena's testimony. He also thought she would make a terrible prosecution witness. Frankly, I agreed with him."

"So, you had no concerns about his diagnosis?"

"No. Dr. Lanaro knows his stuff."

"Did anyone else have any concerns?"

"About the Athena Gibson case? No."

"Was there another case that raised a concern?"

"Not any involving his assessment of victims or suspects. However, two of our homicide detectives thought he may have had something to do with his wife's death."

"Huh? I thought she died from a sleeping pill overdose while he was traveling."

"She did. She drank wine from a bottle laced with a large overdose of sleeping pills. Therefore, some think it could have been the doctor who put the drug in the wine before he left. She liked her wine."

"Was he investigated?" asked Shaw.

"Well, we interviewed him. There were some problems in the marriage, but there was no evidence the doctor put the drugs in the bottle. The coroner ruled the death a suicide."

"No one else lived in the house?"

"Umm, I believe he had one son, but I'm unsure if he still lived there."

"Interesting. Thank you, Dan. I appreciate your help."

After the call, Shaw sat at her desk, frustrated. Detective Benson confirmed Dr. Lanaro was correct about Athena, at least initially. However, in his layman's opinion, Benson believed Athena improved over time. And then the information that some detectives thought Lanaro may have been involved with his wife's death was a surprise. Shaw wasn't about to share that with anyone. Sharing that information could really get her in hot water.

"Caro, what's up?" asked Nichols.

"Huh?"

"You look lost in another world."

"Oh, nothing. I'm just tired."

Chapter 20

Della had just been through another rough night. At least, she believed it was night. It could have been daytime. Della was cut off from the world, never knowing what time of day it was. She estimated she had not seen daylight for at least seven weeks. The light in her dungeon had been on for well over twenty-four hours, and the loud pounding music had played for hours. The man in the hood had warned her the next day would bring another round of what he called electric shock therapy. This was worse than getting tased. During electric shock therapy, the man would attach two probes to each side of her head with wires leading to a small black metal box. The box looked like a transformer with a dial on top of it. Whenever he turned the dial, pulsating electricity would shoot through her head, causing extreme pain and paralysis. It also affected her memory.

I can't go through more electric shock treatments. This is it. I'm going to die, or I'm going to get out of here.

Once again, Della carefully retrieved the long needle from her mattress, using her body to shield it from the camera. As she had before, Della carefully slid the needle into the side of her shorts along her right leg. Della knew she would have to stab the man before he started the shock treatments. Once they started, she would be helpless. Della lay on the bed and waited. He did not come. Without the pounding music, Della's fatigue took over. She fell asleep on the bed.

"Wake up!" shouted the man.

"Huh?" said a surprised Della. She opened her eyes and saw the hooded man standing over her.

"Get up. It's time for your treatment."

Della took a moment to gain her senses.

"I said get up!" he shouted.

"Okay," said Della as she pulled herself to a seated position at the edge of the bed, moving carefully so as not to expose the needle.

"Go sit in the chair and strap yourself in."

Della knew if she strapped herself in, her chance for escape was over. She hesitated.

"What are you waiting for? Strap in."

Della shuffled over to the chair and sat down. She bent over and fumbled with the ankle straps.

The man was growing angry. "You've done this many times. Get the straps on."

"I can't today."

"What do you mean?" he asked, pulling out his trusty taser.

"You haven't fed me in a long time. I'm weak, and my hands are trembling. Look at them," Della pleaded as she held out her shaking hands.

"Sit back!" shouted the man as he approached her.

As the man bent down to strap in her right ankle, Della reached for the needle. She had difficulty pulling it out while seated in the chair.

"Hold still!" he shouted.

Della worked the needle out as her right ankle was being strapped tight to the chair. The man shifted to strap in her left ankle. It was now or never, thought Della.

Holding the needle in her right hand, Della lunged forward and thrust the needle into the man's lower left abdomen as hard as she could. Fortunately, the needle did not hit bone. It easily penetrated deep into the man's gut.

"Ahhhh!" screamed the man as he rocked backward on his feet, his butt hitting the floor. "You bitch! What have you done?" he cried in obvious pain. The man clasped his hands over the wound as bright red blood soaked through his white smock.

Della quickly bent over to undo the strap on her right ankle. She had to get it off before the man got back on his feet. Her hands were shaking, making it difficult to undo the strap.

The man groaned and slowly rolled to his left, getting onto his left knee, then his right knee. While holding his left hand over his wound, he used his right hand on the floor to steady himself. He placed his right foot on the floor with his right knee in the air, readying himself to stand.

Della saw the man attempting to stand. Her life depended on the next few seconds. Frustrated, Della began screaming for help while still trying to undo the strap holding her leg to the chair. Della no longer focused on the man. She only focused on releasing her right foot. One more hard tug. The strap released! Della looked up, and the man was almost upon her.

Della let out an ear-piercing shriek as she lunged forward, the needle in her right hand. Just as the man put his hands on Della's neck, she plunged the needle in as far as it could go. Della wasn't sure where she had stabbed him, but she knew the needle quickly went in.

The man's hands released their grip on Della's neck as he again staggered backward. The man stumbled to his left, then fell, hitting his left hip on the side of the bed and rolling to the floor. As he fell, he screamed, "You bitch, I will kill you!"

Della didn't wait to find out. She bolted out the open door. It was the first time Della had gotten a look at her dungeon from the outside. It appeared she was in a basement, with timbers built up from the floor to create the room that held her captive for so long. However, Della had no time to waste. She had to find the way out. A set of metal stairs ran up the side of the timbers, leading to a platform above. Della hobbled up the stairs. Once she got to the top, she looked down through the grate she had stared at for weeks. She could see the man lying on the floor, holding his stomach. Della noticed something else. The man had taken off his hood. For the first time, Della saw her captor without his hood. She couldn't see much of his face but noticed he had dark, almost black hair.

Della turned around and found an opening in the wall behind her. It almost looked like a double sliding door that had split open. Della ran through the opening and found herself in a home. She noticed furniture and a table but paid little attention to the décor. Her mind was set on getting out before her captor could recover. Della ran for the first door she found. It was deadbolted. She fumbled with the lock until she unlocked the door. She then reached for the doorknob, opened the door, and ran out. Della ran onto the porch, pushed open the gate and ran down the steps into the street. It was nighttime, and the street she was on was very dark. Della did not know where she was but knew it was a residential area. The cool night air felt like velvet soothing her face, and the smell of fresh air brought tears to Della's eyes.

Della continued to run, causing pain in her injured right knee. She saw people along the sidewalks but was too afraid to approach anyone. Della no longer knew what city she was in or even what state she was in. All she wanted to do was get as far away from the man in the hood as possible. The second thing she wanted was to avoid the police. She didn't want them to take her back to that living hell hole for more treatment.

Della saw a group of people walking toward her on the sidewalk. She quickly stepped behind a parked car and ducked down. Della allowed them to pass before she continued on her journey. She did not know where to go except to get as far away as possible. After hobbling for several blocks, Della was out of breath. She hid in some bushes alongside a house to calm herself down. She bent over, placing her hands on her knees and breathed deeply. It was then she noticed she had no shoes on. Della was so focused on escaping she forgot she was barefooted. Della then saw the blood on her hands, T-shirt and white shorts.

After a few minutes, Della was ready to continue her escape. She didn't know in which direction to run. She just had to keep going. Della looked around trying to recognize anything familiar. A block away, Della could see bright lights, moving cars, and people milling around on the sidewalks. She walked in that direction, hoping she could blend into the crowd. As Della got closer, some buildings looked familiar. Della thought she had been there before. Della tried to remain in the shadows as she walked and avoided eye contact with other pedestrians. However, she could sense that others were looking at her. Della arrived at a busy intersection and looked up at the street sign on the corner. 13th and College. Those streets sounded familiar to Della, but she wasn't sure. Her mind was still very confused.

"Are you okay?" said a female voice.

It startled Della. "Huh?"

A young woman, who was with three other friends, stood in front of Della. "You look like you're bleeding."

Della was frozen in fear. She didn't know whether to run or fight.

"She's hurt," said another woman. "I think she needs help."

"Has she been stabbed?" asked another.

Della was frozen in fear. She didn't know whether to accept help or run.

"I'm calling the police," said one woman.

"No!" screamed Della. She then took off running north on 13th Street from College. She could hear her bare feet slapping the pavement as she ran, and her knee called out in pain. Della then felt a sharp pain on the bottom of her left foot but continued to run until she came to

Pennsylvania Street. The surroundings again looked familiar to Della. There was an open door leading into a place called The Sink. Della ran inside.

"Whoa, not so fast," said a man inside the doorway. "Can I help you?"

The room was noisy and full of people. "Huh?" asked Della.

"You're bleeding," said the man. "Are you hurt?"

Della was too frightened to answer. She didn't know who she could trust.

"Come over here and sit down," said the man, leading Della to a chair. Della was tired, hungry, thirsty, in pain, and scared. She agreed to sit down.

The man then waved over the manager from the bar. "I think this woman needs medical attention. She has blood on her shirt and pants. She also looks like she is in shock."

"I'll call the police," said the manager.

"No!" shouted Della. "No police."

"We're just trying to get you some help," said the manager. "You're not in trouble."

"Please, no police," pleaded Della. "They will take me back."

"Back to where?"

"To that awful place. I don't want any more treatment."

The employee and manager looked at each other. "What awful place?" asked the manager.

"The treatment place. It was horrible."

The manager whispered to the employee, "Get her some water and something to eat. I'm going to call the police."

The Sink employee brought Della a glass of water and a slice of pizza. Della quickly gulped the entire glass of water. She then began eating the pizza. She couldn't remember the last time she ate anything. "I'll get you some more water," said the employee.

He soon returned with another glass of water and noticed Della was almost finished with her pizza slice. Della took another long drink of water.

"What is your name?" asked the employee.

"I'm not sure," said Della. "I think, Amy."

"Are you on any drugs?"

"I don't know."

The employee sat with Della for several minutes before hearing sirens in the distance. When the manager returned, he pulled the employee aside. "The cops and an ambulance are on the way." The employee nodded.

Within seconds, the sound of an approaching siren grew louder.

"What is that?" asked Della in a panicked voice.

"Someone coming to help you," said the manager.

"NO! I said no police. They will take me back!"

"Did you escape from jail or something?"

Della glared at the manager. "Yes! They were going to kill me in there."

"In jail?"

Della quickly stood and ran out the door before the manager could stop her. Della stopped on the sidewalk, not knowing which way to run. She then saw a Boulder Police patrol car approaching northbound on 13th Street from College. Della turned and ran in the opposite direction until she came upon a busy four-lane road. The street sign above her read Broadway. Della looked back and saw the patrol car stopped in front of The Sink. An officer was on the sidewalk talking to the manager. She then looked up and down Broadway. Della was confused. Some things looked familiar, yet she did not know where she was.

Two college-aged men saw Della standing with fresh bloodstains on her shirt and pants. They stopped to offer assistance.

"Do you need help?" asked the first man.

"Where am I?" asked Della.

"You're at 13ᵗʰ and Broadway."

"What city!" screamed Della.

The question surprised both men.

"You're in Boulder. Are you lost?"

"I don't know where I am," replied Della.

By now, both men suspected something was seriously wrong. "Where do you live?" asked the second man.

Della ignored the question. "I need a place to hide."

Both men were confused and concerned. They knew something was seriously wrong. "Let us get you some help," said the second man.

Della looked back and saw the police car was now driving toward her and was only 100 feet away. She spun around and ran north along Broadway. As she approached the intersection of Pleasant Street, Della saw a second police car driving southbound on Broadway, nearing Pleasant Street. Della and the officer locked eyes. Della made a quick left turn and began running westbound on Pleasant Street. The officer quickly turned onto Pleasant, stopped his car, and then gave chase on foot.

"Unit 1232, I'm in a foot pursuit with the female subject, westbound on Pleasant. White female wearing a white shirt and white shorts."

"Unit 1264, I'm right behind him."

Dispatch: "All units standby. We have officers in a foot pursuit on westbound Pleasant from Broadway."

"Unit 1302, I'm at 10ᵗʰ and Pleasant heading eastbound."

Della was weak from a lack of food and sleep. As she ran, her legs felt like rubber. She continued to feel pain on the bottom of her left foot. A piece of broken glass had pierced through the skin and some muscle in the foot. As Della slowed, the first officer caught up and grabbed her by the shoulder. Della screamed, spun around and hit the officer in the face with a hard slap.

"Let me go!" Della screamed.

The officer grabbed Della's right arm and pulled it behind her back. Della began kicking the officer's shins with the heel of her right foot, the whole time screaming for the officer to let her go.

"Unit 1264, I'm with 1232. Subject is resisting."

As the second officer grabbed Della's left arm, she leaned over with her head turned and bit him hard on the arm. The officer yelled and yanked his arm back.

The first officer then threw Della to the ground on her stomach, placing his right knee on her back.

"Help me!" screamed Della. "I don't want to go back! Someone, please help me!"

The third officer pulled up in her patrol car as the officers were handcuffing Della's hands behind her back. Della continued to scream and kick.

"Stop it!" yelled the first officer.

Della was now crying while screaming. "Please, I don't want to go back. I'll do anything you want. Just don't take me back."

"What is she talking about?" asked the female officer.

"I don't know," said the first officer. "Tie up her legs so she stops kicking."

"No, no!" yelled Della. "I'll stop kicking."

Della stopped resisting. "Please don't take me to the dungeon."

"You're not making any sense, lady," said the second officer.

"Why is your nose bleeding?" asked the female officer to the first officer.

"The bitch smacked me good in the nose. And then she bit Jack on the arm."

"Are you taking her to mental health?"

"Absolutely not. She's going to be charged with assaulting two police officers. Our cars are a couple of blocks back. Can you take her to the jail for us?"

"She needs to go to the hospital first," said the female officer. "She has blood all over her. I'm calling for an ambulance."

Once the ambulance arrived, the officers assisted in getting Della into the ambulance. One of the EMTs asked if they could take the handcuffs off.

"No," said the arresting officer. "She assaulted two of us. She's under arrest."

They arrived at the hospital at 12:45 am, Friday, June 2nd. They took Della into an exam room in the emergency center of Boulder Community Hospital. The female officer remained with Della until the arresting officer, Bret Lockett, arrived.

By the time Officer Lockett arrived at the hospital, they had given Della a sedative to calm her down. Both of her wrists were handcuffed to the railings on the bed. The medical examination of Della revealed some old wounds, an injured right knee, and a cut on the bottom of her left foot. The doctor could not explain the blood on Della's clothing. Lockett asked the doctor when the suspect would be released. He was told they wanted to observe her for at least an hour before releasing her.

"She's been talking nonsense since I got here," said the female officer. "And she is clearly afraid of us."

"I told her we just wanted to ensure she was okay," said Lockett. "It didn't matter. She went ballistic once I stopped her."

"Where are you going to take her?"

"She assaulted us."

"Yes, but she is clearly not in her right mind. She needs help. You can always charge her later."

"I'll think about it," replied Lockett.

The female officer left while Lockett waited for Della to be released. The emergency room doctor walked into the waiting room to talk with Lockett.

"Do you know who this woman is?" asked the doctor.

"No. She had no ID, and I couldn't make sense of what she was screaming."

"We'll enter her as Jane Doe number seven in our system. Please let us know once you identify her."

"Jane Doe number seven?"

"That's how we separate all the John and Jane Does in our system. We assign a number."

Lockett nodded. "Yeah. Once I know, I'll let you know."

After 40 minutes of waiting, a nurse advised Lockett that the woman's vitals had been stable for over an hour. He was free to take her. Lockett walked into the exam room and saw Della asleep on the bed. Her right knee was wrapped, and a bandage covered the bottom of her left foot. Lockett uncuffed Della's wrists. The nurse assisted Lockett in getting Della seated with her legs hanging over the edge of the bed.

"She will remain groggy for another two hours," said the nurse. "She shouldn't give you any trouble now."

Lockett thanked the nurse as he handcuffed Della's wrists behind her back. The nurse and Lockett lifted Della up and sat her in a wheelchair. The nurse then wheeled Della out of the emergency room to Officer Lockett's patrol car. They lifted Della up and sat her in the back of the vehicle. Della mumbled something unintelligible. Lockett seatbelted Della in, thanked the nurse, and then walked around to the driver's seat. He sat for a minute, thinking without starting the car. Lockett heard Della mumbling in the back seat. Lockett turned to look and saw Della with her head down, her chin almost touching the top of her chest, and he heard her repeating, "Please stop, don't hurt me. Please don't hurt me anymore."

Lockett turned back around and started the car. He sat there for another minute. Della continued to mumble behind him.

"Screw it," said Lockett out loud. He picked up his microphone. "Unit 1232, I'll be en route to mental health from the hospital with one female subject."

"Copy, Unit 1232."

Chapter 21

Later that Friday morning, June 2ⁿᵈ, Shaw arrived at work at 9:10 am. She had slept in for an extra hour.

"Where have you been?" asked Detective Jordan.

"I needed some extra sleep. I feel much better now."

"That's good, because another stack of tips came in overnight."

"As long as this case goes unsolved, I'm sure we will keep getting tips," said Shaw.

"Here's a good one," said Jordan. "This woman calls in and claims she had an epiphany of who the killer is."

"Yeah? Who is it?"

"Some volleyball coach at the high school. He was dating this woman's daughter and recently ended the relationship."

"And mom had an epiphany he was our serial killer?"

"Yes."

"I'll tell you what," said Shaw. "Put that one on Tom's desk."

Jordan laughed. "Okay."

Shaw began going through the tips on her desk when Commander Greenberg called Shaw into her office.

"What is it, Commander?"

"I had a strange call from Janice Brooks with Boulder County Mental Health a few minutes ago. Last night, officers picked up a distraught young woman near Broadway and Pleasant. She was hysterical and had to be restrained and taken to the hospital. From there, Officer Lockett took her to mental health."

"Okay," responded Shaw.

"There's more. The woman had blood on the front of her clothing, but only the bottom of her left foot was cut. She was very frightened by our officers and was screaming not to take her back."

"Back to where?"

"We don't know. But according to Janice, this woman has said things that concern her. The woman claims to have been taken somewhere by the police for treatment. This woman's description of treatment involved torture. Janice said there are old injuries on her body that corroborate her story. The difficulty is that this woman's story is all over the place."

"What's her name?"

"They don't know for sure. She didn't have any identification. They think her first name might be Amy or Della."

"Did Janice get a description of the person who tortured her?"

"The woman kept referring to someone in a white hood."

Shaw's jaw dropped. "Athena described her attacker as always wearing a hooded mask over his face. We may have found a survivor of our serial killer."

"I thought the same thing," agreed Greenberg. "I want you and Tom to go interview this woman."

"Thank you, Commander."

Shaw walked back to the work area. "Where's Tom?" yelled Shaw. Nobody knew. Shaw dialed his number on her cell phone.

"Hello."

"Tom, where are you?"

"I'm upstairs having a coffee with some patrol buddies. What's up?"

"We have a major break in the case. I need you down here right now."

"On my way."

Once Nichols arrived, Shaw filled him in. Within minutes, they were on their way to Boulder County Mental Health. Upon arrival, they met with mental health crisis worker Janice Brooks, a fifty-four-year-old white female with dark wavy hair and plastic dark-rimmed glasses to match. She was dressed in a white blouse and casual dark blue pants.

"What can you tell us about Amy?" asked Shaw.

"Not much, other than her being distraught and untrusting of the police. They sedated her at the hospital before bringing her here. I talked to her at eight o'clock this morning for over an hour."

"Did she say what happened to her?"

"It's hard to follow her story. One minute, she talks about bright lights. The next, she hears loud music."

"Do you know if she has any family?" asked Nichols.

"She said her parents are dead."

"No last name?"

"She doesn't remember."

"May we talk to her?" asked Shaw. "We believe she might have escaped from our serial killer."

"You can try. We still have her on a mild sedative. However, I wouldn't tell her you are with the police. She's deathly afraid of you guys. She's down the hall in room 103."

"Thank you," said Shaw. "Do you have someplace where we can lock up our guns? I wouldn't want her to see them and freak out."

"Sure, you can lock them in my filing cabinet."

Nichols looked at Shaw and quietly said, "I'm uncomfortable giving up my gun."

"I know, but we are in a locked facility, and this is a special situation. I can go in there alone if you prefer."

Nichols thought for a moment. "No, I get it. I'm going in with you."

After securing their weapons, Shaw and Nichols entered room 103. Della was sitting in a chair with her feet on the floor and rocking back and forth. She was wearing blue cotton pants and a blue cotton shirt that had been provided by Mental Health. White cloth slippers were on her feet. Tangled and dirty, her long blond hair hung down past her shoulders. Her eyes were bloodshot.

"Amy, my name is Caro, and this is Tom. We are here to help you."

"Are you the police?"

"Right now, we're just two people working with mental health. We are here to help you. We understand you have been through a traumatic experience."

"Why am I locked up again?"

"You are in a mental health facility. As soon as you are better, you can leave."

"I want out of here now."

"Amy, if you help us, we can get the person who did this to you."

Della looked directly at Shaw. "I want him dead."

"Then let us help you, Amy."

"I don't know who I am."

"What do you mean?" asked Nichols.

Della's eyes watered. "I don't know. Sometimes, I think my name is Della."

"Della? Why is that?" continued Nichols.

"I don't know."

"Do you have family we can call?" asked Shaw.

"I don't know."

"You don't remember?"

"He messed up my mind. He convinced me they were dead."

"Well, maybe they are still alive," suggested Shaw. "We can help you. Were you held captive somewhere?"

"The police took me there."

"Took you where?"

"To the dungeon."

"The dungeon?"

"Yes. A small wooden room with no windows, a crappy bed and a bucket to pee in!" screamed Della.

Nichols and Shaw looked at each other. "Please excuse us a minute, Amy," said Shaw as she motioned Nichols to follow her out of the room.

Once in the hallway Shall said, "This is almost exactly what Athena told us happened to her five years ago."

"You're right," agreed Nichols. "If she can tell us where this place is, we can solve this case."

"I don't believe her name is Amy. That is the name our suspect gave to her."

"Again, I think you're right. She's warming up to you. You need to be the lead."

"Okay, let's go back in."

"Thank you for waiting, Amy. Is there anything we can get for you?" asked Shaw.

"I could use another water."

"I'll get it," said Nichols as he left the room.

"Tell me more about this room you were in," continued Shaw.

"It had a grate on top where he would shine a bright light or play loud music. I still have ringing in my ears."

"That sounds awful."

"You can't imagine."

"Did this man abuse you?"

Della stared at Shaw. "Did he abuse me? Every day."

"If you can, describe how he abused you for me."

Della spoke softly. "It was like a torture chamber. Electric shocks, needles, cold temperature, music, lights, everything."

Nichols re-entered the room and handed Della a bottle of water.

"Thank you," Della said softly.

"Amy, what did he do with the needles?" continued Shaw. Shaw noticed Della's eyes filled with tears. "It's okay, Amy. We can talk about something else right now. How did you get away?"

Della looked down at the floor. "If I tell you, will you tell the police?"

Shaw glanced at Nichols, who shrugged his shoulders.

"Amy, we need to find the man who did this before he hurts someone else. How did you escape?"

"I stabbed him with a needle," cried Della.

"Where did you stab him?"

"In his stomach. I stabbed him two times."

"Did you kill him?"

"I don't know," cried Della.

"Is that how you got blood on your clothing?"

"I had blood on me?"

"Yes."

Della groaned.

"Where were you when you stabbed him?"

"In the room I described."

"Yes, but is it in a house?"

"I think so."

"Where is the house?"

"I don't know."

"According to the reports, you were first seen near 13th and College. Do you remember that?"

"Yes."

"Okay, how did you get to 13th and College?"

"I ran."

"From the house?"

"Yes."

"How long did you run?"

"I don't know. I was so scared he was coming after me."

"Did you run several blocks? A mile? Two miles?"

"I can't remember. Much of it is a blur. I just wanted to get as far away as possible."

"But you remember 13th and College?"

"Yes. It looked familiar to me, and I saw the street sign."

"Do you believe you had been there before?"

"Yes. The area looked familiar."

"Okay, good. Try to remember how long you were running before you got to 13th and College."

"I don't know. My mind is so foggy right now. Maybe fifteen minutes. I remember hiding in some bushes for awhile."

"Were you hiding from your attacker?"

"No. I was hiding from other people. I was afraid."

"Let's go back to the man who kept you captive. What did he look like?"

"I don't know. He always wore a mask and a white jacket."

"What type of mask?"

"Like a hood. I could only see his eyes."

"Do you remember what color his eyes were?"

"I'll never forget those eyes. They were very dark and evil."

"You never saw anything else? His hair or skin color?"

"He was white."

"This is good, Amy."

"I'm not sure my name is Amy."

"I don't think it is," agreed Shaw. "You were conditioned to believe your name was Amy."

"I think my real name is Della."

"Do you know your last name?"

Della sat and thought for several seconds. "I believe it is Kemp."

"I'm going to call you Della," said Shaw. "Do you know where you are from?"

"Denver."

"Is that where your family is?"

"No, wait. Let me think."

Della bowed her head and shut her eyes. Shaw and Nichols patiently waited.

"Can you shut off the music?" asked Della.

"What music?" asked Shaw.

"It's pounding in my head."

"There is no music right now," explained Shaw. "You're under a lot of stress, Della. You're having a flashback. I think we will stop for today. You've been very helpful, Della. Would you mind if Tom took a small swab from your mouth for DNA testing? It might help us identify who you are and where your family is."

"Okay."

Nichols took a swab kit from his inside jacket pocket. He carefully swabbed the inside cheek of Della's mouth.

"Just one more question," said Nichols. "Can you remember anything else about your attacker?"

Della thought for a moment. "Yes. After I stabbed him, he pulled off his mask. I saw he had black hair."

"Did you see anything else?" asked Nichols.

"No."

"Thank you, Della," said Shaw. "We will let you get some rest now."

"When can I get out of here?"

"As soon as the staff here believes you can care for yourself. I don't think it will be long."

On the drive back to the police department, Shaw and Nichols were excited to finally have the break they needed.

"Our killer is right here in Boulder," said Nichols.

"Yes," agreed Shaw. "What she described is very similar to Athena's story. It has to be the same guy."

"How are we going to find the house she talked about?"

"I don't believe Della was running for long before people noticed her. That house must be in the Hill Neighborhood somewhere. We just need to find it," said Shaw. "Call Gates at the Sheriff's Department and have him meet us at the police department. Then call the commander and tell her we have important news to share."

"On it," replied Nichols.

Chapter 22

All those most involved in working on the Boulder Creek Murders were present in the first-floor conference room at the police department. Seated at the conference table were Police Chief Ken Atkins, Commander Stella Greenberg, Sergeant Luca Martinez, Sheriff Commander Joel Clark, Sheriff Detective Owen Gates, and Boulder Detectives Caroline Shaw, Tom Nichols, and Kevin Jordan. Commander Greenberg led the discussion.

"As you all know by now," said Greenberg, "patrol officers picked up a distraught young woman last night. Further investigation today revealed her name is probably Della Kemp. From what we've gotten out of her thus far, we believe she had been held captive for some time, during which she was tortured. She claims to have stabbed her captor to escape. Della fits the description of our three murder victims. She is young, pretty, and has long, blond hair. We've checked local hospitals and have found no one being treated for stab wounds. Because of our victim's state of mind, it is difficult to know fact from fiction."

"Have we done a canvass of the hill neighborhood yet?" asked Sheriff Commander Clark.

"We have not had time to put that together. We interviewed our victim just this morning."

"Has this woman been able to describe where she was being held?" asked Chief Atkins.

"She described a room, Chief. Our victim is not even sure the house is on the Hill. We believe it is, only because we don't think she could have gotten far in her condition with blood over the front of her clothing and a cut on her foot. Remember that she was so afraid last night she assaulted two of our officers because she believed they would take her back. She is also still under sedation."

"Based on what you are telling us, how can we be sure of anything she says?" asked the Chief.

"We can't. However, Caro spoke to a past victim of kidnapping and torture that closely resembles Della's story. The suspect in that case was never caught."

"We need to bring Dr. Lanaro back in on this," said Chief Atkins. "He helped profile our suspect. Maybe he can get additional information out of our victim."

"We can arrange that," responded Greenberg.

"Let's do that right away," demanded the Chief.

"As soon as I'm done here, I will call him."

"What are the next steps, Commander?" asked Sergeant Martinez.

"I propose we assemble a team to canvass a twelve-block area from 13th and College. The sooner, the better. We still have a suspect at large, and for all we know, he may be lying dead somewhere. We'll have copies of our suspect sketch for people to show to those in the neighborhood. I can pull some detectives and patrol officers to assist."

"We can add some people as well," offered Sheriff Commander Clark.

"Okay, it's almost noon. Let's plan to meet back here at two o'clock to brief everyone. We will then send everyone out to find our suspect," said Greenberg.

"Thank you, Stella," said the Chief.

After the meeting, Shaw pulled Nichols aside. "I don't think having Dr. Lanaro interview our victim is a good idea."

"Why not?"

"I just got a bad vibe from him as he described Athena. He dismissed everything she told us. And remember how pissed he got with me?"

"Yeah, but you challenged him."

"I asked him a simple question. And ever since Benson told me about Lanaro's wife, I've felt uneasy about him."

"He seems to know his stuff, Caro. And besides, the Chief made it clear he wants Dr. Lanaro to interview our victim."

"Yeah, I know."

"Be positive. He might be helpful in getting our victim to open up. Do you want to get some lunch?"

"No, you go on. I'm not hungry."

Commander Greenberg called Dr. Lanaro's cell phone.

"Hello," snapped Dr. Lanaro.

"Is this Dr. Lanaro?"

"Yes, it is."

"Hi, Doctor. This is Commander Greenberg with the police department. I'm unsure whether you heard, but we have a victim at Boulder County Mental Health who claims to have been held captive for weeks. We believe she is a victim of our homicide suspect. The Chief wanted me to ask if you would be willing to interview our victim. She is very troubled."

"When?"

"He would like it done this afternoon."

"Ummm. I would be happy to help, but not today. I have too many appointments today. How about tomorrow?"

"We can make that work. What time?"

"Uh, one o'clock."

"Thank you. I'll let the Chief know."

Shaw sat at her desk, searching the computer for information on Dr. Anthony Lanaro. She wanted to know as much about him as possible. Shaw discovered Lanaro received his doctorate in psychiatry from UCLA in Los Angeles, CA. Soon after, he married Lilly Stevens. Lanaro practiced for several years in California before moving to Colorado Springs and opening his own office. Twenty-six years ago, he and his wife had a baby boy. They named him Angelo. Dr. Lanaro was well known in the field of psychiatry. Shaw found multiple articles written about him and some written by him. She also found news stories about the death of his wife six years ago. According to the reports, Dr. Lanaro returned home from a conference in California and found his wife dead from an overdose of sedatives. Lanaro's son, Angelo, was not home at the time. He was attending the University of Colorado in Boulder. According to statements made by Dr. Lanaro, Lilly suffered from depression. Her death was ruled a suicide. Four years ago, Dr. Lanaro sold his practice in Colorado Springs and moved to Boulder, where he opened a new office.

Shaw then logged into the Department of Motor Vehicles to search for a driver's license for Angelo Lanaro. Within seconds, a photo of Angelo Lanaro popped up on the screen with his identifying information. Shaw couldn't believe it. Angelo was five-nine, 170 lbs., with dark brown eyes and black curly hair. It was difficult to see if he had a scar in the black-and-white photo. *He fits our profile perfectly,* thought Shaw. *It can't be him. This is just a crazy coincidence. Or is it?* Shaw felt a pit in her stomach, and her mouth turned dry. *Maybe he is our suspect and was under our nose the whole time. If so, does Dr. Lanaro know?*

Shaw briskly walked to the commander's office. "Commander, you won't believe this."

"What is it, Caro?"

"I think Dr. Lanaro's son might be our suspect."

Greenberg pushed herself back in her chair, away from her desk. "What the hell are you talking about?"

"I just looked him up. He fits the description."

"Yeah? And so do about ten thousand other men in this city. What do you have against Dr. Lanaro?"

"I don't have anything against him. I just had a strange feeling about him, so I did some research. Come to my desk; I'll show you."

Greenberg followed Shaw to her desk.

"See? Look at his photograph."

"Yes, Caro. I see a young man who fits our description, just like many other men in this city. Why him and not any of the others?"

"Don't you see the resemblance to the sketch?"

"Some. Not enough to call him a suspect. Until you have more evidence than this, we are not calling Dr. Lanaro's son a suspect. Hell, Dr. Lanaro would turn him in himself if he thought his son had any involvement in our murders. Our suspect is probably lying somewhere in a room dead."

Shaw didn't respond as the commander walked away. *She's probably right. But I need to be sure.*

Shaw printed a copy of Angelo Lanaro's picture and stuck it in a file folder.

At 2:00 pm, the team met again in the conference room for assignments. Before the commander could give out the assignments, Shaw raised her hand.

"Commander."

"What is it, Caro?"

"I would appreciate it if you would assign Tom and I to Eleventh Street between College and Aurora."

"Any particular reason?"

"I was looking at the map, and based on our discussion with Della, I think that's a good starting point."

Nichols furrowed his brow and looked at Shaw. Shaw did not notice his look.

"Okay, you and Tom can take those two blocks," agreed the Commander. She then continued assigning teams of two detectives or officers to two-block areas in the surrounding neighborhood.

"Be sure to take a copy of the sketch of our suspect with you," reminded the Commander. "And be careful out there."

Shaw insisted on driving. Once they were in the car, Nichols turned to Shaw. "Where did you come up with the idea that 11th Street would be the best place to start? Della had no clue where she ran from."

"Look in my file folder."

Nichols picked up the folder tucked next to the console. He opened it up and saw the driver's license photograph of Angelo Lanaro.

"What is this?" asked Nichols.

"That's Lanaro's son."

"You think Dr. Lanaro's son has something to do with this?"

"Well, look at him!"

"Yeah, he matches the description, but still...."

"I have a hunch," said Shaw.

"I don't know, Caro."

"I just want to show his photo to the neighbors. If he lives there, someone will know him."

"Okay," replied Nichols. "I hope you know what you are doing."

Shaw found a parking space on 11th Street. Both detectives exited the car, and Nichols followed Shaw south on 11th to the block where Dr. Lanaro lived. They started with the first home on the block. An older gentleman answered the door. Shaw explained their presence and showed the man the suspect sketch and photo ID of Angelo Lanaro. "I'm sorry, I don't recognize either of those men."

At the second home, a young college-age woman named Cindy came to the door. Shaw showed Cindy the photograph and sketch drawing.

Cindy studied the drawing and photo ID. "He looks familiar, but I don't know for sure."

"Where do you think you've seen this person?" asked Shaw.

"Wow, it could have been anywhere. A party, a bar. I just don't know."

"Could this person live in the neighborhood?" asked Shaw.

"Um, I don't know. I've seen the drawing on TV. Maybe that's what I'm thinking of."

"Thank you for your time," said Shaw.

At the third home, a middle-aged African American woman answered the door wearing a paint-stained smock. Shaw showed the woman both the sketch and driver's license photo.

"Well," said the woman. "That looks like many of the young men I see in this neighborhood."

"Look closely," said Shaw. "Have you seen this person in the neighborhood?"

"I'm sorry, I can't say. Too many of these college kids look alike."

"Thank you," said Shaw.

At several homes no one answered the door. Eventually, the detectives came upon the home belonging to Dr. Lanaro. Shaw and Nichols walked past his house to the one south of Dr. Lanaro. It appeared to be another home used as student housing. Nichols knocked on the door. A young college-aged man with blond hair answered. His name was David. Shaw again explained their purpose and showed David the pictures.

"I just moved in for the summer," said David. "I don't know anyone yet. Some other roomies might know him, but they are on summer break now."

"Damn," said Shaw as they walked away. "I was afraid of this. Most of the students have already left."

"Let's try across the street," suggested Nichols.

"Good idea. Let's try the house directly across from Lanaro's."

Nichols knocked on the door. A white male in his forties answered the door. He identified himself as Rick Russell. Shaw showed him the drawing and photograph. After looking at the driver's license photograph, Russell nodded his head.

"This looks like Dr. Lanaro's kid," said Russell.

Shaw turned and pointed to Dr. Lanaro's home. "Is that where he lives?"

"If this is the same kid, yes. He lives with his father."

"Do you know his name?"

"I think the doctor told me his name once, but I can't remember it now."

"Does Angelo sound familiar?"

"Yes, that's it. Angelo."

"Have you ever seen Angelo with a girlfriend?" asked Shaw.

"No, I can't say I have," replied Russell. "Other than patients occasionally coming and going, I rarely see anyone else over there."

"Thank you, Mr. Russell. You've been a big help."

After Shaw and Nichols walked away, Shaw turned to Nichols. "We need to get into that house."

"Caro, we don't have enough for a search warrant. You already knew Angelo probably lived with his father. This doesn't prove anything."

"I know, but we have to try."

"You won't get a search warrant, Caro."

"We'll talk our way in."

"You think Dr. Lanaro will let you search his house?"

"It's worth a try."

"Okay, but it's on you if this goes badly," warned Nichols.

"I know," agreed Shaw.

The detectives walked across the street and knocked on the door leading to Dr. Lanaro's office. Nichols looked into the office through the large window in the tower. He didn't see anyone inside.

"I don't see any activity inside," said Nichols.

"Let's try the resident side," replied Shaw.

They walked to the residential entrance, and Shaw rang the doorbell. Nichols tried looking inside, but all the curtains were drawn shut. Shaw continued to ring the doorbell. After three rings, the door flung open.

"Detectives," said Dr. Lanaro. "What do you want?"

"Sorry to bother you, Doctor, but we are canvassing the neighborhood looking for the location where our victim was held captive. We are checking every home."

"And you think this is where the woman was held captive?" asked Lanaro in a disgruntled voice.

"No," said Shaw. "Of course not. But your son matches the description of our suspect."

"As do thousands of other males," interrupted Lanaro.

"You are right, Doctor," agreed Shaw. "But because of that, we must eliminate him from suspicion."

"Well, you missed him by a week, Detective Shaw. He is probably somewhere in California right now. You see, he is a doctorate student at the university in psychiatry and is on his summer break, like most students. You happy now?"

"Thank you, Doctor," said Shaw. "Would you mind if we look around your home?"

"Why?"

"To eliminate your house as a location. We are checking all homes in the hill neighborhood."

"You are searching all homes in this neighborhood?"

"If someone lives in the home matching our suspect description, then yes, we will ask to look through the home. We need to be thorough. Please let us do this, and we will leave you alone."

Dr. Lanaro stepped aside. "Go on, have your look around. However, I will talk to your chief about this."

Shaw and Nichols walked into the living room. The room was elegantly decorated with leather furniture and antique tables. Dr. Lanaro sat in a leather recliner and picked up a book.

"You don't mind if I read, do you?"

"Not at all," said Nichols.

A large floor-to-ceiling bookcase was on the west wall, divided by an ornate wood center from the floor to the top of the shelves. Books of all types filled each shelf. The dining room and kitchen were off to the left. Shaw walked through the kitchen looking for signs of blood on the floor, walls and fixtures. Nichols followed behind her. Down the hallway on the left were a study and a bathroom. Nothing looked out of the ordinary. A locked door was on the right of the hallway.

The detectives then walked up the stairs to the second floor. There, they found three bedrooms and a second bathroom. One bedroom obviously belonged to the son, Angelo Lanaro. Shaw took her time in looking through Angelo's bedroom. The bed hadn't been made, and the room was a mess. Clothing was piled in a corner. Shaw carefully examined the clothing, looking for blood. She then studied Angelo's college graduation photograph sitting on his dresser.

"There's nothing here," said Nichols. "You may have gotten us in a heap of trouble."

Shaw didn't say a word. She knew Nichols may be right. When they returned to the living room, Shaw asked what was behind the locked door.

"That is the passage to my office. Do you want to search that as well?"

"We would appreciate it, Doctor."

Dr. Lanaro stood and walked to the door. He removed a key from his pocket and opened the door. He even held it open for Shaw and Nichols to walk through.

The office looked the same as when the detectives first talked to Dr. Lanaro. Shaw found the door leading to the basement and walked down. Nichols followed her. The narrow basement ran the length of the house. It was unfinished and carried a musty smell. In one corner were the furnace and water heater. The rest of the basement was used as storage for old furniture, tools, an old mattress, boxes of records, and other miscellaneous items. The detectives returned to the living room, where Dr. Lanaro was back in his chair.

"Satisfied, Detectives?" asked Dr. Lanaro in a condescending tone.

"Thank you, Doctor," said Shaw. "We will just do a walk around outside, then we will leave you alone."

"Detective Shaw."

"Yes?"

"After today, I don't want you coming here again. Are we clear?"

"Yes, sir."

They walked out onto the white porch as Dr. Lanaro shut the door behind them. Shaw took a minute to study the porch.

"Dammit, Caro. You've got me caught up in your wild ideas."

Shaw ignored the comment. "Do you have any saline swabs in your jacket?"

"Yeah, I always carry a few. Why?"

"Look at this," said Shaw, pointing to a spot on top of the white porch gate. "This looks like blood."

"Caro, we looked through the entire house. There's nothing here. That could be from anyone."

"You're probably right but swab it anyway. Do it quickly."

Nichols took out two swabs and ran them across the red stain on the gate. He then placed the swabs in a sealed envelope. Just as he finished, the front door opened.

"What are you two still doing here?" asked Dr. Lanaro in a loud voice.

"We're leaving now," replied Shaw. "Just one more question. The basement was only under half of the house. Why is that?"

"Many of these homes were built with half basements. The other half is a crawl space. Now leave."

Shaw and Nichols left without another word. Nichols was quiet as they walked to the next house.

"Are you okay?" asked Shaw.

"I'm worried you may have gotten us into a load of trouble."

"Don't worry, Tom. I'll take all the blame. But did you look at the graduation picture?"

"No."

"You can't tell in this driver's license photo, but I thought I detected a scar above the right eye in the graduation photograph."

Nichols didn't respond. He was still thinking about the trouble Shaw may have gotten them into.

Chapter 23

Most of the task force returned to work on Saturday morning, June 3rd. At 9:05 am, Commander Greenberg called Shaw and Nichols into her office.

"Would one of you like to tell me what you did to Dr. Lanaro yesterday?"

Nichols looked at Shaw.

"It was my idea," admitted Shaw. "Tom was just along as my partner."

Greenberg frowned. "Did you search Dr. Lanaro's house?"

"Yes, we did," said Shaw.

"According to the chief, Dr. Lanaro is not happy. He wants the chief to suspend both of you."

"Commander, we did nothing wrong. We asked for consent to look around, and Dr. Lanaro consented."

"Why would you ask to search the doctor's home and office?"

Shaw pulled out the driver's license photograph of Angelo Lanaro from her file and handed it to Greenberg. "Look at this."

"You already showed me that," said Greenberg sternly.

"I know. Look how closely he matches the sketch. It's hard to see in this photograph, but while in the house, I saw a graduation picture of Angelo in his bedroom. It wasn't a large photo, but I could see a mark above his right eye, like a scar."

"Caro, the man described by your two witnesses may or may not be our suspect. It's a lead, but we won't know for certain until we find the person who killed our victims. Did you find a room as described by our victim?"

"No."

"How do you explain that?"

"I can't. He could have another location he uses."

"Did you talk to Angelo Lanaro?"

"No. He wasn't home."

"I know," said Greenberg sternly. "Dr. Lanaro told the chief his son has been vacationing since school ended. If that's true, he can't be the person our victim stabbed early Thursday morning."

"Yes, if he is truly out of town, he is not our suspect. But we need to confirm that."

"The doctor didn't know where he was?"

"He just said somewhere in California."

"That would be a solid alibi," said Greenberg. "Is there anything else?"

"There was something strange about that house. It's been remodeled into two halves, but the layout is unusual. We also found what appeared to be a blood smear on the front porch gate. Tom swabbed it for DNA. We need to test it against the blood on our victim's clothing."

The commander thought for a moment. "You think it was blood on the gate?"

"I do."

"Get that submitted immediately, and I will have CBI (Colorado Bureau of Investigation) get it tested against our victim's sample as a priority. In the meantime, I'll explain things to the chief. But I don't want you returning to the doctor's house unless we have a search warrant."

"We won't," agreed Shaw.

"Caro, you know Dr. Lanaro is meeting with our victim today at one o'clock, right?"

"No, we can't allow that," said Shaw.

"Until you get better evidence that he or his son is involved, I have no basis for asking the chief to remove him as a consultant. Think of the media backlash if we remove him now."

"Think of the harm to the victim if the doctor is involved," said Shaw.

"Caro, Dr. Lanaro is one of mental health's consulting psychiatrists," said the commander. "There isn't enough evidence to have him removed as a consultant. If his son were involved, why has he not shown up at a hospital, doctor's office, or morgue? Where is this dungeon the victim talked about? Dr. Lanaro told you his son was in California somewhere. If true, it couldn't have been him. Maybe you should try to track him down. We just don't have enough right now. Hopefully, the DNA will clear things up."

Shaw walked out of the commander's office disappointed. While the commander supported her and Nichols, she disagreed that the evidence was strong enough to identify Angelo Lanaro or Dr. Anthony Lanaro as a suspect.

"I can't believe the commander is allowing Dr. Lanaro to remain involved," complained Shaw.

"Caro," said Nichols, "she supported you more than I thought she would. All we have right now is a photograph of someone who matches a general description."

"Are you forgetting the scar?"

"Honestly, I can't tell if it is a scar or just a blemish on that driver's license photo."

"Didn't you see a scar on the graduation picture?"

"I don't know, Caro. It was hard for me to see. And to be honest, it's difficult for me to believe Dr. Lanaro would be involved in such a thing."

At 12:55 pm, Dr. Lanaro arrived as scheduled at the mental health facility, dressed in a light blue long-sleeved shirt, beige sport coat and brown dress pants.

"Good morning, Dr. Lanaro," greeted the female crisis worker seated at the desk. "Are you here to see Della?"

"Yes, I am."

"She's in room 103. She's still under some low-level sedation."

"Thank you," said the doctor.

Dr. Lanaro knocked on the door to room 103. "It's Dr. Lanaro." Hearing no response, he slowly opened the door.

Della sat on an orange cushioned chair. The room also had a twin bed, an end table, a wall-mounted TV, and a second chair. Della was wearing a blue scrub outfit and white slippers. Her blond hair was clean and pulled back in a ponytail.

"I'm Dr. Anthony Lanaro. You're looking good today. How are you feeling?"

"I'm feeling better."

"Do you know who you are?"

Della looked at the doctor. "I believe I'm Della."

"But you're not sure?"

"Who are you?" asked Della.

"I told you. I'm Dr. Lanaro."

"Do I know you?"

"No, but I'm here to help you get home. The police brought you here, but you would benefit from being around friends and family. Would you like to go home, Della?"

"I can leave here?"

"Yes, that's why I'm here. I want to help you get home."

"I would like that. Your voice sounds familiar," said Della.

"I don't know why that would be. We've never met. Let me take you home, and you will feel better."

"You know where I live?"

"Yes, I do. You live in Denver, remember?"

"I'm not sure."

"You have friends who miss you and are waiting for you. Would you like to go home and see your friends?"

"Yes."

"Wait here. I'll get you checked out, and we'll get you home."

Dr. Lanaro walked out of the room and back to the reception desk. "Della is doing well, but I'm going to check Della out and take her to my office for additional therapy that I can't do here. Then I will take her home."

"Are you sure?" asked the crisis worker. "Our staff didn't believe she was ready to be released."

"I will take responsibility," said Dr. Lanaro. "My setup at the office is better for the type of therapy she needs. I will see that she gets home safely."

"She doesn't know where she lives."

"I found some friends she was living with in Denver. I will take her home after her therapy. And if I don't think she is ready, I'll bring her back here. Just give me the paperwork."

The crisis worker handed Dr. Lanaro the release form. He filled it out, signed it, and handed it back. He then walked back to room 103.

"Are you ready to go home?"

"Okay."

"Let me help you," said Dr. Lanaro, lifting Della by her left arm. He then walked her down the hallway, to the lobby, and out the door to his white Lexus GX. He opened the passenger door, seat-belted her in, and then shut the door. Dr. Lanaro walked to the other side and entered the driver's seat.

"You feeling okay, Della?"

Della knew she had heard his voice before. "Who are you?"

"I told you, I'm Dr. Lanaro."

The way he said it struck Della. Then it hit her. She HAD heard the voice before. It was the voice of the larger man with the low voice from the dungeon.

"LET ME OUT OF HERE!" screamed Della as she fumbled with the seat belt latch.

Dr. Lanaro quickly pulled a syringe from his inside coat pocket and plunged it into Della's left arm.

Della screamed louder, hoping someone would hear her. Dr. Lanaro grabbed Della by the hair and pushed her head toward the center console, holding her tight. Della flailed her arms as she screamed for help. Within seconds, Della felt lightheaded. Her arms weakened until she could no longer fight back. Her vision faded until she was completely out. Dr. Lanaro looked around to see if anyone had seen them. Not seeing anyone, he started the car and drove out of the parking lot with Della slumped in her seat.

After doing some more canvassing in the hill neighborhood, Shaw and Nichols returned to the police department. It was 4:35 pm. Shaw was interested to know how the interaction between Della and Dr. Lanaro had gone earlier in the afternoon. She called the mental health facility.

"County Mental Health, Mike speaking."

"Hello, this is Detective Caro Shaw with Boulder PD. I was calling to see how Della Kemp was doing."

"Apparently, well. She was released earlier this afternoon."

"Released? Who picked her up?"

"I'm not sure. Let me check."

Shaw waited for about thirty seconds.

"Dr. Lanaro signed the paperwork allowing her release."

"What?"

"I said Dr. Lanaro signed her out."

"How could he do that!?"

"He's a doctor. He has the authority."

"Damn it!" shouted Shaw as she slammed down her phone.

"What is it, Caro?" asked Nichols.

"Dr. Lanaro picked up our victim this afternoon from mental health!"

Sergeant Martinez walked over to see what the commotion was about. "What's going on?"

"Dr. Lanaro signed our victim out of mental health."

"Maybe she was ready to be released," suggested Martinez.

"He might be a suspect!"

"Calm down, Caro," said Martinez. "This indicates to me he is not involved. He has to know we would find out."

Shaw calmed down. "That makes some sense. He's not stupid. I'm going to drive to his office to check on her."

"Why don't you call him?" suggested Martinez. "If you go over there, it will only aggravate things. And if the chief or commander find out about it, you will definitely be suspended for not following orders."

"Okay," agreed Shaw. She knew Sergeant Martinez was right. After Martinez walked away, Shaw dialed Dr. Lanaro's cell phone.

"Hello."

"Dr. Lanaro, this is Detective Shaw. I understand you checked Della out of mental health."

"I thought I told you not to bother me again, Detective."

"I'm not trying to bother you. I want to know where Della is."

"Right now, she is probably with her friends."

"Where?" asked Shaw.

"Detective, as you know, she believes the police had something to do with her captivity. I think I have her convinced that is not the case, but I don't want you calling her right now. Once I believe she can handle it, I will have her contact you."

"She is our victim and has valuable information. We need access to her."

"And you will have it when she is ready."

"Where is she, Doctor?"

"Goodbye, Detective." The phone then went silent.

"Asshole!" yelled Shaw.

Nichols looked toward Shaw's desk. "Is everything okay, Caro?"

"Lanaro signed our victim out of mental health earlier today, and now he won't tell me where she is."

"Yeah, I know. Maybe he is trying to protect her," suggested Nichols.

"Or maybe she's dead," said Shaw. "I'm going to drive over there."

"Caro, you can't. You better ask the commander first," replied Nichols.

"Are you coming with me or not?"

Nichols sighed. "Caro, please."

"If I ask the Commander, she will say no. I have to find out if Della is okay. Now, are you going to help me?"

Nichols thought for a moment. "Yes, but under duress. Just don't do anything stupid."

Shaw drove quickly toward Dr. Lanaro's home. When they arrived, the house was quiet, with a dim light shining in the office side of the house. Shaw knocked on the entrance to the office. No response. Shaw then grabbed her cell phone and tried calling Dr. Lanaro. No answer.

"Let's try the residence side," said Shaw. Nichols followed behind as Shaw approached the front door and knocked loudly. She knocked several more times and rang the doorbell. No response.

Shaw walked down the porch steps and headed toward the south side of the house.

"Where are you going?" asked Nichols.

"I just want to look around."

Nichols followed as Shaw looked into windows. Most of the curtains or blinds were closed. "Look at these basement windows," said Shaw. "They are boarded up."

"Many people black out or board up basement windows," said Nichols as they continued to walk around the house.

When they got to the north side of the house, Shaw pointed to the basement windows. "The windows on this side aren't boarded up."

"The sun comes in on the south side, not the north side, Caro."

"I don't know," responded Shaw. "Something's not right."

"There's nothing we can do right now," said Nichols.

"Even the garage windows are blacked out," observed Shaw.

"He probably doesn't want people snooping around seeing what he has in his garage. Obviously, no one is home right now. Let's go, Caro."

Shaw again dialed Dr. Lanaro on his cell phone. Again, there was no answer.

"Can we go now?"

"Yes, we can go," said Shaw.

By the time they returned to the detective bureau, everyone else had gone home. It was after 6 pm.

"I'm tired, Caro, and I need some family time. I'm going home."

"Sorry to keep you out so late. Unless something happens tomorrow, I'll see you Monday."

After Nichols left, Caro called Alani Taylor.

"Hello?"

"This is Detective Shaw. Is this Alani?"

"Yes, it is."

"Alani, would you be available tomorrow to look at a photograph of someone?"

"I'm out of town tomorrow, but I can come in on Monday."

"Would ten in the morning work?"

"Yes, I can be there."

"Thank you, Alani."

Before leaving work, Shaw made one more call. This one was to Mick Collier.

"Mick, would you be willing to come over tonight? I've had a tough day and would prefer not to be alone."

"I'd love to. I will see you at eight o'clock," replied Mick.

Chapter 24

Sunday, June 4th

Caro woke up, rolled over, and placed her right hand on Mick's chest. Mick opened his eyes, looked at Caro and smiled.

"Thank you for staying," said Shaw.

"My pleasure."

"Would you like some breakfast?" she asked.

"Yeah, I could eat some breakfast. However, I promised my mom I would help her with the yard today. Ever since my father died, I've tried to keep the yard looking nice for her."

"That's sweet," said Shaw. "Do you like pancakes and bacon?"

"That'll work."

Shaw swung her legs off the side of the bed, stood up and put her bathrobe on. "You can use the shower if you'd like. Breakfast should be ready when you come out."

"Thank you, Caro."

After his shower, Collier joined Shaw for a breakfast of pancakes, bacon and black coffee. "Are you feeling better about your case this morning?" he asked.

"Physically, I feel much better. Mentally, I can't stop thinking about Angelo being our suspect. And the way Dr. Lanaro is behaving, I think he is covering it up."

"That would be a bombshell," said Collier.

"Yeah, I know. But I can't seem to convince anyone else."

"What I can't understand," said Collier, "is why would he pick the victim up if he was involved? He had to know that would raise questions."

"Maybe to kill her?"

"Come on, Caro. That would be too obvious. Even if you are right about Angelo, Dr. Lanaro isn't going to kill the woman now. She's probably safe with her friends. And hasn't Angelo been out of town?"

"According to the doctor."

"Try not to worry about it, Caro. Once you get the DNA results, it will help clarify things. Now, let's enjoy our breakfast. Do you think the Rockies will win today?"

"They're playing the Yankees. So probably not."

****

Della opened her eyes but felt groggy with a pounding headache. The muscles in her body were lethargic. She could not move her arms or legs. Della blinked a few times to gain focus on her surroundings. To her horror, she found herself sitting back in her dungeon with her legs and wrists strapped to the wooden chair. Della screamed in terror. "NOOOOO! SOMEONE HELP ME!"

It was then that Della noticed a man lying in the bed she had used for weeks. He was a white male wearing a light green hospital-type gown. An intravenous tube ran from his left arm to a bottle of solution hanging from an I.V. pole. The man was glaring at her with his dark brown eyes. Dark, wavy hair covered his head. Della immediately knew it was him. The man in the hood who had tortured her for so long. She could never forget his eyes. Della stared back with hatred.

"It's good to see you again, Della," said the man.

"Who are you!" shouted Della.

"I'm the man who nurtured and treated you for weeks."

"You tortured me!"

"And you tried to kill me."

"I should have done a better job."

Just then, an older man walked through the open door. "I thought I heard something," said Dr. Lanaro.

"YOU!" screamed Della. "I knew it was you! Let me out of here!"

"You were on your way to getting out of here," said Dr. Lanaro. "But you eliminated that chance by being stupid."

"You plan to keep me here forever?"

"No. You sealed your fate when you escaped. Once he is well enough, Angelo here will kill you, just like the others who failed the treatment."

"I told people about this place. They will come to find me. Let me go, and I won't say anything."

"Who will come? The police? They're the ones who brought you here in the beginning, remember?"

"I was told they took me to that hospital to help me."

"They told me where to find you, Della."

A wave of fear came over Della. Dr. Lanaro bent over his son and lifted his shirt to check his wounds. He folded back the large bandage covering Angelo's two puncture wounds.

"Your wounds are healing well," said Dr. Lanaro. "It won't be long before you are up and about."

"Thank you, Father," replied Angelo.

As Dr. Lanaro walked out the door, Della screamed, "I have to pee!"

Dr. Lanaro turned around. "Then pee." He was then gone.

Della held the urine in her bladder until she could no longer hold it. Warm yellow urine soaked her gown, some dripping onto the floor beneath her chair.

Monday, June 5th

At 8:30 am, Commander Greenberg approached Shaw at her desk. "Come with me, Caro."

"Where are we going?"

"To the chief's office."

"Am I in trouble?"

"We might both be in trouble."

Once Greenberg and Shaw reached the upstairs office of the Police Chief, his administrative assistant informed him they were there.

"Send them in," barked Chief Atkins.

Greenberg and Shaw walked in. The chief was seated behind his desk. Various awards and plaques filled the shelves behind the chief. "Have a seat," he said.

Greenberg and Shaw each sat in a chair opposite the chief.

Chief Atkins looked directly at Shaw. "I understand you had another conversation with Dr. Lanaro and returned to his house to look around. Is that true?"

"Um, yeah, I had a phone conversation with him when I found out he checked our victim out of mental health."

"He says you challenged his actions and then searched around his home office after he told you the victim was safe with friends."

"Chief, let me explain..."

The chief cut her off. "Yes, please explain because I'm about to remove you from the investigation."

"Chief, have you seen the photograph of Angelo Lanaro, the doctor's son?"

"Commander Greenberg has told me he has dark hair and brown eyes. That doesn't make him a suspect."

"It's more than that, Chief. I saw a graduation photograph of Angelo when we were in the house. It's not a large photograph, but I'm sure he has a scar or blemish above his right eye. One of our witnesses in the Melanie Quinn homicide described the suspect as having a scar above the right eye. I have that witness coming in today to see if she can positively identify Angelo Lanaro as the man who befriended Melanie just before she disappeared."

"Even if he was the man in the bar, it doesn't prove he kidnapped her, held her hostage, and then killed her."

"No, not by itself," agreed Shaw. "However, we collected what looked like fresh blood on Lanaro's front porch. Is that just a coincidence? If that DNA matches the blood on Della's clothing, that will certainly give us probable cause."

"But I thought you searched the entire house. Did you find a so-called torture chamber or dungeon, as our victim called it?"

"No, but here's something else that has been bothering me. The house has a strange floor plan, and the basement is a half basement. I didn't think much of it at the time, but three walls of the basement are poured concrete. The south wall was made of concrete blocks painted the same color. There could be a hidden room in that basement."

"That's a big leap, Caro."

"It may be at the moment, but not if the blood DNA from the porch matches the DNA on Della's clothing. And honestly, Chief, Dr. Lanaro has been an asshole toward Tom and me. He won't even tell us where the victim is right now. I don't find that very cooperative with a kidnapping investigation."

The chief sat back in his chair. Nothing was said for several seconds. Finally, he spoke. "Caro, given Dr. Lanaro's help to police departments in the past, I have difficulty believing he is involved. However, when I put my detective hat on, I have to admit you've raised some valid questions. Where do you think our victim is right now?"

"I don't know, Chief. If I'm right, she could be locked up in that house somewhere. If I'm wrong, maybe she is safe with friends. I have a question. If that is okay?"

"Sure, what's your question?"

"No one was home at the house Saturday night. How did the doctor know we were there?"

"He told me he has two security cameras that recorded you walking around and looking into windows."

Shaw nodded. "That makes sense. I didn't think of that."

"Here's what I'm going to do," said Chief Atkins. "I'm going to allow you to continue on the case. However, any further contact with Dr. Lanaro must be cleared by your commander beforehand. Can you live with that?"

"Yes, sir."

"Weren't you already told that by the commander and yet you failed to consult her?"

Shaw looked down. "Yes, sir. I'm sorry for creating problems for you and the commander. Things just aren't adding up."

"Stella, are you willing to give Caro another chance?"

"Normally not," replied Greenberg. "But in this situation, I think it would be a mistake to take Caro off the case. Other than not following orders, she has done a tremendous job."

The chief looked at Shaw. "Do you give us your word you will consult with the commander before contacting Dr. Lanaro in the future?"

"I do. And again, I'm sorry. I know this must be hard for you to deal with."

The chief laughed. "I've dealt with a lot worse, Caro. Now, the two of you should get back to work. Is that okay with you Stella?"

"Yes, Chief. I think you made the right call."

As they were walking back to the detective bureau, the commander turned to Caro. "I'm supporting you, Caro, but you must do what the chief said. No more contact unless I know about it and approve it."

"Don't worry, Commander. I got the message loud and clear."

"Good. Round up Luca, Tom, and Kevin and meet me in my office."

Ten minutes later, Sgt. Martinez and Detectives Shaw, Nichols, and Jordan were meeting with the commander in her office. Greenberg had Shaw give everyone an update on the case. Greenberg then opened it up for questions and ideas.

Sgt. Martinez started. "If I followed correctly, no one has had contact with our victim since Saturday?"

"No one. Dr. Lanaro would not tell me where she is," answered Shaw.

"After this meeting, I will call Dr. Lanaro for additional information," said Greenberg. "We need to know where she is and her welfare."

"Do you know when our DNA results will come back?" asked Jordan.

"That's the second call I'm going to make," said Greenberg. "The DNA is crucial."

"What happens if our witness doesn't positively identify the photograph as the person she knows as Steve?" asked Nichols. "Doesn't that put us back to square one?"

"Most likely," admitted Shaw. "But we still have the DNA."

"I wish we had a better photograph of Angelo," said Martinez. "Those black and white driver's license photos are crap."

"He's a student at the university, right?" asked Jordan.

"As far as we know," said Shaw.

"They have color photographs of every student. Why don't we ask the University Police if they could get us one?" said Jordan.

"Damn. I should have thought of that," said Shaw. "That's an excellent idea."

"I'll call them right after this meeting," volunteered Jordan.

"Any more questions?" asked Greenberg. "Okay then, let's get back to work."

Shaw immediately called Alani Taylor. "Alani, this is Detective Shaw. Are you working today?"

"No, it's my day off."

"Would it be okay if I delayed our meeting? We are trying to get a better photograph to show you."

"Sure. What time do you want me there?"

"Once I have it, I will come to you. I don't want to disrupt your day any further."

"Okay, just call me."

"Thank you, Alani."

Chapter 25

Dr. Lanaro's cell phone buzzed. He noticed it was Commander Greenberg calling.

"Hello, Commander. I hope you're calling to tell me I won't have to deal with Detective Shaw's nonsense anymore."

"You won't, Doctor. But I'm calling for another reason."

"What is it?"

"We are concerned that you released our victim without notifying us."

"She made a dramatic improvement. In my assessment, she was ready to be discharged."

"A heads up would have been appropriate, Doctor. We have many more questions to be answered."

"Okay, I'm sorry about that. I should have told you."

"Where is she now?"

"Well, I held a session with her at my office. She responded very well. In fact, she remembered her roommates in Denver."

"We thought she lived in Boulder."

"I think she stayed with someone for a few nights in Boulder, but she lives in Denver."

"And where is that?"

"Let me look. It was a large apartment or condo complex in Denver. Here it is. She said it was the Grove near Stapleton."

"Do you have an address?"

"She had it. I don't have it."

"How did you get her there, Doctor?"

"I called her an Uber."

"You sent a mental health patient home to Denver with an Uber driver?"

"Commander, she was fine."

"Two days ago, she didn't know who she was."

"Well, she did Saturday when I met with her. If you don't believe me, call Uber. They can confirm a pick-up on Saturday at my place."

"I will do that," snapped Greenberg. She then hung up the phone. Greenberg looked up the number for Uber and made the call. She talked to a male named Seal. Greenberg provided Dr. Lanaro's address and a description of Della. She was put on hold. After approximately 8 minutes on hold, Seal came back on the line.

"Yes, we show a pickup at that Boulder address on Saturday at 4:40 pm for a female passenger. She was dropped off at The Grove apartment complex in Denver."

"Do you have the passenger's name?" asked Greenberg.

"It says here the name was Della Kemp."

"What did she look like?"

"I'm sorry, ma'am, we don't keep that information."

"How about an apartment number?"

"No, I don't have that either."

"Thank you," said Greenberg.

Greenberg walked to Shaw's desk. "The Uber office confirmed a female passenger named Della Kemp was picked up on Saturday afternoon from Dr. Lanaro's."

"Where did she go?" asked Shaw.

"An apartment complex called The Grove near Stapleton."

"Do we have an apartment number?"

"No."

"We have no apartment number, and Della has no phone," said Shaw in exasperation.

"I'll call the complex management. Maybe Della's name is on the lease," said Greenberg. "Then I will call CBI to check on those DNA results."

"Thank you," said Shaw. "I'm still waiting on a photograph from the University Police."

Shaw was antsy while waiting. From memory, she sketched the inside of Dr. Lanaro's home and office. As best she could, Shaw made the sketch to scale as she remembered it, including the basement. The side of the house most curious to her was the south side, or residence side. The office side made sense, and all the space was accounted for. However, as Shaw remembered, there was a long hallway on the south side leading to a bedroom and a bathroom. The dimensions didn't make sense. There should have been another room along the hallway. Furthermore, she wasn't convinced there wasn't another part to the basement. It was mid-afternoon when Jordan finally approached her.

"I just received this photograph of Angelo Lanaro from the University Police."

"Excellent work, Kevin. Look here, I can clearly see a scar in this photo."

"Yes, me too."

Shaw got on the phone with Alani Taylor. "Alani, I have the photo I want you to look at. Where are you?"

"I'm on the Pearl Street Mall with some friends."

"Can you meet me in fifteen minutes in the parking lot behind the old courthouse building?"

"Yes, I can do that."

"You know where I'm talking about, right?"

"Yes, between 13th and 14th streets, correct?"

"Yes, I'll see you soon," said Shaw.

"Tom!" shouted Shaw.

"What?"

"Let's go. I'm meeting Alani to show her this picture. I need a second witness. You drive. We're going to the old county courthouse."

Shaw and Nichols met with Alani Taylor in the parking lot behind the old courthouse building at 3:35 pm.

"Thank you for meeting with us," said Shaw.

"Sure, anything I can do to help," responded Taylor.

"I have a photograph to show you. It may or may not be the person you saw with Melanie. If it's not the same person, don't be afraid to tell us it's not. Just do your best, okay?" instructed Shaw.

"Yes, I get it," said Taylor.

Nichols opened the file folder and handed Taylor the color photograph of Angelo Lanaro.

Taylor studied it closely for what seemed like a long time to Shaw.

"He has a scar above the right eye," said Taylor. "It looks very close to the man I knew as Steve."

"Very close, or is it Steve?" asked Shaw.

Taylor studied the photo some more. "I think it's him."

"You're not positive it's him?" asked Nichols.

"It's been several months, and I only saw him a few times. I think it's him, but I can't say one hundred percent. But the scar looks the same."

"Thank you, Alani. We appreciate your help," said Shaw.

After Taylor had left, Nichols said, "She was as close to being sure as possible."

"Yes, and she said the scar was the same. I think it will be good enough," said Shaw. "It is for me."

"Why don't we have Trina Perez look at it?" asked Nichols.

"She didn't have the recall Alani had," said Shaw.

"No, but you never know. Another witness saying it looks like Steve would help."

"You drive. I'll call her," said Shaw.

Shaw called Trina's cell phone.

"Hello."

"Trina, this is Detective Shaw. Where are you right now?"

"I'm at work. The carwash."

"Would you mind if we came by to show you a photograph? I want to know if you recognize the man you know as Steve."

"How long will it take?"

"Five minutes."

"Okay. When?"

"We will be there in twenty minutes," said Shaw.

When Shaw and Nichols arrived, they went into the office. Trina Perez was already waiting.

"The manager allowed me to take my break," said Perez.

"Thank you, Trina. We really appreciate it. This won't take long. We have a photo to show you of someone who may or may not be the man you know as Steve. You just tell us what you think, okay?"

"Sure."

Nichols opened the folder and showed Perez the photo. "Take your time," said Nichols.

"Oh, yeah. That's Steve."

"That was quick," said Shaw. "Are you sure?"

"Yes. Steve looks just like that."

"You didn't remember a scar, though, correct?"

"No, but now that I see it, I remember a mark above one of his eyes."

"Thank you, Trina. You've been a big help."

"Is that who killed Melanie?" asked Trina.

"Maybe," said Shaw. "We have more work to do, but I will let you know one way or another."

When they returned to the police department, Shaw and Nichols met with Commander Greenberg. They informed her of the identifications made by Taylor and Perez, noting that Taylor wasn't entirely sure.

"This gives us enough for a search warrant on the house," said Shaw.

"Not yet," advised Greenberg. "You have already searched the house and did not find any room as described by Della."

"I believe the room is hidden," protested Shaw.

"Maybe," said Greenberg. "But this doesn't give us enough for a search warrant. We need those DNA results."

"Well, when are they coming?" asked Shaw.

"I talked to Natalie Abbott with CBI earlier today. She hopes to have them done by tomorrow morning."

"That may be too late," said Shaw.

"Caro, Uber confirmed a woman named Della Kemp was picked up from Lanaro's address and taken to Denver. While you were out, I found out who the driver was and contacted him. He confirmed he picked up a woman named Della. He described her as a white female with long blond hair wearing hospital scrubs. How would you explain that in an affidavit to the court?"

The room was silent as Shaw digested what she had just been told. "I don't know, Commander. None of it is making sense right now."

"That's why we need to wait," emphasized Greenberg. "In the meantime, you may start writing an affidavit for a search. But we aren't taking it to a judge until we have the DNA results."

"Do we want to give Angelo's photograph to the media, asking for help in locating him?" asked Nichols.

"I'm afraid that would only alert Dr. Lanaro and his son to what may be coming. It would then give them time to destroy evidence if they haven't already," said Greenberg.

"You're right," agreed Nichols.

****

Della had fallen asleep. Her head hung down and to the left. She was jolted awake by the voice of Dr. Lanaro. Her mouth was dry, and her stomach ached from hunger.

"How are we doing today?" asked Dr. Lanaro to his son.

"I'm feeling better," said Angelo.

"You look better," agreed Dr. Lanaro. "Let me check those wounds. Ah, yes, they are looking good. I think the antibiotics worked. I don't see any infection. Here, I brought you some breakfast."

Dr. Lanaro had brought with him a tray of food. He gave Angelo a bowl of hot oatmeal with cream and blueberries, a muffin, and coffee.

"I need something to drink," said Della.

"You don't deserve anything," said Dr. Lanaro. "But I've got water for you and a granola bar. It's enough to keep you alive until Angelo is strong enough to deal with you."

Dr. Lanaro unhooked Della's right wrist and placed a bottle of water and the granola bar on the arm of the wooden chair.

"If you try anything, I'll strap you back in, and you won't get another thing to eat or drink."

Della grabbed the water and guzzled down half the bottle. She then used her teeth to open the granola bar. She ate the bar, using the rest of the water to wash it down. After she was done, Dr. Lanaro asked if she needed to go to the bathroom.

"Yes, please," said Della.

Dr. Lanaro walked over and unhooked Della's left hand and both ankles. "If you try anything at all, I'll kill you right here. Do you understand?"

"Yes. Where is the bathroom?"

Dr. Lanaro pointed to the bucket in the corner.

"I can't go with you two in the room."

"Then go sit back down."

Della stared at Dr. Lanaro. He stared back. Della couldn't wait any longer. She walked to the bucket, lifted her gown, then sat on the bucket. She cried as she relieved herself.

Dr. Lanaro turned to his son. "Do you need the bedpan, or can you get up?"

"I can get up."

Dr. Lanaro unhooked the I.V. and helped his son up and off the bed. Angelo then slowly walked out the door.

After Della finished, Dr. Lanaro ordered her back to the chair.

"Can I have a change of clothing? I stink from the urine."

"Just sit down," ordered Dr. Lanaro. Della did as she was told. He then strapped her wrists and ankles to the chair.

"What are you going to do to me?" asked Della.

"Honey, your little escape adventure sealed your fate. I would love to release you, but we have no choice now but to kill you."

"I won't tell anyone," pleaded Della.

Dr. Lanaro laughed. "You already did. Had you completed the program, we would have released you alive."

"What kind of program is this?"

"We study the human mind's ability to be manipulated into believing alternative facts to one's life experiences. Then, once the human mind becomes convinced of alternative facts and life experiences, we work to bring the mind back to reality. We also study what it takes to break down the human mind."

"What happened to the other woman that was here?"

"There was no other woman here."

"I heard her. I know someone else was here. You're going to kill me, so why not tell me the truth?"

"Good point, Della. Yes, there was another patient here for a while. However, she was stronger than you, and we could not alter her memory, no matter how hard we tried. It happens sometimes. We never start out to kill anyone. We are only interested in furthering our research. However, in those unfortunate instances when it doesn't work, we must eliminate the subject. Otherwise, our work would shut down. And that would benefit no one."

"How did you kill her?"

"You don't want to know, Della."

"You're going to kill me. So, tell me the truth. At least give me that."

Dr. Lanaro looked off to the side, staring at the wood-timbered wall. "I liked Melanie, but she was tough to crack. She was a pretty gal like you. Melanie came to us from Kansas. We tried, Della. I was pulling for her. But, once it was clear our methods weren't working, we couldn't just let her go."

"So, what did you do?"

Dr. Lanaro kneeled down next to Della, looking her straight in the eyes. It was a look that frightened her. His eyes were dark and cold. He reached out with both arms and put his hands around Della's neck. He slowly squeezed tighter.

"What are you doing?"

"You wanted to know what happened to Melanie."

Della felt her throat and windpipe collapsing. She had difficulty taking in air and could no longer speak.

"Dad, what are you doing?" shouted Angelo as he shuffled back into the room.

Dr. Lanaro immediately released his grip while Della gasped for air.

"I was showing Della what happened to Melanie."

"It looked like you were killing her," said Angelo. "That's for me to do. I'm the one she stabbed."

"I wasn't going to kill her, Angelo. She just wanted to know."

Della continued to gasp. "I need some water," she said in a raspy voice.

Dr. Lanaro lifted the water bottle to Della's mouth to give her a drink. "He's going to do worse than what I just showed you," whispered Dr. Lanaro. Della shuddered with a chill running down her back. Her eyes watered. She was now sure she wasn't getting out alive.

****

Detective Shaw worked into the evening hours putting together a search warrant affidavit for Dr. Lanaro's office and residence. By 8:10 pm, she was satisfied with her work. All she needed to add was the DNA test results. Shaw was counting on the results confirming the blood on the porch railing matched that found on Della's clothing. If not, her theory would fall apart.

On her drive home, she called Mick Collier. She ran through the events of the day.

"It sounds promising to me," said Collier. "But how do you explain the Uber pick-up?"

"I'm thinking they may have dropped her off, hoping in her confused state she just disappears. The management at the apartment complex told Greenberg no one named Della Kemp was in their database of residents."

"Do you believe Della is safe now?"

"My gut is telling me she is in danger. I don't know how, but I can feel it. We have not been able to find her, Mick. She could already be dead."

"Let's hope not, Caro. Do you need me to come by tonight?"

"No, I'm fine. And I'm exhausted. I need my sleep. Tomorrow could be a long day."

"All right, you take care of yourself, Caro."

"You too, Mick. Good night."

Chapter 26

Tuesday, June 6th

Della hardly slept during the night. Strapped to a wooden chair was highly uncomfortable and painful. Her butt cheeks hurt, her legs hurt, and her neck and back ached. She looked up, and Angelo was gone. The bed was unmade and empty. The I.V. pole stood alone, and the door to the room was still open. It didn't matter. Della was strapped tight to her chair. Della's genuine memories slowly began to return. *I'm not from Denver. I'm from Erie, Pennsylvania. My father is dead, but my mother is still alive.*

As Della continued to recall her true memories, Angelo slowly walked through the open door. "Good morning, Della," he said in his all too familiar voice. It made Della shudder. She noticed Angelo was no longer in a hospital gown. He was now dressed in black sweatpants and a loose-fitting light blue T-shirt with a pocket on the front. She looked down at his feet and saw he was wearing white tennis shoes. She wondered where the suede shoes were. Angelo moved slowly as though he still felt some pain.

"I'm getting better, Della. I'm lucky you didn't pierce my liver. Your time is short. It's sad, really. I liked you more than most of them. Too many were just big crybabies. You? You were tough. Father thought you were too tough and wanted me to end the experiment. I fought for you, and you know what? You were going to make it out alive. But no, your toughness became your death sentence. Why did you attack me like that?"

Della didn't answer.

"Well, it doesn't matter now," continued Angelo. "You're going to pay dearly for what you did to me. I'm not going to choke you to death, Della. I'm going to slowly cut you a thousand ways."

Della saw evil in Angelo's eyes. It was almost like his eyes were hollow with no emotion.

"I remember you now," said Della softly. "You're Steve, the guy I met at the bar. You don't have to do this."

Angelo laughed. It was a laugh that sent chills down Della's spine. "You sealed your own fate, Della."

"The police didn't bring me here. You brought me here."

Angelo didn't respond. Instead, he pulled a sharp eight-inch knife from a sheaf Della hadn't noticed. He stepped closer to Della. Della tried to coil away from him, her straps holding her tight. Angelo held out his hand and ran the blade across his left thumb. Blood ran down his thumb, dripping onto the concrete floor.

"You see that, Della? Your whole body will be a thousand cuts like this."

Angelo then slightly bent over Della, grimacing as he did. He reached down with his blood-covered left hand and moved Della's smock until her left thigh was exposed.

"What are you doing!" shouted Della.

Angelo lowered the knife's sharp edge until it rested on Della's thigh.

"Please don't," begged Della. "I'm sorry. I won't try to escape again," she cried. "Just tell me what you want."

Angelo slid the blade across Della's thigh. Blood immediately flowed onto her leg as the knife effortlessly cut into the skin. Della screamed as loud as she could.

Angelo lifted the knife and stood straight. "Death by a thousand cuts, Della. That's what's coming." Angelo then turned and walked out of the room.

Della could only watch the blood flow down her left leg onto the floor. She hung her head and sobbed.

****

It was almost noon when Commander Greenberg emerged from her office. She approached Shaw.

"You did a great job on this affidavit, Caro. If the DNA results come back in our favor, we should have no problem getting a warrant."

"I'm not as optimistic as I was earlier," replied Shaw.

"What do you mean?"

"I keep thinking about what you told me about the Uber driver. About him confirming he picked up a woman named Della. If Della is not being held, where is she?"

"It sounds damning to our case," said Greenberg. "But let's not get ahead of ourselves. Angelo may torture women without Dr. Lanaro knowing. Maybe he saved her."

"If it's not Angelo, we go back to zero," lamented Shaw.

Thirty minutes later, Nichols approached Shaw. "Do we have any results yet?"

"No, still waiting."

"Let's go get a coffee at Starbucks."

"Huh? I have to be here when we get the DNA results."

"No, you don't, Caro. You're eating yourself up. Starbucks is just down the street. I'll buy you something, and we can relax a bit. The commander will let us know as soon as they come in."

"Yeah, I could use a break. Let's go."

At Starbucks, Shaw ordered a latte, and Nichols ordered a mocha and cinnamon muffin. "You sure you don't want a muffin?" asked Nichols.

"Um, yeah, why not? Get me the blueberry."

Shaw and Nichols sat at a small round table towards the back and in the corner.

"How are you holding up, Caro?" asked Nichols.

"I was a mess on Saturday, but I'm better now. I have to accept that I could be wrong about Dr. Lanaro."

"Because of what the Uber driver told the commander?"

"Mostly. It matches what the doctor told the commander."

"It doesn't mean Angelo isn't our killer."

"True," agreed Shaw.

"Let's change the subject," suggested Nichols. "Have you gone out to eat again with Mick?"

"Why are you asking me that?"

"I'm interested in your romantic relationships."

"We are not dating. I told you that."

"Caro, if you spent more time talking to the patrol officers, you'd be much more aware of what is happening in the department."

Shaw looked at Nichols. "You heard about Mick and me from patrol?"

Nichols smiled.

"Oh, all right. We are seeing each other."

"Yeah, I know," smiled Nichols. "Nothing is secret around here."

"Tell me about your family," said Shaw.

"This case has been hard on them. My late hours take a toll on Kristin. The kids do well, but they miss their father. Having Sunday off was nice. We took the kids to the Rockies game. Brian loved it. I think Lisa was more thrilled with the snow cone."

"Did the Rockies win?"

"Oh, hell no. We lost twelve to three. We play the Pirates next, so we might win a game or two."

Just then, Shaw's phone beeped. It was a text message from the commander. "The DNA results are in," said Shaw. "Let's go."

They rushed back to the police department and into Commander Greenberg's office.

"What are the results?" Shaw anxiously asked.

"The blood DNA samples taken from Della's shirt and pants match the blood DNA you recovered from the porch of Dr. Lanaro's house," said Greenberg.

"YES!" screamed Shaw. "I knew it!"

"Now finish up that affidavit and go get your warrant."

"Thank you, Commander."

"Congratulations, Caro," said Nichols as they left the office.

"You had just as much to do with this, Tom."

"Not really, but thank you."

Shaw quickly worked on adding the new information to the affidavit while Nichols called the DA's office to prepare them for what was coming. Within 45 minutes, they were ready to go to the District Attorney. They arrived just after the lunch hour.

It took Assistant District Attorney Marilyn Anderson thirty-five minutes to read the affidavit.

"This is very detailed and quite the investigation," said Anderson. "I will sign off on this, and I believe Judge Morgenstein is in his office. I will call and let him know you are coming."

"Thank you, Marilyn," said Shaw.

Shaw and Nichols rushed over to the Judge's office.

"Come on in, detectives. I've been waiting for you."

Shaw handed the judge the affidavit. He took his time going over every detail. After about forty-five minutes, he put the affidavit down.

"You make an interesting case," said the Judge. "I know Dr. Lanaro, and this doesn't sound like something he would be involved in."

"He might not be, Your Honor, but his son certainly is," said Shaw.

"It sure looks like it," said the judge as he picked up his pen and signed the warrant. "Go find out."

"Thank you, Judge," said Shaw and Nichols simultaneously.

"Now let's go back and put a team together to do this search," said Shaw.

Shaw and Nichols met with the commander and Sgt. Martinez at the police department. Sgt. Martinez had already assigned other detectives and patrol officers to assist with the search.

"What time do you want them to meet you at the scene?" asked Martinez.

"Can they be there in thirty minutes?" asked Shaw.

"I'll let everyone know," replied Martinez. "I'll be there as well to help coordinate."

"Thank you, Sergeant," said Shaw.

****

Dr. Lanaro entered the hidden room where Della sat strapped to the wooden chair. Della looked up.

"What happened to you?" asked Lanaro.

"You know what happened."

"I brought you another energy bar and some water."

"What for? Your deranged son is just going to kill me."

Dr. Lanaro unlatched Della's left wrist. He then set the bottle of water and energy bar on the armrest. "I'll give you ten minutes to eat and drink. Don't waste the time."

Della ate the energy bar and drank half the water while Dr. Lanaro watched over her.

273

"Allowing your son to kill me makes you just as guilty."

"No one will find out, Della. The police believe you left here in an Uber on Saturday. They are looking for you in Denver right now."

"You're lying."

Dr. Lanaro smiled. "How did you end up in Boulder?"

"Why do you care?" snapped Della.

"It might explain how you ended up in here."

"You've messed with my head so much, I can't remember everything yet."

"You were a runaway," said Dr. Lanaro. "You ran away from your home in Erie, Pennsylvania, when you were seventeen. You haven't been back since."

"How do you know this?"

"We do our research, Della."

"You're evil, just like your son," Della said softly.

"No. We're simply doing the necessary research that would never be acceptable to the outside world. The Chinese do it all the time. That's why they are more advanced than us."

Della's eyes watered, and she felt a tear run down her right cheek. "Please let me go."

"I would like to, Della. But I can't."

"Then just kill me now. Don't make me suffer any longer."

"Angelo will be strong enough soon. Maybe tomorrow."

With that, the doctor re-secured Della's left wrist and left the room. Della sobbed uncontrollably.

Chapter 27

By the time everyone had assembled around the corner from Dr. Lanaro's home, it was 3:40 pm. Sgt. Martinez assigned two patrol officers as security on the outside of the house. A third officer would secure the front entrance. Sgt. Martinez and Detectives Shaw, Nichols, and Jordan would search the inside of the home and office.

Dr. Lanaro was in his office when he observed two patrol cars and two unmarked cars pull up to the front of his house. He got up and quickly ran to Angelo's bedroom.

"Angelo, you need to get to the hiding room now."

"What's up?" asked Angelo.

"The police are here. Go now. Go, go, go."

Angelo hobbled quickly to the stairs leading to the south side of the basement. Dr. Lanaro then closed the entrance to the basement. Five seconds later, there was a loud knock on the front door. Lanaro took his time getting to the door. A second knock sounded, and he heard someone shouting. "We have a search warrant. Open up."

Lanaro opened the door to find Shaw, Nichols, two other detectives, and a uniformed officer on his porch.

"What can I do for you?" he asked.

"Dr. Lanaro," said Shaw. "We have a signed search warrant for your home, office, and premises."

Shaw handed him a copy of the warrant. "Please step aside."

Dr. Lanaro backed up and stepped to the side. The four detectives entered the house.

"Caro, you and Tom take the back half. Kevin and I will take the front half," directed Sgt. Martinez.

"This is absurd," said Lanaro. "I'm going to sue the city and each one of you."

"That's up to you, Doctor," said Martinez. "But right now, we are in charge, and we are searching."

"Am I under arrest?"

"No sir, not yet."

"Then I'm leaving. I won't stand here and watch you rummage through my house."

Dr. Lanaro grabbed his car keys from the kitchen table and walked out the front door. He went to the north side of the house and entered his garage. Within seconds, he backed his white Lexus GX onto the street and sped away.

The detectives thoroughly searched the residential side of the house. They looked through every drawer, closet, and shelf for evidence. They were also looking for secret passageways. Shaw collected toothbrushes from the main bathroom and two T-shirts from a dirty clothes pile in Angelo's bedroom. She knew getting Angelo's DNA was crucial to compare to the blood on Della's clothing.

After searching the residential side, all four detectives entered the office side and conducted the same thorough search. Nichols found two saline bags, medical bandages, and painkillers in one of Dr. Lanaro's desk drawers.

"Why would a psychiatrist need this stuff?" asked Nichols.

"Maybe to treat his injured son?" asked Shaw. "Collect all of it."

Next, all four detectives entered the basement. They found nothing unusual.

"Look at this south wall," said Shaw. "It's made of concrete blocks. Why would a builder use poured concrete on three basement walls and blocks for the fourth wall?"

"They wouldn't," said Martinez. "This was put up sometime after construction."

"Which means something is behind this wall," said Shaw.

"There's no access," said Nichols. "We've looked everywhere."

"Let's go look outside," suggested Shaw.

The four detectives walked the perimeter of the house. Shaw pointed out the two narrow blacked-out windows on the south side.

"Dr. Lanaro said this side was a crawl space," said Nichols.

"Who puts windows on a crawl space?" asked Jordan.

"Exactly!" said Shaw. "These windows are hiding something."

"I don't see any outside access," said Jordan.

"Let's check the yard for a trapdoor or tunnel," suggested Nichols.

"How about we just break a window?" asked Shaw. Everyone looked at Sgt. Martinez.

Martinez sighed. "Yeah, let's do it. We need to know what's in there."

Nichols sat on the ground adjacent to one window. He reared back his right leg and kicked at the window with the bottom of his foot. The glass broke, but there was a board behind the glass. Nichols kicked again. The board gave some but did not break away.

Inside the dungeon, Angelo and Della heard a pounding sound. "Don't say a word," warned Angelo. The sound was like a hammer banging against a board. Della's heart raced.

Nichols kicked repeatedly. Each time, the board would give a little more. Finally, after another hard kick, the board broke away from the window frame and fell to the floor. Using his flashlight, Nichols looked through the opening. He saw what looked like a large wooden box extending from the floor of the basement up through the floor above. The box consisted of thick, dark square timbers. There was approximately a four-foot space between the basement wall and the wooden structure.

"Boulder Police!" announced Nichols. "Anyone in here?"

"HELP!" screamed Della.

Angelo lunged toward Della, slapping her in the face. "I told you to shut up!"

Della then let out a blood-curdling scream.

"Della, is that you? It's the Boulder Police. We're going to get you out of there," shouted Nichols.

"Oh my god," said Shaw. "Someone's down there. Can you fit through there, Tom?"

"I don't know. It's a tight fit."

After Della's scream, Angelo knew he had to get out before the police got inside. He left Della and hobbled up the stairs on the side of the wall to the floor above. He then pushed the button to open the wall. On the other side, the large bookcase split in the middle and the two sides began moving apart. Each side of the bookcase slid along the floor, opening a passage to the secret basement room. It startled the officer guarding the front door to see the large bookcase moving. Not knowing what was on the other side, he drew his sidearm and held it at a 45-degree angle toward the ground. Once the opening was large enough, a dark-haired white male quickly moved through the opening into the living room.

"Stop! Boulder Police," shouted the officer.

It startled Angelo. He looked left, then right. He briefly thought of jumping through the south living room window.

"Get down on the ground now!" shouted the officer as he raised his gun and pointed it at Angelo's chest.

Angelo had no way out. He dropped to his knees.

"Lay down," directed the officer.

Angelo got all the way down onto the floor. The officer walked over and handcuffed Angelo's hands behind his back. He then pulled him up to a sitting position.

"Careful, that hurts," protested Angelo. "I have stab wounds."

As Nichols attempted to squeeze through the basement window, Martinez heard the officer on the radio say that he had Angelo in custody.

"Where did you find him?" asked Martinez.

"The wall just opened up, and he came out. You need to see this."

"Tom, stop," said Martinez. "You don't need to crawl through there. I think we found the way in."

Nichols yelled into the window. "We are coming to get you! Just hang on."

Shaw was the first one to re-enter the house. She could not believe what she saw. The large bookcase was split in half, revealing a passage into another room. Angelo Lanaro was sitting on the floor with his hands cuffed behind his back. Shaw walked to the opening in the wall and looked in with amazement. She saw a large wooden box-like structure made with 8 by 8-inch square logs extending approximately four feet above the floor line. It was centered in the middle of the room, with floor space wrapped around both sides. On the right side, a metal stairway extended through the floor to the basement level.

Shaw observed two metal grates on top of the box. She stepped forward and looked through the grate on the left. She was stunned to see the room extended deep into the basement. It was a prison-like room with a single bed and wooden chair. As she was mentally recording what she saw, Shaw heard a yell. "I need help!"

Shaw moved to the grate on the right side and looked in. There sat Della, in a similar room, strapped to a wooden chair.

"Della!" yelled Shaw. "I'm Detective Shaw with the Boulder Police Department. You're going to be okay."

Della looked up, recognizing the familiar face. "Get me out of here!"

"We're coming."

Just then, Sgt. Martinez ran up beside Shaw. "Did you find her?"

"Yes, take a look."

Martinez looked through the grate. "Oh, my god."

"Follow me," said Shaw, carefully working her way down the metal steps. The metal door into the room was still open. Shaw ran to Della, who was now crying. Martinez followed her into the room.

"It's okay, Della," said Shaw. "You're safe now."

Della nodded but could not speak. She was overcome with emotion. She began shaking. Shaw and Martinez worked to undo the straps as Nichols ran into the room.

"Is she okay?" asked Nichols.

"Her leg is cut, and she's traumatized," said Shaw. "Get an ambulance here."

Nichols got on the radio and requested medical assistance while Shaw and Martinez helped Della out of the chair. She was too weak to walk. They helped her to the bed and laid her down. Shaw held Della's hand while they waited.

"Patrol wants to know what to do with Angelo," said Nichols.

"Tell them to take him to jail," answered Martinez. "He's under arrest. And have Jordan go with him. See if he will talk."

"Got it," said Nichols.

"Oh, and have patrol seal off the property with crime scene tape."

"Okay."

Within five minutes, Shaw and Martinez could hear sirens approaching. "It won't be long now, Della," said Shaw.

Shaw could see Della was shaking as though she had a fever. She covered Della with a blanket.

"God, this place smells," noted Shaw.

"Yeah, it's disgusting down here," agreed Martinez.

After several more minutes, EMTs arrived from the fire department and ambulance company. Shaw and Martinez backed off to let them attend to Della.

"We need to get her to the hospital," said one of the EMTs. "She is dehydrated and in emotional shock. We will have to carry her up the stairs."

With the help of firefighters, they carried Della up the stairs and into the living room. Della was placed on a wheeled gurney covered with warm blankets and taken to a waiting ambulance.

Nichols was ecstatic about finding Della. He was confident they had found the serial killer. He looked over at Shaw to congratulate her. She was wiping tears from her eyes.

"Caro, what's wrong? We just saved Della."

"I know. I'm happy. I'm also angry we didn't protect her better. I knew Dr. Lanaro was involved in this."

"If not for you, Caro, we might still be looking for her."

"I know," agreed Shaw. "Now let's go get that son-of-a-bitch doctor."

Just about then, Police Chief Atkins and Commander Greenberg walked through the front door.

"Congratulations, everyone," said the Chief. "You are all to be commended."

"Yes, great job," agreed the Commander.

"We're not done yet, Chief," said Shaw. "Now we need to arrest Dr. Lanaro."

"I agree," said the Chief. "Go find him."

"Martinez," barked Commander Greenberg, "why don't you take Caro and Tom and start work on finding our doctor? Our crime scene techs will soon be here to photograph and process this entire house."

"Will do, Commander."

After the three left, the chief and commander walked through the opening in the wall to look around. They were careful not to touch anything.

"My god, can you believe this?" asked Chief Atkins.

"No. This is worse than I could have imagined," said Greenberg.

They both walked down the steps to look into the room that had held Della for almost six weeks. The Chief took a handkerchief from his pocket and covered his nose.

"How could anyone have lived down here?" asked the Chief.

Greenberg shook her head. "Let's get out of here, Chief."

Back at the police department, Martinez, Shaw, and Nichols were strategizing how to arrest Dr. Lanaro.

"Let's take two approaches," said Martinez. "We need to work on an arrest warrant. Tom, can you do that?"

"Yes."

"Caro, what do you think about calling the doctor? Maybe he will tell you where he is, and perhaps you can talk him into turning himself in."

"I can try," said Shaw.

Nichols returned to his desk to get the affidavit for arrest started while Martinez began to work on an all-points bulletin to go out to patrol and surrounding agencies in the hunt for Dr. Lanaro.

Shaw sat at her desk, pulled out her cell phone, then punched in Dr. Lanaro's phone number and activated the record function on her phone. To Shaw's surprise, he answered.

"What is it, Detective?"

"We found your torture chamber, Doctor."

The phone was silent.

"Did you hear me?" asked Shaw.

"I don't know what you are talking about."

"Cut the crap. You are just as involved as your son. He couldn't have built that hidden room without your knowledge. No one on earth will believe that."

"Well, congratulations, Detective. You've solved your case. Now what?"

"You can save everyone a lot of trouble by coming to the police department to turn yourself in."

"I'm not going to do that, Detective."

"Then tell me why."

"Why what?"

"Why did you or your son torture and kill these women?"

There was a pause.

"We were conducting important research into creating alternative realities and then bringing the subjects back to actual reality. No one had ever done this type of research."

"You killed women."

"Not all of them. Only the ones in which we could not alter their minds."

Shaw could not believe the doctor was so open and frank about his evil activities. She continued to play along.

"How many are we talking about?"

"How many have we treated? Or how many weren't successful?"

"How many have you treated?"

"Thirteen."

"And how many were not successful?"

There was another pause. "Seven."

Shaw tried not to reveal her shock over the phone.

"And by not successful, you mean they were murdered, correct?"

"I don't like that word, Detective."

"What would you call it?"

"Terminated from the program."

"Okay, so seven women have been terminated. Over what time period?"

"Six years."

As Shaw spoke with Dr. Lanaro, Commander Greenberg returned to the office. Martinez told her Shaw was on the phone with Dr. Lanaro. Greenberg walked over to Shaw's desk. Shaw wrote a note letting the commander know the doctor had confessed to murder. Greenberg told everyone in the room to be quiet, then motioned Shaw to put the phone on speaker mode.

"You've terminated seven women in six years?"

"Well, not me. Angelo did."

"You're putting this all on Angelo?"

"The terminations, yes. I haven't terminated anyone."

"But you knew about them."

"Of course. I was supervising the program."

"What was your intent with this program?"

"To uncover the secrets of mental illness. If we could learn how to manipulate the mind into believing alternative reality, maybe we could one day cure mental illness."

"By torturing people?"

"Stop with the insults, Detective. We were finding alternative ways to treat people."

"Once someone failed your treatment plan, how would Angelo terminate them?"

"Through strangulation. It seemed the most humane way."

Greenberg and Shaw looked at each other and shook their heads.

"And you would dispose of those bodies along creek beds?"

"Recently, yes. I believe two of them have never been found. Unfortunately, Angelo got careless with the last few."

"Where are the two that haven't been found?"

"You'll have to figure that out yourself, Detective. I'm not doing your work for you."

"I'm curious about something. We talked to an Uber driver who claimed he picked up a blond woman named Della in front of your house on Saturday and then drove her to Denver. Obviously, we now know that not to be true. How did you pull that off?"

"Finding a local blond-haired college student willing to make a few extra bucks wasn't hard. For five hundred dollars, they will do just about anything."

"Was she aware of why you were doing this?"

"Oh, heavens no. She asked why, and I told her it was not her concern. She decided to take the money and do it."

"You even dressed her in scrubs. That was brilliant."

"Yes, it was, wasn't it?"

Shaw rolled her eyes at the commander.

"Why don't you come in now, Doctor? We can continue this discussion more comfortably at the police department."

Dr. Lanaro laughed. "Do you actually think I would tell you all this if I intended on coming into the police department? You will never arrest me, Detective. You think you're so smart, yet all you are is a punk-ass, know-it-all detective. I never did like you."

"We will find you, Doctor. The entire country will look for you once this hits the news."

"I didn't say you couldn't find me. I said you would never arrest me."

"You've got a big ego. I'll give you that. Let me ask you this. Did you kill your wife?"

"My wife? She killed herself."

"I don't think she did. She was your first, wasn't she?"

There was silence for several seconds. "Why do you care, Detective?"

"Well, you're already going to prison, so why not tell the truth now? Don't you want the credit?"

Dr. Lanaro laughed in a manner that sounded wicked to Shaw. "She drank the wine. I didn't force her to drink it."

"But you put the barbiturates in the wine, didn't you?"

"If she hadn't been an alcoholic, she never would have died. She drank two bottles of wine that night. That's what killed her."

"You're one son of a bitch, Doctor. If you were a real man, you would turn yourself in. But no, you want your son to take all the blame. You're a coward."

"You don't know what you're talking about, Detective."

"Then come tell me, face to face."

"I'll show you I'm no coward, Detective. You want me? Come up to Flagstaff Mountain."

"Is that where you are right now?"

The phone went dead.

"He's going to kill himself," said Greenberg. "Call dispatch right now and get patrol up there before he has the chance."

"On it," said Shaw.

Shaw called dispatch and gave them the information, including the vehicle and suspect description. "He said he's on Flagstaff Mountain. Let officers know he may be armed and dangerous."

Flagstaff Mountain is a prominent landmark offering panoramic views of Boulder and the surrounding area. It is located just west of Boulder and is part of the Boulder Mountain Parks system. At the top, the elevation is approximately 6,983 feet. The mountain is renowned for its scenic overlooks and breathtaking views of the city. It is a popular spot for taking photographs and sightseeing. It can be reached by driving westbound on Baseline Road. The road turns into a winding crawl up the mountain. Drivers must be careful navigating the hairpin turns.

Martinez, Shaw, and Nichols gathered in Commander Greenberg's office to await news from patrol. The time was 5:15 pm. Time seemed to creep along as they waited for any information. They listened to the police scanner in the commander's office.

At 5:24 pm, they heard the first radio traffic.

"We see the suspect vehicle," said Officer One. "A white Lexus GX with Colorado plates. He's parked facing the overlook."

Several more minutes passed. It was 5:30, and still no news.

Finally, the radio crackled.

"We see movement, but he is not responding to our orders to get out of the vehicle," reported the officer. "We are going to approach the vehicle. Standby."

"I hope they take him alive," said Shaw. "I want him to rot in prison."

Another three minutes passed.

"We heard a gunshot!" the radio cracked.

"That doesn't sound good," said Nichols.

Two more minutes of silence. Then it came.

"Suspect is deceased. Single gunshot wound to the head."

Shaw dropped her head and slumped her shoulders.

"What a coward," mumbled Nichols.

Chapter 28

Friday, June 9th

After attending the arraignment of Angelo Lanaro, Shaw and Nichols met with Sgt. Martinez and Commander Greenberg in her office. Greenberg could tell Shaw was upset.

"How did the arraignment go?" asked Greenberg.

"He pleaded not guilty by reason of insanity," grumbled Shaw.

"Don't worry about it, Caro," advised Greenberg. "What he did was too detailed and calculated. He will never win by pleading insanity."

"Well, the District Attorney only charged him with kidnapping, Second Degree Assault, and False Imprisonment."

"That's all we have right now," said Greenberg. "We haven't completed our review of the records our crime scene investigators found in the basement. Dr. Lanaro took very detailed notes on each victim. And I just received a report from our DNA analysts."

"What were the results?" asked Shaw.

"The blood DNA on Della's clothing matched Angelo's DNA."

"That doesn't prove murder. Della is still alive."

"True, but DNA swabs taken from the other room in the basement matched the DNA of Melanie Quinn, our victim from Eben G. Fine Park. It proves she was there. We have him for murder, Caro."

"Melanie is likely the one Della heard screaming," said Shaw.

"What about the other two women?" asked Nichols.

"Well," said the commander, "the DNA we got from underneath the nails of Jennifer Bryant matched Angelo's DNA. And while we couldn't find any DNA on Aubrey Leaver, our CSIs found her identification in the basement filing cabinet. I think that gives us three murder convictions."

"And there are four other victims somewhere," said Shaw. "Lanaro admitted to killing seven women."

"There is certainly more work that needs to be done for the families and other victims," admitted Greenberg. "We'll get there. With all the media attention, we're getting calls from all over the country."

After their meeting, Shaw drove to Boulder Community Hospital on Arapahoe Road to visit Della Kemp. On her way to the room, Shaw stopped to buy a bouquet of carnations from the gift shop. Upon walking into Della's room, she found Della awake and sitting up in bed.

"Good afternoon," said Shaw.

"Hi, Detective. Are those flowers for me?"

"They are. How are you feeling?"

"Much better. The doctors think I'll be strong enough to leave tomorrow."

"Where will you go, Della?"

"My mom flew into town yesterday. She just left twenty minutes ago. She will take me back home to good ol' Erie, Pennsylvania."

"Isn't that where you ran away from?" smiled Shaw.

"Yeah, back when I was stupid. But I can't stay in Colorado. Too many horrible memories."

"Speaking of memory, how is yours coming along?"

"I still get confused, but it's better every day."

"I wanted to tell you we have enough evidence to charge Angelo with murder."

"Really? Oh, that is such good news. Thank you for telling me. What about the other families?"

"We've identified all our victims and notified the families."

"Detective?"

"You can call me Caro."

"Caro, I have nightmares. Do you think they'll ever go away?"

"The mind and body have an incredible way of healing themselves. It will take time, Della. But I think you'll get there."

"Thank you for coming to see me, Detective. And tell the officers I'm sorry for how I acted."

"Don't be. It's all understandable. You worry about healing your mind and body."

"I will."

"I have to go now. Keep in touch, Della."

"Thank you, Detective."

Shaw then drove to Eben G. Fine Park. She walked toward the spot on the creek's bank where Grizzly found Melanie Quinn. The creek gurgled and bubbled as the water swirled among the boulders. Shaw stood for several minutes thinking about the horrors Melanie must have suffered. She had saved a flower from the bouquet she had bought for Della. Shaw placed the pink carnation on a rock near the shoreline where Melanie's body had been.

A gray-haired woman in her sixties walking eastbound on the concrete path observed Shaw placing the flower. She approached Shaw.

"Is that for the woman who was found here?"

Shaw looked at the woman. "Yes," she said softly.

"That's a sweet gesture. Are you family?"

"No, I'm just a detective with the police department."

"You're Detective Shaw, aren't you?"

"Yes, ma'am."

"I read about all the work you did in the newspaper. Thank you so much, Detective. The whole town thanks you and police department."

The woman's words brought tears to Shaw's eyes. Shaw faintly smiled and nodded. The woman then placed her right hand on Shaw's shoulder and squeezed before continuing her walk.

Shaw looked back at the carnation in time to see a wave of water wash the flower from the rock. Shaw watched as the carnation was slowly carried away in the current.

Nine Months Later:

Angelo Lanaro, age 26, lost his attempt to plead insanity. A court-ordered psychiatric examination determined Angelo was not insane. Evidence of his ability to distinguish right from wrong included several notebooks of documentation, much of it written by Angelo, of the methods used to torture young women in a misguided effort to alter their minds. Second, he took many well-thought-out steps to avoid detection and discovery by the police. Third, he was well-educated and carried a 3.75 grade point average at the doctorate level of study. The examination found Angelo to be extremely disturbed but not legally insane.

Motions by Angelo's attorney to exclude much of the evidence against him for police misconduct were denied. Angelo was eventually charged with three counts of First Degree Murder, four counts of Second Degree Assault, four counts of Kidnapping, and four counts of False Imprisonment. He was charged with the murders of 18-year-old Jennifer Bryant (found near Boulder Falls), 23-year-old Aubrey Leaver (found near Central Park), and 22-year-old Melanie Quinn (found in Eben G. Fine Park).

The trial was extensively covered by both FOX News and CNN. It lasted for nine days. Most of the time was spent on the testimony of multiple prosecution witnesses, including Athena Gibson, Alani Taylor, and Trina Perez. While each primary detective who worked on the case testified, the star prosecution witnesses were Detective Caroline Shaw and victim Della Kemp. Della's vivid descriptions of her time in the "dungeon" brought tears to the eyes of several jurors. After Della's testimony, the judge called for a recess to allow the jurors to compose themselves.

Another dramatic moment in the trial occurred when video and photographs of the house on 11th Street were presented to the jury. When pictures of the rooms in which Melanie Quinn and Della Kemp were held prisoner were shown, one older female juror audibly gasped. A crime scene investigator carefully described each item as seen in the photographs, including blood stains on the wooden chair and concrete floor. In addition to DNA evidence, records detailing Dr. Lanaro's and Angelo's "research" were presented in court. Prosecutors had CSIs read some of the most gruesome procedures documented in the papers. Family members in attendance often cried in the gallery as they listened to the details.

Angelo's defense attorney attempted to put all the blame on Angelo's father, Dr. Anthony Lanaro. According to the defense, Angelo was just as much a victim as the women killed. The defense claimed Angelo played no role in the captivity and torture of the victims and that he was just as fearful of his father as the women. Angelo did not testify in his own defense.

After the closing arguments by both the defense and prosecution, the judge gave the jury final instructions and sent them to the jury room to deliberate. The jury only took three hours to reach a verdict. GUILTY ON ALL CHARGES.

Under Colorado law, First Degree Murder carries a penalty of life in prison with no parole. The judge had no choice but to sentence Angelo to three life sentences with no parole. Melanie Quinn's family was in the courtroom. Upon hearing the sentence, Mom, Dad and her sister broke down in tears as they hugged each other.

Later that same day, a press conference was held in the police department's training room on the second floor. The Boulder County District Attorney, Boulder Police Chief Ken Atkins, and Sheriff Alex Higgins hosted the press conference. They faced a bank of bright lights and cameras from every local and national news station.

Shaw and Nichols sat in the back of the room and watched the commotion. About halfway through the news conference, Shaw told Nichols she was leaving.

"Where are you going?" asked Nichols.

"I've seen enough of this. I have to make a phone call," answered Shaw. "I'll see you back downstairs after this is over."

Shaw walked downstairs to her desk in the detective bureau. She then called Athena Gibson.

"Hello, Athena. This is Detective Shaw."

"Hi, Detective. What's up?"

"I take it you heard about the verdict?"

"Oh yes. It's on every channel. Thank you for finding the man who kidnapped me."

"No, Athena. I'm calling to thank you. You were the first to give us information that sent me down the right track. I'm so grateful for that call from you. We might still be looking if not for that call."

"That's nice of you," said Athena.

"Are you doing okay?" asked Shaw.

"I'm doing really well. When I heard about the guilty verdict, I felt relief that I haven't had in a long time."

"That's good to know, Athena. If you ever need anything, don't hesitate to call me."

Shortly after the call, Nichols was at Shaw's desk.

"Are you okay?" asked Nichols.

"Yes. I'm relieved it's finally all over. I take it the news conference is over?" asked Shaw.

"Yes, and it's almost three o'clock, and I haven't eaten lunch. Come on, I'll treat, and you can pick," said Nichols.

"I can pick?"

"Yes."

"Hmmmm. Moe's Bar-B-Que?"

"Seriously? You're picking Bar-B-Que?"

"I never said I didn't like it. Just try not to get any sauce on your shirt this time."

Nichols laughed. "I'll try my best."

Thank You

I would like to thank my readers for supporting me in my book writing endeavors. I hope you enjoy my stories as much as I enjoy writing them. It would be greatly appreciated if you would leave an online review of my book. It really does help. Thank you.

And if you haven't yet read my first three books, please check them out. They are titled **Behind The Lies,** a book of three novellas full of action and drama; **Death From Desire,** two short novels of more crime action, mystery, and suspense; and **Naked Evidence,** two more crime thrillers with mystery and intrigue. They are available from various vendors, both online and through bookstores.

What's next?

Please look for additional future releases of crime thrillers.

For further information, please visit my webpage at:

Becknerbooks.com

Email: becknerbooks@gmail.com

You can sign up for notifications of new releases and offers. I also display some of my scenery and wildlife photography on the website.

Thanks again.

Mark R. Beckner